A DENAZEN NOVEL

TOUCH

BOOK ONE

For Kevin…
Every miracle in my life is because of you.

1

I couldn't see them, but I knew they were there, waiting at the bottom. Bloodthirsty little shits—they were probably *praying* for this to go badly. "What do you think—about a fifteen-foot drop?"

"Easily," Brandt said. He grabbed my arm as a blast of wind whipped around us. Once I was steady on my skateboard, he tipped back his beer and downed what was left.

Together, we peered over the edge of the barn roof. The party was in full swing below us. Fifteen of our closest—and craziest—friends.

Brandt sighed. "Can you really do this?"

I handed him my own empty bottle. "They don't call me Queen of Crazy Shit for nothing." Gilman was poised on his skateboard to my left. Even in the dark, I could see the moonlight glisten off the sweat beading his brow. Pansy. "You ready?"

He swallowed and nodded.

Brandt laughed and tossed the bottles toward the woods. There were several seconds of silence, then a muted crash, followed by hoots and hysterical laughter from our friends below. Only drunk people would find shattering bottles an epic source of amusement.

"I dunno about this, Dez," he said. "You can't see anything down there. How do you know where you're gonna land?"

"It'll be fine. I've done this, like, a million times."

Brandt's words were clipped. "Into a pool. From a ten-foot-high garage roof. This is at least fifteen feet. Last thing I want to do is drag your ass all the way home."

I ignored him—the usual response to my cousin's chiding—and bent my knees. Turning back to Gilman, I smiled. "Ready, *Mr. Badass*?"

Someone below turned up one of the car stereos. A thumping techno beat drifted up. Hands on the sill behind me, drunken shouts of encouragement rising from below, I let go.

Hair lashed like a thousand tiny whips all along my face. The rough and rumbling texture of the barn roof beneath my board. Then nothing.

Flying. It was like flying.

For a few blissful moments, I was weightless. A feather suspended in midair right before it fluttered gracefully to the ground. Adrenalin surged through my system, driving my buzz higher.

The crappy thing about adrenalin highs, though? They never last long enough.

Mine lasted what felt like five seconds—the time it took to go from the barn roof to the not-so-cushy pile of hay below.

I landed with a jar—nothing serious—a bruised tailbone and some black and blues, maybe. Hardly the worst I'd ever walked away with. Stretching out the kink in my back, I brushed the hay from my jeans. A quick inspection revealed a smudge above my right knee and a few splotches of mud up the left side. All things the washing machine could fix.

Somewhere behind me, a loud wail filled the air. Gilman.

Never mix tequila and peach schnapps with warm Bud Light. It makes you do stupid things. Things like staying too long at a party you were told not to go to or making out in the bushes with someone like Mark Geller.

Things like skateboarding off the roof of a rickety barn…

Well, that's not entirely true. I tended to do these things without the buzz. Except kissing Mark Geller. That was *all* alcohol.

"You okay?" Brandt called from the rooftop.

I gave him a thumbs-up and went to check on Gilman. He was surrounded by a gaggle of girls, which made me wonder if he wasn't faking it—at least a little. A scrawny guy like Gilman didn't warrant much in the way of female attention, so I'd bet all ten toes he'd run his mouth tonight to attract some.

"You are one crazy ass, Chica," he mumbled, climbing to his feet.

I pointed to the pile of hay I'd landed in—several yards farther than where he'd crashed. "*I'm* crazy? At least I aimed for the hay."

"Wooooo!" came Brandt's distinctive cry. A moment later, he was running around the side of the barn, fist pumping. He stopped at my side and stuck his tongue out at Gilman, who smiled and flipped him off. He punched me in the arm. "That's my girl!"

"A girl who needs to bail. Ten minutes of kissy face in the bushes and Mark Geller thinks we're soul mates. *So* don't need a stalker."

Brandt frowned. "But the party's just getting started. You don't want to miss the Jell-O shots!"

Jell-O shots? Those were my favorite. Maybe it was worth… no. "I'm willing to risk it."

"Fine, then I'll walk with ya."

"No way," I told him. "You're waiting for Her Hotness to show, remember?" He'd been trying to hook up with Cara Finley for two weeks now. She'd finally agreed to meet him at the party tonight, and I wasn't ruining his chances by having him bail to play guard dog.

He glanced over his shoulder. In the field under the moonlight, people were beginning to dance. "You sure you're okay to go alone?"

"Of course." I gestured to my feet. "No license needed to drive these babies."

He was hesitant, but in the end, Cara won out. We said goodbye, and I started into the dark.

Home was only a few minutes away—through the field, across a narrow stream, and over a small hill. I knew these woods so well, I could find home with my eyes closed. In fact, I practically had on more than one occasion.

Pulling my cell from my back pocket, I groaned. One a.m. If luck was with me, I'd have enough time to stumble home and tuck myself in before Dad got there. I hadn't meant to stay so late this time. Or drink so much. I'd only agreed to go as moral support for Brandt, but when Gilman started running his mouth… Well, I'd had no choice but stay and put up so he'd *shut* up. I had a rep to worry about, after all.

By the time I hit the halfway point between the field and the house—a shallow, muddy stream I used to play in as a child—I had to stop for a minute. Thumping beats and distant laughter echoed from the party, and for a moment I regretted not taking Brandt up on his offer to walk home with me. Apparently, that last beer had been a mistake.

I stumbled to the water's edge and forced the humid air in and out of my lungs. Locking my jaw and holding my breath, I mentally repeated, *I will not throw up*.

After a few minutes, the nausea passed. Thank God. No way did I want to walk home smelling like puke. I shuffled back from the water, ready to make my way home, when I heard a commotion and froze.

Crap. The music had been too loud and someone must have called the cops. Perfect. Another middle-of-the-night call from the local PD wasn't something Dad would be happy about. On second thought, bring on the cops. The look on his face would be so worth the aggravation.

I held my breath and listened. Not sounds coming from the party—men yelling.

Heavy footsteps stomping and thrashing through the brush.

The yelling came again—this time closer.

I crammed the cell back into my pocket, about to begin what was sure to be a messy climb up the embankment, when movement in the brush behind me caught my attention. I whirled in time to see someone stumble down the hill and land a few feet from the stream.

"Jesus!" I jumped back and tripped over an exposed root, landing on my butt in the mud. The guy didn't move as I fumbled upright and took several wobbly steps forward. He'd landed at an odd angle, feet bare and covered in several nasty looking slices. I squinted in the dark and saw he was bleeding through his thin white T-shirt in several places as well as from a small gash on the side of his head. The guy looked like he'd gone ten rounds with a weed whacker.

Somewhere between eighteen and nineteen, he didn't look familiar. No way he went to my high school. I knew pretty much everyone. He couldn't have been at the party—he was cute. I would have remembered. I doubted he was even local. His hair was too long, and he was missing the signature Parkview T-shirt tan. Plus, even in the dark it was easy to make out well-defined arms and broad shoulders. This guy obviously hit the gym—something the local boys could've used.

I bent down to check the gash on the side of his head, but he jerked away and staggered to his feet as the yelling came again.

"Your shoes!" he growled, pointing to my feet. His voice was deep and sent tiny shivers dancing up and down my spine. "Give me your shoes!"

Buzzed or not, I was still pretty sharp. Whoever those guys yelling in the woods were, they were after him. Drug deal gone south? Maybe he'd gotten caught playing naked footsie with someone else's girlfriend?

"Why—?"

"Now!" he hissed.

I wouldn't have even considered giving up my favorite pair of red Vans if he hadn't looked so seriously freaked. He was being chased. He thought having my shoes would somehow help? Fine. Maybe as a weapon? Rocks would have worked better in my opinion, but to each his own.

Against my better judgment, I took several steps back and, without turning away from him, pulled them off. Stepping up, I tossed him the sneakers—and teetered forward. Instead of trying to catch me, he took a wide step back, allowing me to fall into the mud.

My frickin' hero!

I struggled upright and flicked a glob of mud from my jeans as he bent down to snatch the shoes—without moving his gaze from mine. His eyes were beautiful—ice blue and intense—and I found it hard to look away. He set the sneakers on the ground and poised his right foot over the first one. A giggle rose in my throat. No way he'd be jamming his bigass feet into them.

He proved me wrong. Cramming his toes in, heels poking

obscenely over the edges, he wobbled with an odd sort of grace to the embankment and wedged himself between a partially uprooted tree and a hollowed-out log. He teetered slightly as he walked, and I remembered the nasty gashes on his foot. Great. Now on top of *borrowing* my kicks, he was going to bleed all over them.

My gaze dropped to the spot he'd been standing. It was dark and the moon had tucked itself behind the clouds so I couldn't see very well, but something about the ground didn't look quite right. The color seemed off—darker than it should be.

I squinted, bending to brush my fingers along the dark spot, but more rustling in the woods had my gaze swinging hard left, heartbeat kicking into high gear. The next thing I knew, a group of four men exploded from the brush and came storming down the embankment like ravers on crack. Dressed in dark blue, skintight body suits that covered them from fingertips to toes, little was left to the imagination. Mimes. They reminded me of mimes.

Mimes with what looked a lot like Tasers.

"You!" The one in the front called out as he skidded to a stop. Looking at the ground, he surveyed the trail leading to the shallow water. "Has anyone been past here?"

From the corner of my eye I saw the boy, face pale, watching us. All the men would have had to do was turn to the right and they'd surely see him.

"Some punk came barreling through a few minutes ago." I stomped my sock-clad foot. Mud sloshed through the material and oozed between my toes. Ick! "Stole my damn shoes!"

"Which way did he go?"

Was he serious? I was about to make a joke about not being allowed to talk to strangers, but the look on his face made me think twice. Mr. Mime didn't seem like he was rocking a sense of humor. I threw my hands up in surrender and pointed in the direction opposite the one I planned on going.

Without another word, the men split into two groups. Half of them heading the way I'd directed, the other half taking off opposite. Huh. Guess they didn't trust a semi-drunk chick with a nose ring and no shoes.

I waited till they were out of sight before making my way over to where the boy crouched, still hidden behind the brush. "They're gone. I think it's safe to come out and play now."

He held my gaze and maneuvered out of the hiding spot. When he made no move to remove my sneakers, I nodded to his feet. "Planning to give my kicks back anytime soon?"

He shook his head and folded his arms. "I can't give them back to you."

"Why the hell not? Because seriously, dude, red is *not* your color."

He looked at the ground for a moment, then let his gaze wander over the path he'd traveled earlier. "I'm hungry." He was staring again. "Do you have any food?"

He gets my shoes then asks for food? The guy had some serious nerve.

The gash on his head still oozed a little and the faint bluish-purple of a bruise was beginning to surface across his left cheek, but it was the haunted look in his eyes that stood out above everything else like a flashing neon sign. He kept flicking his fingers, one at a time. Pointer, middle, ring, and pinky—over and over.

An owl hooted and I remembered the time. Dad would be home soon. This might work to my advantage. I knew bringing the guy home would royally piss him off. He'd have puppies if he found a stranger in the house. Hell, he might even have a llama.

But while the thought of pushing Dad closer to the edge gave me warm tingles, it wasn't my only motivation. I kind of wanted a little more time with the guy. Those arms… Those *eyes*. We were all alone out in the middle of the woods. If he'd wanted to go serial killer on me, he would have made a move by now. I didn't believe he was dangerous. "My house isn't far from here—Dad went to the grocery store the other day. Lots of junk food if that's your thing."

The look in his eyes made me think he didn't trust me—which I didn't get. I'd given him my *shoes* for crap's sake. "I don't know who your friends were, but they might double back. You'll be safe at my place for a while. Maybe they'll give up."

He looked downstream and shook his head. "They are not the type of men who give up."

2

It was a straight path through the woods and across to Kinder Street. The small cul-de-sac bordered the Parkview Nature Preserve and was home to five houses, all painfully similar except for their color. As we walked, I tried to get the guy to talk a few times, but all I got were simple, one-word answers that told me jack-shit. Eventually, I gave up and settled on counting the heavy fall of my shoes—still on his feet—as they clomped against the earth.

By the time the house came into view, I was dying of curiosity.

"So, ready to fill me in yet? Who were those guys in the fruity leotards?" I fought with the front door lock. Damn thing always stuck. "Did you piss off a herd of male ballet dancers?"

Silence.

The door finally gave way and I stepped aside, waving him in. He didn't move. "Well?"

"You first."

Alrighty then. Someone had a serious case of paranoia.

I stepped in and waited. It took a few moments, but finally, he crossed the threshold.

"Can you at least tell me your name?"

He wandered the room, running his fingertips along the edge of the couch and over some of Mom's old knickknacks. "Sue calls me Kale," he mumbled after a minute of hesitation. He picked up a small crystal horse, held it to his ear, then shook it several times before setting it back down and continuing on.

"Kale what?"

The question halted his inspection and earned me a funny look. In his hand was the tile ashtray Mom made at an arts and crafts fair the week before I was born. It was cheesy and cheap looking, but I was still afraid he might drop it.

"As in your last name?"

"I don't need one," he said, and returned to his surveillance. It was like he was searching for something. Picking apart each item in the room as if it might contain the clues to a mass murder — or maybe he was looking for a breath mint.

"How very Hollywood of you." I hefted the laundry basket off the floor, set it on the couch, and rummaged through it till I found a pair of Dad's sweatpants and an old T-shirt. "Here. The bathroom is upstairs — second door on the right. There should be clean towels in the closet on the first shelf if you want a shower. Take your time." *Please* take your time.

This would be the perfect payback for the ass-chewing Dad gave me for sneaking out last week. That, and it didn't hurt that Kale was a total hottie.

He made no move to take the clothes from me.

"Look, no worries, all right? Dad isn't due home for awhile and you're covered in mud and gunk." I set the clothes down on the seat in front of him and took a step back to grab a pair of my jeans from the basket.

Without taking his eyes from me, he gathered the clothes in his arms and stared. His expression was so intense I had to remind myself to keep breathing. Something about the way he watched me caused my stomach to do little flips. The eyes. Had to be. Crystalline blue and unflinching. The kind of stare that could make a girl go gaga. The kind of stare that could make *this* girl go gaga—and that was saying a lot. I wasn't easily impressed by a pretty face.

He seemed to accept this because he gave a quick nod and slowly backed out of the room and up the stairs. A few minutes later the shower hissed to life.

While I waited, I changed out of my muddy clothes and started a pot of coffee. Even if Dad didn't find a strange guy in the house when he got home, he'd be pissed about the coffee. I couldn't count the times he'd told me the El Injerto was strictly *hands off*. He even tried to hide it—as if *that* would have worked. If he wanted me to leave his coffee alone, he should go back to drinking the Kopi Luwak. No way—no matter how much I loved coffee—would I drink anything made from a bean some tree rat crapped out.

I'd almost finished folding the laundry when Kale came down the stairs.

"Much better. You look almost human." The pants were a little baggy—Kale was a few inches shorter than Dad's six three—and the shirt was a bit too big, but at least he was clean. He still had his feet crammed into my favorite red Vans. They were soaked. Had he worn them in the *shower*?

"Your name?" he asked once he'd reached the bottom, the sneakers sloshing and spitting with each step. He *had* worn them in the shower!

"Deznee, but everyone calls me Dez." I pointed to the soggy Vans. "Um, you ever gonna take my sneakers off?"

"No," he said. "I cut myself."

Maybe something wasn't screwed on right. There was a mental facility in the next town—it wasn't unheard of for patients to get out once in a while. Leave it to me to find the hottest guy in existence and have him be a total whack job. "Oh. Well, that explains it all then, doesn't it…?"

He nodded and began wandering the room again. Stopping in front of one of mom's old vases—an ugly blue thing I kept only because it was one of the few things still in the house that belonged to her—he picked it up. "Where are the plants?"

"Plants?"

He looked underneath and inside, before turning it over and shaking it as though something might come tumbling out. "This should have plants in it, right?"

I stepped forward and rescued the vase. He jerked away. "Easy there." I carefully placed the blue monstrosity back on the table and stepped back. He was staring again. "You didn't think I was going to hit you or something, did you?"

In eighth grade I'd had a classmate who we later found out was being abused at home. I remembered him being skittish—always twitching and avoiding physical contact. His eyes were a lot like Kale's, constantly darting and bobbing back and forth as though attack was imminent.

I expected him to avoid the question, or deny it—something evasive. That's what abused kids did, right? Instead, he laughed. A sharp, frigid sound that made my stomach tighten and the hairs on the back of my neck stand straight up.

It also made my blood pump faster.

He crossed his arms and stood straighter. "You couldn't hit me."

"You'd be surprised," I countered, slightly offended. Three summers in a row at the local community center's self-defense classes. No one was hitting *this* chick.

A slow, devastating smile spread across his lips. That smile had probably ruined a lot of girls. Dark, shaggy hair, tucked behind each ear, still dripped from the shower, ice blue eyes following every move I made.

"You couldn't hit me," he repeated. "Trust me."

He turned away and wandered to the other side of the room, picking up things as he went. Everything received a quizzical, and almost critical, once-over. The trio of *Popular Science* magazines sitting on the coffee table, the vacuum I'd left leaning against one wall, even the TV remote sticking between two cushions on the couch. He stopped at a wall shelf full of DVDs, pulling one out and examining it. "Is this your family?" He brought the box closer and narrowed his eyes, turning it over in his hands several times.

"You're asking me if" — I stood on my tiptoes and looked at the box in his hands. Uma Thurman glared at me from the cover, wearing her iconic yellow motorcycle suit — "Uma Thurman is a *relative*?" Maybe he wasn't loony. Maybe he had been at the party. I'd missed the Jell-O shots, but obviously he hadn't.

"Why do you have their photograph if they're not your family?"

"Seriously, what rock did you crawl out from under?" Pointing to a small collection of frames on the mantle, I said, "Those are pictures of my family." Well, except my mom. Dad didn't keep any pictures of her in the house. I nodded to the DVDs and said, "Those are actors. In movies."

"This place is very strange," he said, picking up the first picture. Me and my first bike — a powder-pink Huffy with glitter and white streamers. "Is this you?"

I nodded, cringing. Pink sneakers, Hello Kitty sweatshirt, and pink ribbons tied to the end of each braid. Dad used it on a daily basis to point out how far I'd fallen. I'd gone from fresh-faced blonde with perky pigtails—his sunshine smile girl—to pierced nose and eyebrow with wild blonde hair highlighted by several chunky black streaks. I liked to think if my mom were alive, she'd be proud of the woman I'd become. Strong and independent—I didn't put up with anyone's crap. Including Dad's. That's how I imagined her when she was alive. An older, more beautiful version of me.

I looked at the scene in Kale's hands again. I hated that picture—the bike was the last gift Dad ever bought me. The day he gave it to me—the same day the picture was taken—had been a turning point in our lives. The very next day my relationship with Dad started to crumble. He started working longer hours at the law firm and everything changed.

Kale set the picture down and moved on to the next. His hand stopped mid-reach and his face paled. The muscles in his jaw twitched. "This was a setup," he said quietly, hand falling slack against his side.

"Huh?" I followed his gaze to the picture in question. Dad and me at last year's Community Day—neither of us smiling. As I recall, we weren't happy about taking the picture. We were less happy about being forced to stand so close to each other.

"Why not let them take me at the water's edge? Why lead me here?"

"Let who take you?"

"The men from the complex. The men from Denazen."

I blinked, sure I'd heard him wrong. "Denazen? As in the law firm?"

He turned back to the picture on the mantle. "This is *his* home, isn't it?"

"Do you know my dad?" This was priceless. Score another point for my megalomaniacal Dad. One of his cases, no doubt. Maybe some poor chump he'd sent to the happy house, because that's clearly where he belonged.

"That man is the devil," Kale replied, lips pulled back in a snarl. His voice changed from surprised to deadly in a single beat of my heart and, crazy or not, I found it kind of hot.

"My father's a shit, but the Devil? A little harsh, don't ya think?"

Kale scrutinized me for a moment, taking several additional steps back and inching his way closer to the door. "I won't let them use me anymore."

"Use you for what?" Something told me he wasn't talking about coffee runs and collations. Acid churned in my stomach.

His eyes narrowed and radiating such hatred, I actually flinched. "If you try to stop me from leaving, I'll kill you."

"Okay, okay." I held out my hands in what I hoped was a show of surrender. Something in his eyes made me believe he meant it. Instead of being freaked out—like the tiny voice of reason at the back of my brain screamed I should be—I was intrigued. That was Dad. Making friends and influencing people to threaten murder. Glad it wasn't only me. "Why don't you start by telling me who you think my dad is?"

"That man is the Devil of Denazen."

"Yeah. Devil. Caught that before. But my dad's just a lawyer. I know that in itself makes him kind of a dick, but—"

"No. That man is a killer."

My jaw dropped. Forget balls, this guy had boulders. "A killer?"

Arms rigid, Kale began flicking his fingers like he had by the stream. Pointer, middle, ring, and pinky. Again and again. Voice low, he said, "I watched him give the order to *retire* a small child three days ago. That is not what a lawyer does, correct?"

Retire? What the hell was that supposed to mean? I was about to fire off another set of questions, but there was a noise outside. A car. In the driveway.

Dad's car.

Kale must have heard it too, because his eyes went wide. He vaulted over the couch and landed beside me as Dad's keys jingled in the lock on the front door and the knob turned. Typical. The damn thing never stuck for *him*.

He stepped into the house and closed the door behind him. Eyes focused on mine, he said, "Deznee, step away from the boy." No emotion, no surprise. Only the cold, flat tone he used when speaking to me about everything ranging from toast to suspension from school.

I used to be sad about it—the fact that his career seemed to have sucked away his soul—but I was over it. Nowadays, it was easier to be mad. Trying to get a reaction from him—any reaction—was my sole purpose in life.

Kale stepped closer. At first, an insane part of my brain interpreted this to mean he was protecting me from Dad. It made sense somehow. According to him, Dad was the enemy, and I, the one who helped him back by the stream—the one who gave him my shoes and lied to those men—was a friend.

But then Kale spoke; his menacing words were delivered in a cold, harsh tone that obliterated the crazy theory.

"If you do not move aside and let me leave, I will kill her."

Some friend.

Despite Kale's threat, Dad remained in the doorway, blocking his path. "Deznee, I'm going to say this one last time. Step away from the boy."

Everything Kale said about my dad rushed bounced in my head like a bad trip, churning in my stomach like sour milk.

"What the hell is going on?" I demanded, glaring at Dad. "Do you know him?"

Dad finally made a move. Not the kind of move you'd expect

from a father fearing for his teenaged daughter's life, but a simple, bold step forward. One that screamed *I dare you.*

He was playing chicken with Kale.

And he lost.

Kale shook his head, and when he spoke, he sounded kind of sad. "You should know I don't bluff, Cross. You taught me that."

His hand shot out, lightning fast, and clamped down on my neck. Warm fingers brushed my skin and curled around my throat. They were long and callused and wrapped more than halfway. He was going to snap my neck. Or choke me. In a panic, I tried to pry his fingers away, but it was no use. His grip was like a vice. This was it. I was a goner. All the stupid stuff I'd done and survived, and a random, almost-hookup was going to do me in. Where was the fair in that?

But Kale didn't crush my windpipe or try to choke me. He just turned toward me—staring. His face pale and eyes wide. Watching me as though I was a fascinating first-place science project, mouth hanging open like I'd presented the cure for Cancer.

On my neck, his fingers twitched, and then he let go. "How—?"

Movement by the door. Dad reached into his pocket—and out came a *gun*? Things had gone from really weird to *I-fell-down-the-rabbit-hole*-surreal. My dad didn't know how to shoot a gun! He lifted the barrel and aimed it at us, hand steady.

Then again, maybe he did.

"What the hell are you doing, Dad?"

He didn't move. "There's nothing to worry about. Stay calm."

Stay calm? Was he crazy? He was pointing a gun in my general direction! If anything about that situation said calm, I was missing something.

Thankfully, my normal catlike reflexes saved our asses. Yeah. More like dumb luck. Dad squeezed the trigger and I dropped to the floor, pulling a very surprised Kale with me. I nearly ripped his arm out of its socket in the process, but it didn't seem to bother him. He wasn't concerned about the gun either, his attention still fixated on me. We hit the ground as a small projectile embedded itself into the wall behind us with a dull thud. A dart. A tranq gun? Somehow this didn't make me feel any better. I could console myself with the fact that the dart hit the wall closer to Kale than me, indicating I hadn't been the target, but still. Bullets or not, a gun was a gun. And guns freaked me the hell out.

"Move!" I hauled Kale to his feet and shoved him through the door and into the kitchen. He stumbled forward but managed to keep himself upright. Impressive considering he still had on my ill-fitting, soggy sneakers.

"Deznee!" Dad bellowed from the living room. Heavy footsteps pounded against the hardwood as he chased after us. No way was I stopping.

Dad had a specific tone he used when mad at me—which was like, ninety-eight percent of the time—and it never fazed me. In fact, I found it kind of funny. But tonight was different. Something in his voice told me I'd gone above and beyond and it scared me a little.

Something shattered—probably the half-full glass of Coke I'd left on the coffee table last night while watching "SNL" reruns. "Get back here! You have no idea what you're doing!"

What else was new? Truthfully, even if the gun hadn't freaked me out, it was obvious Kale, despite the badass vibe, was afraid of my dad. He'd been through something brutal—and Dad had somehow played a part in it. I wasn't sure why this guy's past was so important, but I needed to find out.

I propelled him out the back door and into the cool night air. We didn't stop—even when we came to the property line. And even as we put distance between Dad and us at a breakneck speed, I could still hear my father's angry words echoing in the cold night, "This isn't one of your goddamn games!"

"We're almost there," I said. We'd stopped running a few minutes ago so we could catch our breath. Kale hadn't spoken since he'd threatened to kill me, only continued to stare as though I'd grown a second—and third—head. I was full of questions, but they could wait for now.

We finally reached the mustard-yellow Cape Cod on the other side of the railroad tracks and followed a small stone path around the back, to a set of bilko doors that had been spray painted black. Written across the front in bulbous white graffiti was *Curd's Castle*. I kicked the hatch twice, then waited. Several moments later, with an ear-piercing clatter, the doors opened, and a spiky, blond- and purple-streaked head popped out. Curd. With a nod and a too-eager smile, he waved us inside as if we were expected.

We descended the dark cement staircase and stepped into a dimly lit room. It was surprisingly clean—none of the typical staples you'd expect to see when walking into a seventeen-year-

old guy's room were visible. No half-eaten plates of food or empty
soda cans. No scattered piles of video games or magazines. There
weren't even any posters of skanky women in obscene poses on
the wall. Not that Curd wasn't a dog. The place may have looked
clean, but it smelled of sex and pot.

Kurt Curday—Curd to his adoring public—was the go-to
guy for all your partying needs. Kegs, pot, X, Curd could get it all.
A big name on the raver scene and fellow senior-to-be, Curd was
one of the organizers of Sumrun. The party, one of the biggest
raves in four counties, was a week away, so Curd was a busy guy.

"Dez, baby, I'd be much happier to see you if you weren't
towing along a little pet." He ran a finger up my arm, then curled a
lock of my hair around his thumb, "But hey, I'm up for whatever."

"This isn't a social call, Curd." I glanced at Kale. He stood
stiffly by the door, eyes fixed on Curd's finger running along my
skin. His gaze lifted to mine, and I felt a shiver skitter up my spine.
Shaking it off, I shuffled away from Curd and into the room. "I
got into some trouble with my dad again. I need a place to lay
low. You were the closest."

He shot me a disappointed frown and flopped onto the futon,
kicking his heels onto a small, rickety table. "Not to worry, baby.
What'd ya get caught doing this time?"

I forced a sly smile and shrugged. "Oh, you know, the usual."
I hitched my thumb back at Kale. "What Dad is thrilled to find a
half-naked guy in his daughter's bedroom?" I hoped that would
explain the clothing Kale wore—clothing that obviously wasn't
his.

"Such a little hellcat." He blew me an exaggerated kiss. A
grin that told me he was picturing himself in Kale's place slipped
across his face. "Tell me again why we haven't hooked up yet?"

I sank into the chair across from him. "I don't like dealers?"

"Oh yeah, that's right. How could I forget?" He nodded in

Kale's direction. "Who's the mute?"

"Curd, Kale." I waved in Kale's direction. "Kale, Curd."

"I touched you," Kale interjected after a moment of silence.

Curd snickered. "If you were in *her* bed, I certainly hope you weren't touching yourself." He turned to me, right eyebrow cocked. "Is he *special?*"

I glared at him.

He shrugged. "You guys thirsty? I'll go find some soda—or something a little harder?"

I sighed and said, "Soda's fine."

Kale watched Curd disappear up the narrow staircase leading to the first floor and took a step forward. He repeated his previous statement. "I touched you."

"Yes," was all I could manage. His blue eyes pinned me to the chair. A mishmash of emotion raged inside my head. I was torn between checking the exits for men in weird suits and checking out Kale. And then I remembered Dad and the gun…

"You're still alive."

"Should I not be?" There was that look again. Like he was standing in the presence of some mythical creature and had been granted a year's supply of wishes. It made me uncomfortable. It's not like I wasn't used to being stared at, and to be fair, I'd done my fair share of staring tonight, but this was different. Intense in a way I'd never felt before.

He took another step forward, head tilted to the side. "That's never happened. Ever." He reached for me, hesitating for a moment before pulling his hand back. "Can…can I touch you again?"

I probably should have been weirded out by a question like that. Any other day, I would have been, but Kale's eyes sparkled with wonder and curiosity. Gone was the cold expression he'd worn back at my house. His voice was soft, but there was a fierce longing in it that made my mouth go dry. I pushed my discomfort aside, nodded, and stood.

For a big guy, he moved surprisingly fast, darting around the coffee table to stand in front of me. Close. Breathing-the-same-air kind of close. I expected him to grab my wrist, or maybe my arm, but instead he brought his right hand up to cup the side of my face.

"You're so warm," he said in awe as his thumb traced whisper light under my eye—like wiping away tears. "So soft. I've never felt anything like it."

Neither had I. His thumb, barely skating across my skin, left a trail of warm tingles in its wake that spread throughout my entire body. His breath, puffing out softly across my nose and forehead, was warm and sweet, almost dizzying.

A loud clanking rang from upstairs—Curd must have dropped something—snapping me out of it. I cleared my throat. "Um, thanks?"

"You helped me escape Cross," he said, stepping back. "I tried to kill you, and you helped me escape. Why?"

I shrugged. "My dad's a dick. Pissing him off is a hobby. 'Sides, you didn't really *try* to kill me. You were scared."

"I don't get scared."

"Everyone gets scared."

Now wasn't the time to argue. I needed answers. Things started churning in the back of my brain. Strange, late-night phone calls. Oddly timed trips to the office. All things that, had I been paying attention, might have popped up as red flags. "You said my dad was a killer. That's some kind of euphemism, right?"

"I'm one of his weapons."

"Weapons?"

"He uses me."

The way he said it gave me chills. The creepy kind, this time.

"To what? Like, spy on the other side's clients?" Even though I knew it was likely crap now, my subconscious was desperate to hang onto the belief that Dad was a lawyer.

"No."

I folded my arms, getting irritated. "Then give me a hint here. What is it you do for Dad?"

Taking two steps forward, blue eyes bright, he spoke softly. "I kill for him."

I blinked and tried to visualize Dad as the big bad. Couldn't do it. Or wouldn't. Sure, he was a tool and we hadn't really talked in years, but a killer? No way.

Turning his palms upward, Kale raised both hands and flexed his fingers. "They bring death to anything I touch."

I remembered the ground he walked across at the stream had looked wrong. Discolored.

I passed it off on the beer at the time, but…

He jerked away each time I got close enough to touch him…

He wouldn't take my shoes off…

The air caught in my lungs and the room began to shrink. "Your skin…?"

I would've called bullshit, but I of all people knew first hand crazy shit was possible. Plus, there'd been rumors floating through the raver scene for years now, ever since a local boy was arrested during Sumrun seven years ago. Rumor had it, the guy shorted out the electricity with a single touch of his fingers after being chased to the party by police. After they took him away, no one ever saw him again.

"Is deadly to anything living. Except you. How am I able to touch you? Everyone else would have died a horrible death."

I took a step back. It was hard to concentrate with him staring like that. "Let's focus here for a sec. You're trying to tell me that my dad uses you as a weapon? A weapon against what exactly?"

His face fell. "Not what, who."

"Who?" I really didn't want to hear his answer. Either my mysterious hottie was crazy or Dad was... Well, either way his answer was bound to throw another bird at my building.

"People. He uses me to punish people."

"My dad has you touch people? To *kill* them?"

"That is correct." The shame in his voice was like a vacuum, stealing all the air from the room. Eyes rising to meet mine, he reached out and ran his finger along the line of my chin and to my cheek, letting his touch linger for a few moments. I found myself wanting to take it all away. The heavy, sad look in his eyes. The pain in his voice. I could do it, maybe. Tell him something about myself that might make him feel less alone. Less isolated. A secret I've never spoken aloud before.

I opened my mouth, but when the words came out they weren't what I'd expected. "You're wrong. My dad's a *lawyer*." The walls that had been in place for as far back as I could remember stood strong.

"A lawyer kills people?"

"Are you serious?" This so wasn't happening. Dad wasn't part of some super-secret conspiracy theory. He was a stick-up-the-ass control freak workaholic. With weird hours. And, for some reason, a gun. Not a killer.

Kale's face remained blank.

"Of course they don't kill people! They put the bad guys away, get rid of 'em so they can't hurt anyone." Not the most accurate description, but the simplest I could come up with.

"No, that's definitely not what your father does. That's what *I* do. The Denazen Corporation uses me to punish those who have done wrong. I'm a Six. Does that make *me* a lawyer?"

Ugh. So much for simple. "What the hell is a Six?"

"It's what we're called."

O-kaay. "And punish those who've done wrong? Who says what's right and wrong?"

"Denazen, of course." He frowned and turned away. "And I belong to them."

"Where the hell are your parents?"

Voice barely a whisper, he said, "I don't have any parents."

"You're a human being, not a weapon. You don't *belong* to anyone," I hissed. "And of course you have parents, even if you don't know where they are."

Fuming, I ripped the little leather cardholder from my back pocket and tugged out a picture. My mom. I'd found it years ago in Dad's bottom desk drawer. I'd only known who she was because of her name written on the back in scrawling blue ink. Dad refused to talk about her—he told me her name, gave me a brief, watery description—and that was it. As I got older, I'd started looking more and more like the woman in the picture, which was probably why he hated me. I'd catch him watching me once in awhile. Like he might have been imagining it was her sitting there, and not me. Like he wished it was her instead of me. It made sense. It was my fault he'd lost her, after all. She'd died having me. Sometimes I hated myself, too.

"My mom is gone—that doesn't mean I don't have one." I shook the photo at him.

Kale closed the gap between us and took the picture from my hands. He purposefully let his fingers brush my wrist, giving a quick smile. "This is your mother?"

I nodded.

"You don't visit her?"

"I can't *visit* her, she's dead."

"She's not dead. She lives at the complex with me." He wandered away, picture still in his hands, and picked up a pair of Curd's worn boots. Leaning back against the wall, he kicked off my Vans and slipped on the boots. The sneakers fell to the floor with a heavy thud.

The world stopped. The air, the four walls, everything, it all fell away. "What?"

He held up the picture. "This is Sue."

I snatched the picture from him, gaping. "What did you say?"

"I said, that is Su—"

"I know what you said!" I snapped.

"But you just asked me—"

"You're sure?" I held up the picture, jamming it close to his face. My pulse pounded and I was feeling dizzy again—though not in a good way. My buzz, so happy and peaceful, was *totally* gone now. "You're sure this is the same woman?"

"I'd know her anywhere."

"And you're saying she's alive? At Denazen?"

He nodded.

"Her name is Sueshanna. Are you *sure* it's the same woman?"

"I am sure. She is alive. Why do you seem upset?"

I grabbed the side of the chair—it felt like the ground was going to swallow me whole. I couldn't help the shakiness. Dad was a tool, but to lie about Mom being dead? That was a dick move that transcended epic.

A noise came from upstairs, and the hairs on the back of my neck rose in warning. It was taking Curd way too long. I drew in a deep breath, held it, and looked over at Kale. Putting a single finger to my lips and hoping he knew what the heck that meant, I crept to the base of the stairs and listened. Silence. Gesturing for Kale to watch me skip the first step—I'd been at Curd's enough in the past to know it squeaked—I started up.

When I got to the top, Kale was behind me, standing very close. I was about to reinforce *quiet*, but he zipped past me, taking the lead. I reached out to grab the back of his shirt, but he was too quick, already to the other edge of the room. Heart thumping, and a lump forming in my throat, I followed him across the kitchen. He stood in the doorway, and when I tried to look around him, he blocked my way.

"No," he whispered, grabbing my arm.

"No what?" The air grew thin. Something about the way he was looking at me.

"We need to leave now."

"Leave? Why? What's wrong?"

More silence. Kale was trying to nudge me back down the stairs.

The thin, icy air drained from the room. I pushed him aside and ducked my head around the corner. Curd lay in the middle of the living room, face down and still as a snapshot. For a few horrific moments, I thought he might be dead, but finally he stirred.

I jerked my arm from Kale's grasp and lunged for Curd. "Oh my God, Curd! What happened?"

An unfamiliar voice boomed, jarring my attention away from Curd. "Living room!"

Kale was at my side, pulling me to my feet. We made it to the kitchen as footsteps thundered closer, and before I could blink, there were two men standing in front of us. One of them lunged for us as Kale jerked me backward. His fingertips raked across my shoulder, snapping the edge of my shirt. I stumbled, catching myself before losing the battle with gravity.

Kale's fingers were tight on my wrist as the men, one wearing a dark blue suit, the other wearing the same leotard the group by the stream had on, advanced. They matched our steps—us back, them forward.

I turned toward the staircase at the other end of the kitchen that led to Curd's room, where a third leotard clothed man stood, tranq gun in hand, blocking our escape. There had to be something—anything—I could use as a weapon. We'd backed into the middle of the room now, trapped beside a center island. I pulled down a large cast iron pan from the rack above my head and swung it in front of us.

"Subdue and capture them both—Cross' orders," the suit said, his face blank. He lunged for me while the man behind us made a grab for Kale.

Kale was like a ninja, skating easily out of reach and ducking under the man's grasp. Pivoting, he spun full circle and brought his right forearm across the man's chest. He followed hard with an upturned fist, whaling into the man's hip. His attacker crumpled to the floor, howling in pain.

The other leotard man sprinted forward as Suit Guy adjusted his grip on my upper arm. I swung out with the frying pan again, missing his head but catching the edge of his shoulder with a satisfying thwack. He released his grip in surprise, and I stumbled away.

But not far enough.

He recovered quickly and lunged forward again. This time, instead of the cold clinical glare, he wore a heated snarl. With a powerful arc, he slapped me across the face. Everything danced and spun. My cheek felt like it had exploded.

I barely registered the jolt as I landed, jarring my right wrist and knee on the floor. My vision cleared enough to make out the man's hand darting forward again. I aimed for the back of his legs and kicked out, but Kale was faster. In a flash, he stood above me, hand intercepting the man's before it closed around my upper arm.

For a moment, nothing happened. Kale froze. Eyes meeting mine, he wore a horrified expression. Then, like the most high-tech special effect Hollywood had to offer, the man's skin shriveled and grayed. In a matter of seconds, he collapsed inward until nothing was left but a pile of clothing sitting amidst a mountain of ashlike dust.

Behind us, the two other men stirred. "Miss Cross—"

Subdue and capture them both—Cross' orders... Jesus what the hell was Dad into?

I climbed to my feet, the room still spinning a little. Kale grabbed my arm, and we sprinted out the door and across Curd's lawn. Subdue and capture, my ass. "Go, go, go!"

· · ·

An hour later, we were tucked under a tree behind my high school. Could it have been this morning I'd been laying out in the sun, enjoying the first days of summer? It felt like weeks had passed. Was it only hours ago my dad had been merely a self-absorbed, coldhearted lawyer in whose eyes I could do nothing right? Now what was he? The head of some super-secret program that used people with strange gifts as weapons?

"I need to know," I whispered, barely audible. My gut already knew the answer, but still.... Without confirmation there was still a small glimmer of hope—and hope could be a dangerous thing.

"My dad told me she was dead—does he know? That she's there, I mean. Does he know my mom's still alive?"

Kale nodded. "I'm sorry." He looked regretful and sad. Also a little scared. The corners of his lips were turned downward, expression darkening. He stepped closer, taking my hands. "He lied to you. You cannot trust him."

When we'd left Curd's, I was still debating what to do about Kale. Watching him deal with those guys proved he was *more* than capable of taking care of himself. So what was stopping me from wishing him luck and shooing him off on his merry little way? At first it was the look in his eyes when he'd demanded my shoes back at the stream. True fear. That same fear was mirrored in his expression when he spoke about Dad at Curd's and when he told me about Mom being at Denazen. Now that same fear was back, but this time it was for *me*.

That was new and made me feel a little tingly—which was totally unwelcomed. I'd been taking care of myself for a long time. I didn't need anyone watching my back—except maybe Brandt. Still, I didn't pull away.

"And she can't leave, right? He won't let her?"

He frowned and nodded.

What kind of man does that to people? To his *own wife*? The same kind of man who doesn't think twice about using a teenager to kill, that's who. The kind of man who couldn't be trusted. Kale was right. Going home wasn't an option.

Kale had been through hell at Dad's hands—I couldn't walk away from him. A part of me felt responsible while another part felt… something else. Something I couldn't quite explain. Something that, like his concern for me, made me uneasy while at the same time caused my blood to pump a bit faster.

"Tell me about her." My chest ached. Did she know my name or what I looked like? Did she know her own husband was the one responsible for keeping her there? "Tell me what she's like."

"A lot like you—kind, but strong. She taught me to survive." He tilted his head to the side, examining me. My hands still in his, he turned them over. With his thumb, he traced circles across my palms. A shiver ran down my spine. "You have the same hands."

"Is she—" I swallowed the lump lodged in my throat. "Can she do what you do?"

He shook his head. "She can become someone else."

"Become someone else?" A shiver of excitement raced through my body.

"Change her appearance. They use us as a team sometimes. She becomes someone the target knows, leading them someplace quiet so I can punish them."

I got to my feet and turned away. I didn't want Kale—or anyone for that matter—to see the tears trailing down my cheeks.

"How could he do this to her? To me?" I whirled around, voice uneven. Forget the tears—bring on the anger. "How could he lock her away and tell me she was dead! She's been there this whole time?"

Kale didn't answer. When I turned back, he was staring up at the sky, fascinated. "Sue used to tell me of the outside world. Late at night when sleep wouldn't come, she would come into my room and tell me stories about the things I could do and see—the people I could meet. She cries sometimes, in the middle of the night, when she thinks no one is listening. But I hear her. I'm always listening."

The tears came harder now. I'd had it easy. This whole time Mom was nothing more than a ghost to me. A voiceless, bodiless figment of my imagination. How hard must it have been for her to know I was out here, living with the man who kept her locked away like an animal? "I asked her once, not long ago, why, if the outside world held so much wonder, she didn't go back to it. Why she did not go to her child."

"What did she say?"

His hands fell away and he turned to the football field. A deer and her two fawns were frolicking in the moonlight. He watched them for a moment, mesmerized. "They tell us normal people would not understand. That they'd hurt us if we left. Sue said that's a lie. She told me we were really *prisoners*—that Denazen would never *allow* us to leave." Fists tight, his voice darkened. "Denazen has always been my home. It's all I've ever known. I didn't know anything about the outside world or the people in it, but I *knew* what the word prisoner meant."

His voice was so sad. I wanted to reach out and hold him. We made a great pair. The universe had seen fit to screw us both over—big time. "That's why you ran away?"

He shook his head. "It wasn't something I planned. After that conversation with Sue, I started thinking. Started to question things. *Prisoner.* A single word changed everything. I looked at things more carefully. They gave me an assignment yesterday. It started out like every other. I was given my target's name and driven to the kill location. I was escorted to the scene and left to enter, do my job, and return. No questions asked."

"What happened?"

He turned back to me, and the muscles in his jaw tightened. "When I entered the house, she was alone. Asleep in her bed. I was confused at first—she wasn't what I expected. I hesitated. It must have taken too long, because they sent someone in to check on me. When he confirmed that she was the target, I ran."

"What made you hesitate?"

His eyes squeezed closed. Shaking his head, he said, "She was a child—no more than seven or eight. Helpless." He opened his eyes. "Innocent. There was no crime someone that young could commit to be deserving of punishment."

"Jesus."

"I ran. Then I found you." He looked away. "Sue told me once, if I should ever find myself on the outside with no place to go, I should find the Reaper."

"The Reaper?"

"Yes. She said he would be able to help."

"Who is he? How can he help?"

Kale shrugged. "I only know he is like us—like Sue and me. A Six. She said he was revered among our kind. Powerful."

I was about to ask him if he'd thought further then running away from Denazen, but a high pitched, alien-themed hum sounded from my back pocket. Kale tensed, backing away. "It's okay. It's only my cell." I pulled it out, expecting to see Dad's number.

"Brandt?"

"Dez? Where the hell are you? It's three a.m.! Your Dad called the house. He said you ran off with some dangerous guy? He's worried for you."

I snorted. "Trust me, Brandt. He ain't worried *for* me." As much as I hated to drag my cousin into this, we needed help. "Listen, I've got a major favor to ask. Can you meet me tomorrow at noon— at the Graveyard? Bring some of your clothes. Long-sleeved stuff. And a pair of gloves. And something for me to change into. I'm gross."

There was a pause. "Dez, you're scaring me. What the hell is up? Why don't you just go home?"

"I can't really say."

Another pause. "Are you okay? Where are you? Are you alone?"

How much to say? Could someplace like Denazen trace cell phones? "I'm okay," I answered finally. I wanted to add, *for now*, but I knew that'd only worry him. "I'm not alone, but I can't tell you where I am. Not right now."

"Okay," he said cautiously. "What else do you need?"

I thought about it and realized I was starving. I'd found Kale on my way home from the party. Party equaled no wallet. No wallet meant no cash. No cash meant serious case of the munchies. "Some water, definitely. Maybe something to nom? Some spare cash if you've got it, too. I'll totally pay you back."

"Done and done. You gonna be okay till then?"

"Gonna have to be," I sighed. We'd lay low until morning. It'd be easy to stay off the radar for a few hours.

Or would it? Curd's place was close, but there were a hundred other houses between his and mine. He'd never been to the house and Dad had never met him. How the hell had Denazen found us so fast?

My fingers tightened around the cell. Duh. GPS. What a moron.

"Don't try calling me back. I'm ditching the phone. And whatever you do, don't tell anyone you talked to me. Not your Dad, and especially not mine." Without waiting, I pushed *end*.

"I can't believe I'm going to do this," I said to myself. Looking down at the phone, I only hesitated a moment before throwing it at the tree behind me. The cell crashed into the trunk, shattering into several large pieces, and falling to the ground. "Come on, we have to get out of here."

· · ·

We killed the rest of the night and early next day by trying to lay low—which wasn't as easy as one would think. Kale, though cautious, was amazed by almost everything he saw. Everything from skateboards and takeout food to the outfits people wore was a brand new experience for him. He especially liked how people in the outside world dressed—namely, the girls. He really liked their short skirts and high, spiky shoes.

The morning slipped away without incident. We hadn't had any further run-ins with the men from Denazen, leading me to believe I'd been right. They'd been tracking my phone. Without it, we could stay off the grid. For a little while, at least.

The Graveyard was an old junkyard on the edge of town we used for partying. Usually, even in the daylight hours, kids could be found hanging out. Avoiding the home scene, ditching school—when it was in session—and winding down after work. This early, it was a ghost town.

We made our way around the back to the rip in the fence and slipped through. Brad Henshaw, the owner, died two years ago, leaving the place in limbo. The rumor was his daughter, a plastic surgeon in the city, had yet to take the time out of her busy schedule to come up and deal with the property. This meant we were free to come and go as we pleased, some nights partying till dawn. We were never really loud, not that there was anything much in the area, and we didn't hurt anything, so the cops pretty much left us alone.

At the very back of the lot, there was a collection of old vans that had been dragged, cut, and fit together like a makeshift fort. This was where everyone usually met. We made it within ten feet when movement inside caught my eye. I stopped mid-stride.

"It's cool," Brandt called. He stepped from the van into the sunlight. Setting his board down, he ran a hand through his wild, sandy blond hair and nodded. He had on the same jeans he'd worn to the party last night. I knew because of the ink stain above the right knee and the huge gaping hole in the left. He kept saying he was going to toss them, yet he never did. I couldn't understand why guys found it acceptable to wear things more than once without running them through the wash. At least he'd changed his T-shirt. "It's only me."

I fell forward, wrapping my arms around his shoulders. "Thank you so much for coming."

"Like I wouldn't," he said, pulling away. His eyes widened when he spotted Kale. "This is the dangerous guy?"

Kale regarded him with the same cool, but sad, expression he'd given me last night right before he tried to kill me. "I'm not dangerous to her."

"My uncle seems to think you are. If you hurt my cousin, I'll kick your ass from here to Jersey. You what, in a gang or something?"

"A gang? Seriously, Brandt. Less TV from now on, okay?" I inhaled. "I ran into Kale on the way home from the party last night. Some guys were chasing him."

Brandt folded his arms and nudged the skateboard at his feet. He always had to be touching the damn thing. Like a security blanket with wheels. "Okay…"

"So I bring him back to my place figuring, hey, this'll piss Dad off something fierce, only I didn't get the reaction I was hoping for. He *knew* Kale. Like, *knew* the guys chasing him down."

Brandt didn't respond. Instead, he backed away and reached into the van. A moment later, he pulled out a small purple duffle and a plastic bag. Tossing the duffle at Kale's feet, he said, "There are clothes for you in here, and what little cash I could scrounge up last minute. Get the hell out of Dodge. Fast."

Kale picked up the duffle.

Holding out the plastic bag to me, he said, "These are yours. This morning I snuck into your room. I was planning to get some of your own things and bail. The last time I gave you one of my *unclean* shirts to wear you spazzed. But when I got there, I heard voices."

"Voices?"

He shook his head. "Didn't see who it was, but I sure as hell heard enough. They said some really tweaked-out shit."

A lump of ice formed in my stomach. "What'd you hear?"

"Your Dad's a bad dude. Like, *really* bad. I heard him saying something about disposing of bodies." He grabbed my shoulders and shook me. "*Bodies*, Dez—as in dead people. Corpses! Something about the old dump site being full. Then he mentioned you. Something about finding you and bringing you in. Then they left."

I felt kind of sick. Maybe he'd misunderstood something. Dump site could mean garbage. Bodies could mean…okay, I had nothing for that one. "That all?"

Brandt hesitated. "No… When he left, he didn't lock his office. Didn't have long, but I managed to dig up some information." He nudged the board again, flipping it over and resting his right foot on top.

"What did you find?"

"Your Dad's into some crazy shit. That law firm he works for? Denazen? Yeah, so *not* a law firm, Dez. They're something else. They use Sixes—that's what they call people with weird *abilities*—as weapons, rented out to the highest bidder. Political scuffles, personal vendettas, hell, even the mob. Assassins. They use these people as *assassins*."

"I can't believe you went snooping. What if he came back?"

His expression melted into pure mischief. Lips tilted up, exposing a single dimple. That smile drove girls crazy. "I've got Dad's nose for digging up news. I didn't endure every father-son career day at the newspaper for nothing, you know. Picked up plenty of mad stealthing skills."

Uncle Mark was an investigative reporter at the *Parkview Daily News*. If there was deeply hidden dirt to find, he'd find it. I stored the thought away for later use. I had no intentions of dragging anyone else into this unless I had no other choice.

"This is not happening," I whispered. "What about my mom? She's alive. Did you find anything about her?"

His eyes widened. "Your mom's alive? What makes you think that?"

"She is alive." Kale reinforced. "She is a prisoner of Denazen, like I was."

Brandt's eyes went wide and he opened his mouth, but I cut him off. "What about the Reaper? Did you come across anything about him?"

"Nothing on a Reaper, but I didn't have a lot of time. Pretty much skimmed the papers on his desk. Trust me, after what I'd heard, your Dad is the *last* person I want to see." He sighed. "We should head back to my place. We'll tell my Dad. He'll figure out what to do."

"No-can-do. Kale is, um, kinda different."

Brandt folded his arms. Shuffling, he switched feet, placing the left one atop the skateboard and rolling it back and forth. "Define different."

"Kale's important to that place. He's one of those *Sixes*. I can't let Dad find him."

"This isn't a game, Dez."

Why did everyone think I thought that, for Christ sake? "I know!"

"This is bigger than you and me. Bigger than pissing your Dad off. You just met the guy. Why bury yourself in trouble for a stranger?"

"First off, he knows about Denazen and he knows Mom. I'll need all the help I can get if there's any chance to get her out." I took a step forward. "Second, he was a prisoner at Denazen. They used him to kill people."

He paled. "Kill people?"

"My skin is deadly to anything it touches," Kale confirmed as he took my hand.

Brandt stared, horrified. The skateboard stilled under his foot. "Then how come he's touching you? *How* is he touching you?"

"I seem to be immune."

"You seem to be immune," he repeated. "Don't you get it? They'll think you're one of them, too!"

"I can't touch other Sixes," Kale said, voice pained. "They had me try. Over and over again. I killed them all. Every time, I killed them."

Brandt whirled on Kale, shooting him a deadly glare. "Back off, dickhead."

"I'm not leaving him," I said, standing my ground.

"This is stupid, Dez." he snapped, even though I could see from his expression he knew it wouldn't change my mind. "Come back to the house and we'll figure this out."

"I can't. Gotta see this through."

He pulled out a pen. Snatching my hand, he began to write on my palm. "Go here and ask for this Misha Vaugn chick—but be careful. I don't know who she is, or what she does, but her name was in a file on the desk that said *main targets*. If she's one of these people, maybe she can help you. Stay off the grid, Dez. I don't want to have to storm this place to drag your ass out."

That was Brandt. Always had my back. I pulled him into a quick hug, then turned back to Kale. "We should get moving. See if you can find anything else out about that place—but be careful."

He nodded and took a step back.

We made it halfway to the edge of the lot before Brandt cursed. "Crap. Wait, I'll go with—"

Shouting rose in the distance.

We scattered. No time. We were on our own.

5

Kale and I made it into town safely. For all we knew, it wasn't Denazen back at the Graveyard, but no sense in taking chances. This thing was getting bigger by the minute, and the more I found out, the more I wondered how far Dad would go to get Kale back. And what he'd do to me.

The address Brandt gave me was an old hotel about five blocks from the Graveyard. By the time we got there, it was coming up on four p.m. and I was ready to drop. Usually, functioning on little to no sleep wasn't an issue, but the last twenty-four hours had been hell. The woman at the front desk, an overweight brunette wearing way too much perfume, greeted us with a weary smile.

"I'm sorry, but we don't rent rooms to minors." Her eyes traveled over us once, then twice. She gave a curt, dismissive nod and went back to her magazine.

"We're not here to rent a room." I stepped up to the desk, leaning over. "We're looking for Misha Vaugn."

"Have you washed your socks?" the woman asked, standing.

She smoothed her pleated skirt and straightened her dark purple blouse, waiting for our answer.

Confused, I could only stare. Kale answered for me.

"I'm not wearing any." He looked down at his borrowed Timberlands, a worried look on his face. "Is that going to be a problem?"

The woman stammered, obviously not expecting the answer he gave. Huh. Maybe she was one of those people creeped out by bare feet. Or possibly a germaphobe. Either way, the sock thing seemed to be important. "Wait here." She disappeared through a door behind the desk.

Kale watched her go, curiosity evident in his eyes. "What is this place?"

"It's a hotel. People come here to sleep."

"Sleep? But it's so quiet." Confused, he turned and walked away from the desk, inspecting the magazines fanned out across the nearest coffee table. He picked one up and began flipping through it.

I wandered away from the desk, settling down on the couch beside him. "It's not quiet at Denazen?"

"Quiet," he repeated, and tugged at the hem of his borrowed green T-shirt. After a moment, he shook his head. "No it's hardly ever quiet."

There was no elaboration, and I didn't ask. I didn't want to know. What my dad had done to these people—my mom, Kale— was criminal. Locked away from the real world and brainwashed to think it was for his safety, Kale had lived his entire life in captivity. Like an animal. Watching him sit across from me, alternating between flipping through a magazine and glancing at the door every few minutes, caused an ache in my chest.

My mental roller coaster was interrupted by the slamming of a door. Tired and on edge, I jumped to my feet. Kale was up and standing, ready before I could blink. With his arms crossed and his legs braced apart, he looked ready to take on the world. It was actually kind of impressive. If the situation were reversed, I wasn't sure I'd be handling things as smoothly.

A woman with an obviously fake smile approached from behind the desk. She wore no makeup, blonde hair twisted in a tight bun atop her head. Her crisp white, button-down blouse was tucked neatly into her dark blue jeans. Oh, yeah. This chick was wound tight.

Kale stayed where he was. "You are Misha Vaugn?"

The woman rounded the desk, hand extended toward him. "I'm—"

He backpedaled, tripping over the small coffee table and landing across the couch.

The woman watched in confusion, hand hanging in mid-air. She wasn't smiling anymore. "Is something *wrong*?"

I stepped up and took her hand. "I'm Dez, and that's Kale. We're looking for Misha Vaugn."

"So I've heard." Her gaze lingered on me for a moment before returning to Kale, who was getting to his feet. "What's wrong with him?"

Kale scanned the room, and after a moment, found what he'd been searching for. He approached a small potted tree in the corner of the room. A single finger to the tip of one of the leaves was all it took.

After several seconds, the leaf dried and disintegrated. The dryness spread like a disease—down the trunk, and out to the rest of the leaves. They browned and shriveled, falling away one by one, and collecting in piles of dust at the bottom.

The woman gave a sharp nod. "I must thank you for your quick reflexes." She turned and nodded to the door. "If you'll both come with me."

We followed her around the desk and through the door to an elevator. She stepped in, motioning for us to follow, but Kale stopped short. He glared at her and took a step back. "Are there stairs?"

The woman balked. "Of course there are, but we're going—"

"I'll take the stairs."

She looked to me for help, but I only shrugged, stepping off the elevator. Ten minutes later the woman, who introduced herself as Sira by floor four, stopped in front of one of the rooms and pulled out a set of keys. "If you'll wait in here, someone will be along shortly."

She held the door open and once we were inside, closed it behind us. From the other side, I heard the echo of her heels clacking on the linoleum fade.

Kale stared at the two single beds in the middle of the room. With caution, he approached the first, and dropped to his knees. Once satisfied there was nothing there, he moved to the next.

"What are you doing?"

"Checking under the beds."

I rolled my eyes. "I can see that. Why?"

He stood, face serious, and said, "Because that's the first place I'd hide if I wanted to kill someone."

The way he said it made my skin crawl. Like informing me the forecast called for rain.

He sat down and nodded to the large window. "Tell me about your life. Tell me what it's like to live out there."

"There's not much to tell. I'm a screwup—bad grades, always in trouble." I laughed and sat down beside him. "Hell, Dad probably contemplated sending you to punish me on more than one occasion."

He leaned close and ran a finger over my cheek and down to my chin. "You're a good person."

"So are you," I whispered. Then, making a spur of the moment decision, I brushed the lightest of kisses on his left cheek.

He sat up straight, eyes wide, and touched the tip of his index finger to his cheek. "What was that?"

I blushed. "A kiss."

"*That's* what a kiss feels like?"

"Well, technically. There are a lot of different types of—"

"Show me."

"Show you what?"

"Show me some of the other kinds."

"You're *asking* me to kiss you?"

He nodded, hands curled over the edge of the bed. "Is that not right?"

"I—" I didn't know how to respond. Imagine that. Me. Speechless. Glaciers were probably popping up all over hell.

Kale was sitting next to me, eyes full of surprise and hope. Who was I kidding? The guy was gorgeous. Kissing him would by *no* means be an act of mercy.

I leaned in, blood pounding in my ears like the bass in the back of Brandt's Jeep. Our lips were inches apart, breath mingling, when a noise came from the door. We both jumped as a petite redhead entered. Wow. Talk about crappy timing! "You are Dez and Kale, I presume?"

We nodded.

"Good. I am Misha Vaugn. Please, may I ask who sent you to me?"

"My cousin." I stood. Kale did the same. "He…found your name…" …while sneaking thorough some super-secret files in my dad's home office.

"And what exactly do you need my assistance with?"

I hesitated. If Misha wanted to help, then she was against my dad. If she was against Dad, would she really help me? Or by extension, Kale? She might see it as a trap. I probably would.

"We need help, and we don't know where else to turn." I took a deep breath. "I'll be honest with you. My name is Deznee Cross. Marshall Cross is my dad. Do you know who he is?" I held my breath and waited for her to kick us out. She didn't.

"I know of Marshall Cross," she said, disgust evident in her tone. Oh, look. Another fan. "Continue."

"Yesterday, Kale broke away from Denazen. He found me by accident and I helped him escape. I didn't know about my dad and I didn't know about Denazen. I brought Kale back to my house, but my dad came home."

She arched a brow. "I bet that was quite a surprise."

"He attacked Kale and we ran."

"Come here, girl."

Misha Vaugn might have been a slim, petite woman, but boy did she have one hell of a presence. I didn't intimidate easily— usually I was the first one to step up and start something—but this woman freaked me out.

"Give me your hands," she said.

I did. She took them, closing her eyes.

"You helped the boy escape," she said, eyes still closed. I wanted to point out that we'd covered that already but decided against it. A few moments of silence passed before she opened them and released my hands. "The Denazen Corporation uses people like Kale and me for their own purposes. They steal children away from their families and brainwash them." She eyed Kale with sympathy. "They do whatever is necessary to rid them of conscience and humanity. Some of the young ones don't survive their methods. The ones that do are locked up and... *coerced* to do Denazen's bidding. If that doesn't work, they're eliminated."

Kale's voice was whisper low, like a puff of smoke hanging

in the air. "When I was younger, Sue told me to do what they wanted. She said I needed to be blank. I had to do my job or they'd keep hurting me." He pushed the sleeve of his shirt up to reveal a nasty-looking scar. "She would cry when they hurt me. I hated when she cried."

My stomach squeezed and acid bubbled in my throat. What the hell had they done to him? To her? Time for answers. "What are they? I mean, is it government-related or something?"

Misha frowned. "We believe the government is involved, yes, but there's still much we don't know."

"The Reaper?" I asked "My mom told Kale to look for someone called the Reaper. Said he could help. Can you tell us anything about him?"

Misha shook her head. "I have heard of him, but I do not know where he is. The rumor is he was once one of the most dangerous of Denazen's weapons. He is the only one to have escaped their facility and survive." She looked at Kale and smiled. "Until now."

This Reaper guy had escaped Denazen—something I was starting to see was no small feat. If I could find him, he could help get my mom out. He might be my only chance of saving her.

"Who would know where to find him?"

"The Reaper is deep in hiding," she said with a frown. "There are rumors of him being spotted all over the country, but no one knows where he really is."

"No offense, but that doesn't help us at all." Rumors were useless. For all we knew, the Reaper was some urban legend made up to make little Sixes eat their veggies and feel safe.

She leaned over and opened the nightstand drawer. Pulling out a pad of paper and a pen, she scribbled something and tore the page off. "Go to this address and speak with Cole Oster. He may be able to give you more information." She stood. "You are welcome to stay the night, but you must leave at first light. It is too dangerous to have you here, Deznee Cross."

I nodded and thanked her, settling back on the bed.

She made it to the door, before turning and giving Kale a stern look. "Because of the dangerous nature of your gift, I'm afraid I'll need to insist you stay in this room at all times. I do not wish to see any of my guests harmed."

Kale nodded and watched her leave. By the time the door clicked closed, he was sitting beside me again. Warmth soaked through my jeans where he rested a hand on my leg.

"Okay," he said.

"Okay?"

"She's gone."

I glanced back at the door. "Yes, she is." I knew what he was hinting at, and for some reason it made me nervous. Another first. I made guys nervous, not the other way around. I wasn't sure I liked this new turn of events. Expect a guy to notice your new shoes or killer pair of jeans, or hell, even remember your name, and you're asking too much. But if you're about to kiss him? He's a dog with a big juicy bone.

He touched my cheek, smiling. "That was nice."

I sucked in a breath. God he was cute… "Was it?"

He nodded enthusiastically. "What's another kind?"

His grin was infectious. I shifted on the bed till I was sitting sideways, facing him. He did the same.

Reaching out, he grabbed my hand and placed it on his chest, over his heart. "Why does my heart pump faster when we're close? How is it you do that to me?"

Under my fingers, his heart hammered a rhythm that matched my own. I smiled. "Nerves, excitement, fear. Could be a lot of things."

"Nerves?"

"Like when you're worried about something. Nervous."

"I know what nervous is." He took his hand off mine and leaned toward me, pressing it over my heart. I tried not to focus on what his hand was curving around. "Yours is doing the same. Are you nervous?"

"Yeah, I guess I am, a little."

His hand stayed there, but his eyes were on mine now, searching. "Nervous because of me?"

"Yes," I said. "No. I mean, it's complicated."

He leaned back, expression sour. "I don't like that word. Complicated."

I laughed. "No one does, trust me."

"Do I make you afraid?"

The laughter died on my lips. What to say? Yes. I was afraid of him. Terrified, actually. But not for the reasons he thought. Moving his hand, I grabbed his chin. Taking one last gulp of air in an attempt to chase away the butterflies going to town in my stomach, I closed the small distance between us.

Our lips met, warm and soft, and I felt him stiffen. Not *quite* the response I normally got. Reaching up, I slid my fingers along the sides of his face and into his hair. When he still didn't move, I pulled away to look at him. His arms stayed at his sides, knuckles white as he clutched the edge of the bed. Breath coming in heavy pants, he looked down at himself for a moment before grabbing my hand and placing it over his heart again.

"It's even faster now."

So was mine. I leaned in again, kissing him until he relaxed. With a contented sigh, he reached for my waist and drew me closer. After what seemed like forever, I pulled away and smiled.

"We should really get some sleep," I whispered.

Kale frowned. "I'm not tired." He ran his finger along my bottom lip. "I'd like to do that again. Please?"

I chuckled and slipped from his arms. "You're a lot more normal than you think."

"That was like nothing I've ever experienced before. Does it feel like that every time?" He leaned back and swung his feet up without taking the boots off.

"With the right person, probably." I pulled off my sneakers and burrowed under the covers of the other bed. The cheap hotel duvet was rough against my skin. I closed my eyes and tried to imagine it was as soft as my down comforter at home with its homemade, jersey covering, and thick, fluffy filling. The pillow was hard—even with the second one stuffed beneath it. The duffle Brandt had given me was about the same size. I could make it a third pillow but it probably wouldn't work and wasn't worth the headache I'd still have in the morning.

"What was it like for you?"

I leaned over and flicked off the light. A car pulled into the parking lot, headlights shining through the small gap in the drapes. The light sent shadows dancing across the walls.

"It was… different," I admitted with caution.

Across from me, Kale gave a satisfied-sounding *hmm*, and I drifted off to sleep with a goofy smile on my lips.

As promised, we'd left the hotel at first light. The same woman who'd been manning the front desk the night before gave us an overly cheerful wave and thanked us for staying as if we'd been on vacation. Then, when we opened the door, she told us never to return.

Way to be hospitable.

The duffle bag Brandt had given Kale at the Graveyard had one of his blue T-shirts—luckily long-sleeved, a pair of black leather gloves, and two changes of clothes for me. Stuffed into the back pocket of my jeans was forty bucks. I felt bad for Kale having to wear a long-sleeved shirt and gloves in this heat, but better to swelter than unwittingly murder an innocent bystander.

We stood under the awning to wait for the bus—which was late as usual. I cleared my throat. "Look, I know you think you need to find this Reaper guy, but what if you skipped town?" The suggestion made my limbs go numb. I didn't want him to leave, but I'd be a horrible person for not at least suggesting it. Selfish was something I'd never done. If Kale could make it on his own, who was I to try and keep him here?

"Skipped town?"

"Yeah, like, left. I can get you cash and you could book. Get a head start on Denazen."

"And you would come with me?"

I started to pace. "Of course not. Now that I know my mom is alive, I can't leave her. I'm going to find this Reaper and get him to help me save her."

Eyebrows drawn, he shook his head. "Then why would I leave?"

"To be safe? To get away? I have a feeling life in that place was no day at the carnival. Why chance getting sucked back in?"

Kale stood and grabbed my hand. I had to remind myself to keep breathing. "If there is a chance to help Sue and see that you remain free, then it is worth the risk."

Tiny prickles of happy sparked a reaction from every nerve ending in my system. A complicated swell of emotion—something I hadn't felt in, well, ever—came rushing to the surface. I wanted him to elaborate. But of course, the bus picked that moment to roll into the stop.

We paid the fare and took a seat in the back. Kale wasn't happy with the situation from the get-go. He scrunched up his nose and pointed to the woman in front of us. "Why is her hair like that?"

The woman, somewhere in her late twenties if I had to guess, turned and flipped us off.

I smacked Kale's arm and whispered, "They're called dreads. It's a hairstyle."

He didn't lower his voice. "They smell funny."

The woman turned again, this time gearing up to tell us off. Before she could get a word out, I mumbled, "He's foreign. First day in America."

She muttered something justifiably rude and turned back in her seat.

"Social Behavior 101..." I said, leaning close. "Don't point out how other people look."

He raised his eyebrows in confusion, and I sighed.

The bus dropped us off about three blocks from the address Misha had given me. The timing was perfect. In the short trip, Kale managed to piss off a pregnant woman by calling her *large* and a goth kid for inquiring about his makeup. If we hadn't gotten off the bus when we did, there probably would have been a riot.

The strip was busy—summer was just getting started, and I felt better about being out in public. No way would Dad send his goons to attack us with all these people here to see it. At least, that's what I hoped.

About two blocks away, Kale reached down and took my hand. At first, I freaked, thinking he'd taken it to pull me out of the way, or possibly to get my attention, but when my gaze skittered to his, panic thick in my throat, he wasn't even looking at me. His eyes were trained on the sidewalk ahead, speed casual.

I waited, positive he'd let go...but he didn't. When he caught me staring at our clasped hands, his brow furrowed. "What's wrong?"

"I—nothing, I—" I felt like an idiot. I hadn't stammered like a moron because of a guy since the age of thirteen. I *definitely* didn't love this new turn of events.

"This is correct, right?" He raised our hands, fingers still laced together. He nodded to an older couple approaching, hands clasped and laughing. "This is what people do here?"

"It's a little more complicated than that."

"Everything seems complicated here," he grumbled.

"That's life," I laughed. "Life *is* complicated."

"And that's good?"

I nodded. "That's good."

He let this settle for a moment before squeezing my hand. "Explain what I did wrong. With the hand thing."

I sighed. If I had to have the sex talk with a guy my own age, I was going to die. Baseball analogies wouldn't work. He probably didn't even know what baseball was. "When two people like each other, they hold hands."

He looked down at our hands, still confused. "You helped me, so I do like you."

Was it this hard for parents? "No, it's a different kind of like. Like when two people want to be more than friends. Like, do *more* than just hold hands."

"More? Like what?"

Oh. My. God. This was so not happening. "There's *like*, as in you enjoy hanging out with someone, and then there's *like*, as in they make you feel special. Happy. The kissing type of *like*."

His eyes lit up. "Should I kiss you instead of holding your hand?"

My heart responded with a thumping, *yes!*

"I'm not explaining this right. People kiss when they're attracted to each other. It makes them feel…nice."

"Touching you makes me happy. It feels nice." His grin widened. "The kiss last night was *very* nice."

I sighed and gave him a small smile. This was a circular conversation and my brain was starting to overheat. All this talk of kissing and Kale looking at me with those amazing blue eyes… *Focus!* "I'm sure it *does* feel nice. But I think you like it because I'm the only person you can touch."

He was quiet for a few minutes before answering. "Possibly."

Something inside me twisted. I'd suggested it because it was logical, but still, I wanted him to insist I was wrong—which kind of bugged me. Now was not the time for crush obsession.

We walked the rest of the way in silence. Parkview was a pretty small place. I'd been to a party a few times in this general area. It was nice. Suburban. Mostly cute houses with well-manicured lawns and tacky plastic animals playing sentry.

As we approached Cole Oster's address, the neighborhood darkened. The homes became dreary and run down. Cole lived in a dilapidated, blue Cape Cod at the end of a cul-de-sac called Last Chance Lane. The name, like the house, didn't fill me with confidence. We made our way up the rickety steps and knocked on the door. After several moments, a short, balding man somewhere in his late forties popped his head out. "Yes?"

"Are you Cole Oster?"

"Who wants to know?" he snapped.

"Misha Vaugn gave us your name. We're looking for the Reaper."

"Go away." He slammed the door in our faces.

I knocked again, this time harder. When he didn't answer, I began kicking at the door with my right foot. "The longer we stand on your front step, the better the chance of Denazen finding us here. Do you really want Denazen dropping by for tea, Mr. Oster?"

That changed his mind. No more than a minute later, the locks on the door jiggled, and he pulled it open. "Hurry up and get inside." As we stepped in, he mumbled something about having a very stern conversation with Misha in the near future. "I'm not inviting you to sit, so make it fast."

I looked past the hallway and into the living room. Scattered takeout containers, beer cans, and plates—all with various stages of mold growth—greeted me. "Well, then let me thank you." I waved at a fly. It was one of many buzzing over my head. Maybe I was wrong. There was a very real possibility that the smell emanating from Cole Oster's home would be enough to keep Denazen at bay. "This place is disgusting."

"Did you come here to insult me?"

"Where can we find the Reaper?" Kale asked.

"I haven't seen him in years." Cole wandered across the hall to the living room. Picking up a questionable-looking piece of cheese, he took a bite. I bit back a gag.

"But you *have* seen him?" I said, hope swelling inside my chest.

Cole gave me an offhanded wave and wandered back into the hall. "Of course I've seen him." He hesitated. "Well, I've spoken to him, anyway."

"Spoken to him?"

"More like written to him."

He'd written to him? Like what, Santa Claus? "Let's go, Kale. This is a waste of time."

We turned to leave, but Cole called to us. "Wait. What do you want with him?"

"Denazen is holding my mom prisoner. Since he's supposed to be the only one to get out alive, I need his help to save her."

"I'll tell you what I know, but don't get too excited. It isn't much."

"Anything you have will be helpful since we've got zilch," I said, looking for a clean spot on the wall to lean. There wasn't one. I'd never rib Brandt about being a slob again.

"The last I heard, he—" Cole stopped mid-sentence. He looked from Kale to me, face going from confused to horrified. Eyes wide, he spread his arms to reveal a slowly spreading stain, bright red, in the middle of his chest. He sputtered something I couldn't quite understand and fell to his knees. I dove to catch him, grabbing his shoulder right before he hit the ground. "Ale…"

"We need to go," Kale said.

Cole gasped for air. "Alex Mo—"

Kale tried to wrestle me from the ground but I pulled away and gripped Cole's stained Metallica T-shirt in my fists. "Alex who?"

A tremor shook him, ending in a body-wracking cough. He sucked in a shallow breath. "Alex Mojourn," he rasped, eyes closing and chest falling still.

"Alex Mojourn?" I stammered, releasing his shirt. Kale yanked me to my feet and dragged me toward the exit, which was a good twelve feet away. "Did he say *Alex Mojourn?*"

The door exploded inward, sending bits and pieces of wood rocketing in every direction. The Denazen flunkies stomped in, armed with tranq guns.

"Down," Kale shouted, and everything slowed.

He wrapped his arm around my waist and spun me away from the front door. We took one step, and the room ahead exploded in a barrage of suits and chaos. Something flew at us. Kale's hand moved up my back and trailed along my spine. His touch was anything but urgent. It skimmed, feather light, stopping between my shoulders. With a single push, he sent me forward, to the floor. I felt the object—another damn dart—disturb the air above my hair, but sail harmlessly by. It smacked against the wall and thumped to the floor with a tiny clink. The duffle slipped from my hand as I reached for the dart. As a last resort, maybe I could use it to help get us out of there.

They were at our front and back now, like at Curd's house, only their numbers had increased. A lot. There were at least five in front of us, and I didn't dare look behind. This was the kind of thing you saw in the movies. It didn't happen in real life.

They held their ground, the ones wearing the protective leotards pushing to the front.

"We're so screwed," I whispered. To our right, the small living room opened up to the hallway we were standing in, and had a single closed door at the other end. I didn't know where it led or if it was locked—or if we'd even make it there before they overtook us. We were trapped.

One of them came forward. Kale's reaction was instant. His right hand snaked out, arcing with lightning speed and connecting with the man's chest. With a strangled cough, he gasped for air and collapsed at our feet. Kale slammed his foot down with frightening force, stopping a fraction of an inch from his attacker's jaw.

Eyes wide, he whispered, "Please…"

Kale made a low noise in the back of his throat. He turned away and snatched the bag from the floor. His hand found mine and, one step at a time, he backed us into the living room. He must have seen the door too, because we were edging our way toward it.

Before I could blink, Kale had the door open and with a sharp tug on my arm, pulled me through. In one quick swoop, he locked the door behind us and we were flying up a dark staircase. It bought us a few precious seconds, but I had no delusions a simple locked door would hamper these men for long.

I lost my footing for a second and reached out to grip the railing. The dart slipped from my grasp. It clattered to the floor and tumbled down the stairs, bouncing when it hit the landing. Crap. I made a move to retrieve it, but Kale pulled my arm and kept us moving forward.

We reached the top of the stairs and had a choice—a room on either side. Kale didn't hesitate. He made a sharp right turn and swept us in. Without as much as a three-second pause, he went to the window, pried it open, and knocked out the screen.

A loud bang rose from the door downstairs. They'd broken through.

I made a beeline for the open window, but Kale stopped me. He pressed a finger to his lips and dragged me to the closet on the other side of the room. We tucked ourselves in and quietly closed the door as feet pounded up the stairwell, and within seconds, tromped across the floor.

"Get people outside, now!" one of them yelled. More rushing feet, then silence.

I didn't dare make a move to open the door. My pulse thundered in my ears and a cool wave of panic washed over me. Still. We just needed to stay perfectly still. After a few minutes, I began to relax. Kale leaned forward, shifting my hair to the side, and rubbed his cheek against mine. Not the kind of nuzzle a guy would try when fishing for a kiss—different. Innocent. But that didn't change my reaction to it. Forget the footsteps downstairs and the yelling outside. I was hyper-aware of Kale standing behind me, breath disturbing the tiny hairs on the back of my neck. I needed to explain personal boundaries to him.

After a few minutes, he slid around me and cracked open the closet door. All clear. We crept to the window and, one leg at a time, climbed out onto the roof of the attached garage. We dropped to our knees and crawled on all fours to the edge. Peeking over, I saw there were still a few men milling about, but the bulk of them seemed to have dissipated.

"Do you think you can make it to the hood of that van?" Kale asked, pointing to a rusting old white VW van beneath us.

I nodded.

"I'll go first. I can catch you."

I didn't tell him I was in no need of catching.

Lowering himself down, he hit the top of the van with a soft but audible thud. Immediately, he dropped to his stomach and peered over the edge to make sure he hadn't been spotted. Once satisfied the coast was clear, he waved to me.

I peaked over the edge. The van was doable, but like Kale, I'd make a sound when hitting it. He hadn't noticed, but two Denazen men had rounded the corner right after he dropped down. Chances were, they weren't within earshot, but it wasn't a risk I was willing to take.

Kale waved again. I pointed to the front of the house where the two men stood, watching the street. His lips twisted into an annoyed frown. When he looked back at me, I motioned for him to stay put and disappeared over the edge. A quick scan through the window and into the room told me there was nothing I could use as a makeshift rope. There were no curtains on the window and the bed had been stripped. I'd have to drop down into the grass and hope for the best.

Back to the edge, I scanned the yard a final time and saw the men were still in the same position. I caught Kale's attention and pointed to the grass behind the van. He nodded and slid off the van roof.

I gripped the outer edge of the roof and lowered myself down. After a second, I let go. The fall was short, but the landing still jarred a bit. Nothing like the skateboard off the barn, though.

We stepped away from the garage and started around the house, but I was paying more attention to what was going on behind us than in front. I ran right into a pair of garbage cans. It wouldn't have been so bad if they'd been the plastic kind— but that would have been too easy. These were the good old-fashioned metal ones, complete with toppling lids that danced and clattered when they hit the concrete.

Shouts from the front of the house told us we'd been caught.

"Hurry," Kale hissed as he dragged me along. I tried my best to keep up, but his legs were longer.

They were behind us—I didn't need to look back to know that. We cut through Cole's yard, hopping the fence and landing in a patch of his neighbor's flowers. Stumbling forward, we were out and running, jumping over toys left strewn about their yard. Just beyond us, a thick patch of forest waited. If we could make it, we might be able to lose them.

Kale paused, looking to his left, then right. "This way," he said, breathing barely labored. Me on the other hand, I was gasping for air. *Note to self—join a gym.*

We made it to the middle of the lawn and skidded to a stop behind an aboveground pool. The smell of chlorine mingling with fresh-cut grass made my nose itch.

"If we head into the woods, we can lose them," I urged.

Kale peered around the edge of the pool, sighing. "I know what those men are capable of. I know what they'll do to get me back. If I run, they will follow. It will allow you to escape."

Anger bubbled in my chest. "We went through this at the bus stop. There's no way I'm walking away from this. Not if my mom is out there. Plus, someone needs to make my dad pay for what he's done. You could have bailed to save yourself, but you stayed. No way am I ditching you now. We're in this together. All the way."

Kale was quiet for a moment. With one last peek, he nodded. "Let's go then."

We began to inch away from the side of the pool when the brush in front of us started to rustle and shake. "Crap!" I flattened myself against the wall of the pool, thinking they had us surrounded again for sure, but what stepped out from the brush wasn't a man in a suit—or a leotard. In fact, it wasn't a man at all.

A scream caught in my throat.

Kale regarded the party's new guest with clinical interest— not fear. "Is that a—"

"Bear!" I squeezed his arm, trying to remember how to breathe. In. Out. In. Hold. "It's a frigging bear!"

7

"It looks much bigger than in the Encyclopedia," Kale said, leaning forward a bit. For a second, I thought he was going to reach out and touch the thing. "Maybe it won't see us."

"Won't see us? It's staring *right at us!* Look at its face! It's thinking about a tasty afternoon snack!" This was the fourth one I'd seen in two weeks. Parkview really had to do something about the growing bear population. Pretty soon they'd be taking over.

The bear ambled forward a few steps, making a loud keening sound. It was about four feet away when the Denazen men rounded the corner of the pool. One of them let out a loud yelp — Denazen must have picked these guys for their bravery — (not) — causing the bear to look from us to them. The man in front, obviously clueless about how to deal with a bear, fired his tranq gun at the large animal. The dart hit the bear in the shoulder. Idiot. One tranq dart was not going to take down a *bear*. It was only going to piss it off. Letting out a roar, the bear rose onto its back legs, swatting paws tipped with wicked long claws at the men.

That was our chance. With their attention on the bear, I grabbed Kale's hand and darted into the woods. Shouts behind us told me we were still being followed, but I was hoping we'd gotten enough of a head start to put some distance between us.

We ran. Kale nimbly dodging bushes and low hanging branches—me, not so much. Several times I stumbled, only to have Kale catch me at the last minute. His reflexes were insane. We came to the edge of the woods, stopping for only a fraction of a second before sprinting across the road to Parkview Mall.

"It's crowded in there. They won't be able to make a scene." I started forward, but Kale hesitated. "What's wrong?"

He looked down at his hands and shook his head. "It's too risky."

"Your skin is mostly covered. Unless you plan on rubbing your face on people, we'll be fine."

He still didn't look sure.

"I promise, we'll be careful." I took his hand and squeezed. "I'll make sure you don't hurt anyone."

After another moment, he nodded, and we speed-walked through the entrance. A woman at the perfume kiosk spritzed customers as they walked by, trying to sucker them into spending their hard-earned cash. As we approached and she held up the bottle, ready to attack, I said, "If you want to keep your fingers, put down the bottle."

She mumbled something about mall security and turned to pounce on the next customer.

When we rounded the corner of the main drag, I took a second to check behind us. Two of the suits were just entering the building. School had officially ended last week, so while not as crowded as a weekend, there were still a fair number of bodies.

But they still saw us.

"Move!" I pushed Kale ahead and we took off into the crowd. Surging forward, he pulled his sleeves down over the tips of his fingers for extra protection. We ducked into the first store we came to—Victoria's Secret. I grabbed a teddy from a rack and pulled Kale into the back by the dressing rooms. After a few seconds, I poked my head around the corner. One of the Denazen guys passed, peeking into the storefront as he went. He walked by without coming in.

"One down," I said, turning to Kale. He wasn't paying attention. His gaze was fixed on the red silk baby doll in my hand.

"What is this?" he asked, rubbing the satiny material between his fingers.

"Clothes," I said. "For women."

His eyes widened. "Girls wear this?"

"Yeah, but usually not for long," I chuckled.

Kale turned as red as the teddy. "Are you going to wear this now?"

"Umm. No," I said, blushing.

He seemed a little disappointed and I stifled a laugh.

"Come on, let's get out of here. Maybe we can double back and hit the exit without being seen."

Of course, that plan failed miserably. No sooner did we step from the shop than the other suit walked by. We stopped and eyed each other. It was easy to see he didn't know what to do. Lunge for us and make a scene? Or let us walk away and follow.

"Kid," he said. "You have no idea what you're getting involved in. This person is a murderer."

I adjusted my grip on Brandt's duffle bag, the straps digging into my palm. Swinging the bag at him was tempting, but it wouldn't do nearly enough damage. A few feet away there was a toy kiosk. Waddling back and forth on the floor was a radio-controlled robot roughly the same size as the duffle. It was probably heavier—which meant more damage—but I couldn't use it. Not in this crowd. "He's a murderer because *you* people made him that way. Something tells me you're more dangerous to me than he is."

He took a step forward, and I smiled.

"One more step and I'll scream my head off that you grabbed my ass. You might be able to talk your way out of it—after a few minutes. We'll be long gone by then though."

The man frowned. "Your father is worried about you."

Somewhere in the closed-off, dark corner of my soul, I wanted it to be true. I ached for it—to be Dad's *sunshine smile girl* again. But I wasn't. And I never would be. He'd turned me into his *big nightmare walking*—the bane of his existence. Now all that was left was for him to reap the benefits. "Maybe he should have thought about that when he lied about my mom."

"You're making a big mistake."

I shrugged and took a step back. "Wouldn't be the first, and definitely wouldn't be the worst. Ask my dad, I've had a few doozies."

He glared at me, but after a few moments of silence, stepped aside. "You still have to leave the mall."

"I'm not worried." I said, taking Kale's hand. I hoped the suit couldn't see the lie. As we walked away two more men join him. Just ahead was a fourth.

He passed us with a simple nod of his head and a wink, and when I glanced back over my shoulder, they were all following. They couldn't have looked less casual if they'd been flipping coins and whistling.

We paused in front of the Jade Panda jewelry kiosk. The girl behind the counter snapped her gum and flipped open a magazine. Perfect. I leaned across the counter, waving my hand to get her attention.

She gave an exaggerated sigh and slammed the magazine shut. "Yeah?"

"Listen, I don't want to freak anyone out, but I think you should call security."

Her expression brightened. "Oh?"

I nodded my head to the left where the group of Denazen guys were huddled, now standing off to the side. "See those suits over there?"

The girl, whose nametag said Frankie, nodded. "The ones in the Armani knockoffs?"

"Yeah. I overheard them talking. Something about"—I leaned in closer and whispered dramatically—"a *bomb*."

Instead of what one might consider a normal reaction—wide eyes and gasping—Frankie grinned and picked up the phone. She spoke quietly into the receiver, sneaking glances at the men who were still standing in a clump to the side.

It only took mall security a few minutes to get down to the kiosk. They spoke with Frankie—who made it seem like *she* was the one who heard them talking about the bomb—and approached the men.

Confusion erupted, and a crowd started to gather. It was exactly what we needed to slip away.

Score one for us!

• • •

Kale leaned back and closed his eyes.

I readjusted myself, trying to get comfortable. Kind of hard to do scrunched inside a plastic playground tube, but I was determined. Luckily, the jeans I'd changed into had gone through the wash with some spare change in the pockets. When we'd left the mall, I found a pay phone and called a few friends, trying to find a place for us to crash but had no luck. Briefly, I thought of heading back to Misha's, but the look on the desk clerk's face as we walked out the door was enough to sink that idea dead in the water. In the end, we ended up at Prospect Park, in the Mill Street section of the playground. We'd gotten in before they locked the gates, so I felt fairly safe no one would find us.

I settled back, across from Kale. "Tell me what Denazen is like?"

"Please don't ask me that," he whispered.

"Is it painful? To talk about, I mean? Bad memories?"

Across from me, he opened his eyes. "It's—unpleasant. Why do you want to hear about it?"

"Were you—I mean, did they keep you in a cage?"

For a minute, I didn't think he'd answer. I felt bad for pushing it, but I wanted to know more. Needed to know. My mom was in there.

Jaw tight, he said, "Not all the time, no."

I swallowed. "But some of the time?"

His fingers twitched. One by one, he started flicking them. "I was... *difficult* as a child. I resisted. Fought them. But they have their *methods* of gaining control."

The quiet fury in his voice made my blood run cold. I wanted to know what *methods* they had, but didn't dare ask.

"After awhile, I was allowed to live with Sue in her unit as long as I behaved." He laughed. "I see now that they were trying to keep me pacified because they couldn't control me."

My stomach twisted. "So my mom wasn't locked up?"

He frowned. "Denazen uses any method necessary to ensure control. Some are brainwashed into thinking their assignments are doing good. Helping people. While others, the not so pliable, are forced. There was no need to keep Sue locked up. Cross kept her a prisoner with a single threat."

What would be enough to keep someone in such a horrible place, doing such horrible things?

Then it hit me. "Dad threatened to hurt me."

"She would have done anything for them to keep you safe, as I would have done anything to keep her safe." He reached across and grabbed my hand. "And now, you as well."

As comforting as it was, I pulled free from his grasp. "Me? Why me?"

"Because you are brave. Strong. Not easily broken." He leaned back, closing his eyes again. "You're like me. You make me feel…nice."

I couldn't stop the smile that threatened to overtake my face. Situation aside, Kale made me feel kind of nice, too.

Despite the cramped space, my eyes grew heavy. Kale's voice, the warmth of his body so close to mine, was soothing. A strange way to look at things considering our circumstance, but there it was. Despite Denazen scouring the city—and from the look on Dad's face when Kale and I ran, I knew they were—I felt pretty safe here with him. Kale was different from anyone I'd ever met. Sure, he'd spent his entire life thinking he was nothing more than a killer, but it was more than that.

Or maybe it wasn't.

Despite the life he'd endured, Kale was a *good* person. Fiercely loyal and courageous. To have lived through what he had and still have those qualities… It was amazing, not to mention miraculous. He'd called me brave and strong? I couldn't hold a candle to him.

I closed my eyes and let my mind wander. The last forty-eight hours of my life had been crazy with a heaping side of fail. How could I have not seen this coming? How could I have not known? The whole thing had been under my nose the entire time. I wondered what the FML post would look like.

Today, when my father tried to shoot me, I found out he was an assassin monger who's been keeping my mom locked away in a secret facility for freaky killers. FML.

Seriously. F.M.L.

8

I woke up the next morning with a serious case of have-to-pee-
now. The rain splashing against the ground outside didn't help.
I'd drifted off to sleep curled up next to Kale. When I opened my
eyes, he was at the edge of the tube, watching the rain. Every few
moments, he'd reach out and let it fall across his skin.

"I've never felt anything like it," he said without turning.
How he'd known I was awake was a mystery. He pushed up the
sleeves of his borrowed blue shirt, now soaked. "It's cold and wet,
yet still pleasant."

"You've never been in the rain before?"

He shrugged, but said nothing.

Never out in the rain? Jesus. Each minute I spent with Kale
made me question my perception of reality. How the hell had I
missed seeing who Dad really was? Maybe, deep down, I hadn't.
I'd chosen to hide things from him at an early age. Keep certain
parts of myself a secret. Suddenly I wondered if maybe—just
maybe—a part of me recognized him for what he truly was right

from the start. A monster. "We better get moving."

"Moving to where?"

I went to pull my phone from my back pocket to text Brandt, but remembered I'd smashed it. Great. Cut off. Digging into the duffle bag I'd miraculously been able to hold onto during everything, I pulled out the remaining cash and stuffed it in my back pocket. "I'm starved. Let's go see what time it is, get some noms, and go find Alex Mojourn."

Kale climbed from the tube, then leaned over to help me out. If possible, the rain fell harder now. We were soaked almost instantly. Fantastic. Now on top of homeless chic, I'd be rocking the drowned rat look.

Kale didn't seem to mind. He shook his head, sending droplets out in every direction. "Where do we look? The man died before telling us where to find this person."

I sighed and brushed soggy bangs away from my face. "I know where he is."

By the time we'd found a clock and gotten breakfast, it was almost ten. The strip was chaos, and normally that would have been a comfort, but today every passing face filled me with suspicion. The sour-faced chick who'd served us our coffee, the homeless man taking a leak on his own shoes, even the little old lady with the warm smile walking her toy poodle. My new sense of paranoia said they were all possible Denazen spies. At one point, I'd been convinced that the two preteen kids trailing behind us, eating ice cream, were Dad's minions.

Roudey's Pool Hall didn't open until noon to the public, but it was a little-known fact that he kept the back entrance unlocked early for regulars. Or at least he used to—I hadn't been to the pool hall in a long time.

Kale trailed close behind as I skirted around the rusted dumpster and stacks of discarded chalk boxes that littered the side of the building. I steered us through the garbage-infested alley with my hand clamped over my mouth as we made our way to the back door. A quick twist of the knob told me little had changed. Pushing it open, I gestured Kale inside and followed.

From the back room, I could hear thumping beats accompanied by a rough voice screaming in tune. I was all for the hard stuff, but Screamo? So not my scene. Laughing and hooting, followed by a distinctly female giggle, floated over the music. I walked into the main room, Kale a hulking presence beside me.

For a moment, no one noticed me. Normally, I'd stroll into a room like I owned the place, but here... Here, things were different. A year ago I swore never to set foot in this place again, and had it not been a matter of life and death I would have kept that pact. This was where I'd first met Alexander Mojourn. This was where it all began.

And where it all ended.

A sharp whistle split the air, snapping me back to the here and now. Time to focus. I was here for a reason—I had a purpose.

"Dez, baby, long time no see," a tall redheaded boy called out, crossing the floor in three sweeping steps. He threw his arms around me, lifting my feet off the floor.

I returned the embrace with a quick squeeze and pulled away when he set me down. "Nice to see you too, Tommy."

At the front, on a stool behind the counter, the owner, Roudey, gave me a small nod and an inconspicuous wink. He watched the room while polishing one of his billiard trophies. I smiled back. Others did the same, calling out greetings and waving in acknowledgment, though thankfully none as enthusiastic as Tommy. Most of the faces were familiar. There were some new additions of course, but the same names were still among them, a little older with more miles of bad road stretching out across their faces. I searched the small crowd until I found the one we were looking for. The one I least wanted to see.

A mop of spiky, white-blond hair, striking hazel eyes, and a labret with a yellow beaded smiley face nicknamed Fred.

Alex Mojourn.

He'd seen me enter the room but remained in the corner. As I approached him, I could feel eyes on me. I tried to come off casual as I strode across the room. Somewhere in the world, pigs were flying, goats were dancing, and little green men were shaking hands with the president. Time to tune it all out.

"I need to talk to you." I kept my face blank while holding his gaze. He'd taught me that. Show nothing.

Still, he didn't speak. He looked from me to Kale, eyes narrowing slightly, before nodding toward one of the private rooms behind the tables and off in the back.

Several familiar faces waved as we walked by, but I ignored them. This was a part of my past. One I had no intention of revisiting. At one time I might have missed these people but not anymore. I was over the whole scene.

"You look good," Alex said as he closed the door behind Kale.

I ignored the compliment. I wasn't here to reminisce. "Cole Oster sent me." I didn't offer anything further because I wanted to see his reaction. His eyes widened—just a bit—before he nodded in acknowledgment of the name. Typical Alex. "We've gotten into some trouble with Denazen, and he said you could help us find the Reaper."

His reaction wasn't what I expected. In fact, he was pretty much reactionless, which proved I never knew him as well as I thought. He gave Kale a casual-once over. "You a Six?"

Kale either didn't notice or ignored Alex's condescending tone and simply nodded.

I felt my fingers twitch. I wanted to hit Alex. Like I'd hit him the last time we'd spoken—ironically, in this very room. "You know about Denazen?" I kept my voice even—not wanting him knowing anything he'd said or lied about in the past bothered me anymore.

This was B-movie perfection. Uber evil corporation, complete with brainless muscle and evil plot to take over the world. Everyone was in on it except the poor, helpless, beautiful girl.

Okay. Not helpless, but definitely beautiful. No. Scratch that. *Hot.*

He ignored my question, still focused on Kale. "What'd you do to get on their radar?"

"Radar?" Kale asked, confused. "Like an ocean ship?"

"He escaped," I snapped, stepping between them.

Alex's eyes went wide. "Escaped?" He jerked forward, seizing my arm to pull me away.

In a flash Kale towered beside me, reaching for Alex.

"NO!" I cried, wrenching from Alex's grasp and pulling back on Kale's shirt simultaneously. Just in time to prevent contact. Kale was wearing gloves, but accidents could still happen. "No," I repeated.

"He was hurting you," Kale said calmly, looking down at my fingers on his wrist. His sleeve had ridden up so my hand rested on bare skin. Turning, he glared at Alex with disgust. "He was going to strike you."

That got a reaction. Alex's face flushed red, and his fists clenched tight at his sides. "Strike her? What the hell is wrong with you?" He stared. "I'd never *hit* her!"

Kale wasn't looking at me anymore. It was all about Alex. "You were hurting her," he snarled, stepping forward. "It *hurts* to be grabbed like that." His voice was low and dangerous. It sent a chill down my spine—and not the scared type, either.

"It's fine, Kale. Alex wasn't going to hurt me. He was

surprised, that's all. Right, Alex?"

Alex's eyes drifted from Kale's face to my fingers still restraining his wrist. "What's his touch do?"

I guess he knew me well enough to know that if it had been simply a matter of Kale pummeling him, I would have stepped back and enjoyed the show. Maybe gone to get popcorn. The fact that I'd stopped him said enough.

"Death touch," I said, easing my fingers off Kale's wrist. Instead of letting my hand fall to the side, Kale laced his fingers with mine.

Alex took it all in, lips pressed tight. "I guess I owe you an apology."

"Yeah," I said softly. "You do." He meant grabbing me—I meant something else. "How do you know about Denazen?"

Alex waved his right hand at a discarded soda can sitting on one of the bar stools across the room. The can shot forward, rocketing into the wall next to Kale's head. Kale didn't flinch.

"Telekinetic." Of course. And the cheesy plot thickens. God. Someone kill me now.

"There are many of you," Kale snorted. "When one disobeys, they *retire* you and pull in another. There is nothing special about you."

A wicked smile spread across Alex's lips. "Yeah? Well at least I can touch—" He looked down at our intertwined hands. "Wait, didn't you say—?"

"When he tried to kill me, we found out I was immune." I said it mostly for shock value. Boy did it work.

Alex froze. The vein on the side of his neck bulged and the top corner of his lip curled upward as he squinted his right eye. I knew that look—the Elvis, I used to call it. There were times that look and the fire that came with it could turn my knees to soft-serve ice cream. Now? It made me angry.

"Tried to kill you? Dez, what the hell have you gotten yourself into?"

"We need to find the Reaper."

Alex shook his head. "Tell me what's going on."

"Like I said, we're looking for the Reaper. Do you know where we can find him or not?"

The stubborn set of his jaw told me he wanted to argue, but I guessed he knew better. Very few people won an argument with me. I'd learned from the best.

"I don't know where he is, but there are some people that might."

I waited, but he said nothing. "Well?"

I could tell he wanted to yell, but he kept it under control. That was new. Self-control wasn't something the guy had in spades. "You're not going to tell me what's going on?"

I glared right back. "Why should I? You didn't feel the need to tell me you were screwing that college girl behind my back."

9

I'd met Alex Mojourn right after I turned fifteen. It was right before he dropped out of school. He was seventeen and a junior, having been left back at one point in grade school, and I was a sophomore.

Honor student, bookworm, good girl—these were all terms used to describe me back then. I was shy and kept to myself—didn't have many friends. I did my homework, and obeyed all the rules. But for some reason, Alex took notice of me. When he deemed me worthy of his attention, well, I just about fell all over myself with excitement. We started dating—he took me to parties, we hung out with all his friends.

He was my first boyfriend, my first love, my first kiss—my first *everything*. When I was sixteen, I caught him undressing some bimbo from the local college in the back room of Roudey's, and he became my first heartbreak.

We'd seen each other plenty since then, mainly because we traveled the same raver circle. Each time, though, we'd stay on opposite ends of the room. Seeing him was hard. Talking to him, that was even harder. Finding out he'd lied about something else? Pretty much devastating.

But was that good enough? Of course not. Fate seemed to have it in for me, because we had to meet him *again*, later that night.

After a bit more arguing—and no apology for past transgressions—he finally agreed to introduce us to the people he knew. We set it up to meet him inside the park behind the pool hall at nine o'clock.

There was no other choice.

"Tell me more," Kale said as he sat next to me on the grass. We'd left the pool hall and grabbed sodas and sandwiches from a sandwich shop in town and settled under a large pine tree behind the building.

"What do you want to know?"

"Tell me what it was like to grow up here." He glanced from the sky to my face, a little sad. "Free."

"How about we have a conversation that doesn't involve me doing all the talking? You can ask me a question, then I get to ask you one."

"Me?" He looked surprised—then worried.

I looked away. "I want to know how *you* grew up."

This seemed to horrify him. "Why? I told you what a horrible place it was."

"Because…"

He scowled and folded his arms. His expression changed—not angry, really—more like frustrated. "My world wasn't pretty. It was dark and loud and full of pain. I do not understand why you keep asking."

"It's what people do. You know, when they're… interested."

"Interested?"

"I want to know about your past. It makes you who you are."

His lips twisted into an angry snarl, and he jumped to his feet. "It doesn't make me who I am. That place has nothing to do with who I am. Sue swore to me—"

I let the turkey sub fall to the grass and sprang to my feet. Grabbing his hands, I said, "You misunderstood me. I didn't mean that as a bad thing." I sank back to the ground and pulled him with me. "All the things Denazen did, all they put you through, it made you strong. You came out of that place in one piece. You're not a drooling zombie or a crazed, machete-wielding maniac. That's a lot more than others can say, I bet."

A glimmer of something danced behind ice blue eyes. Sadness and maybe a small spark of hope. I died a little at the thought of him locked away from the rest of the world. "I couldn't miss what I never had. But now that I know…" He brought his hand to my face and let it trail down my neck and under my shirt to my bare shoulder. Looking away, he said, "Please don't ask me about that place again. I don't *want* you to know what my life was like before."

I could have argued. Hell, I argued about everything. But the agony in his voice made me sick. I needed to know what they did to him—to Mom—but I couldn't stand to see him hurting over it.

Leaning back against the tree, I tilted my head sideways so it rested against his shoulder.

I started by telling him about the first time I'd done something stupid to get Dad's attention. "It wasn't long after Dad started working longer hours at Denazen, and I'd been feeling kind of neglected." I sighed and picked at the edge of my sub. "He was distant and cold—sometimes he was downright mean. I didn't understand. For awhile I thought it was me. That I'd disappointed him somehow… It'd been my brilliant idea that sliding down the stairs on a plastic sled—to show him how brave I so obviously was—would fix all that. I was eight at the time and ended up breaking my right arm."

"Did he think you were brave?"

I laughed. "He thought some colorful things—brave was *not* one of them."

Kale played with a strand of my hair. He wrapped it around his pointer finger, let it unravel, and then wrapped it again. "So you used to be close with him?"

"I wouldn't say close—normal is more like it. He went to work, came home, and asked me what I'd learned in school. I did my homework and watched TV with him." I shrugged. "Normal stuff. But there was always this…barrier…between us."

I pulled a piece of turkey from the sub and popped it into my mouth. It was dry and tasted rubbery. Processed. Nothing beat the real thing. "It was like he was keeping me at a distance on purpose. I used to think it was because I looked so much like Mom—but I guess I know now that wasn't true…" I sighed. "When I started hanging with Alex and his friends, getting into more and more trouble, I thought for sure he'd have some kind of reaction."

"And he didn't?"

I pulled another piece of turkey from the sub, but this time instead of eating it, I tossed it across the lawn. A pigeon swooped down immediately and snatched it away. "Nope. Sure, he'd yell and scream, but it was all empty. You could tell. He wasn't really into it. Like he was doing it because it's what was expected."

Kale thought about this for a moment, then frowned. "Let's not talk about him anymore. Tell me about something else. A secret no one else knows."

A secret no one else knew. I had one—and it was a game changer—but since Alex, trust didn't come easy. With Kale though, the thought of sharing the deepest, darkest part of myself felt exciting and not terrifying. Still, I couldn't get the words out. Not yet anyway. I stopped picking at my sandwich and moved Kale's hand onto my lap. Turning it over, I pulled blades of grass from the ground one by one and watched them disintegrate in his palm. The remains would hover for several seconds before fluttering away in the breeze. Every few pieces, I'd stop and trace circles across his open palm.

After a while, Kale cleared his throat. "School. Tell me about school."

I blinked. "Are you serious?"

"Sue used to tell me about a place where people my own age gather to learn. It always fascinated me." He smiled. "What was your favorite part?"

I gave him a lopsided grin. "Well, there's this class called detention…"

. . .

"I don't like him," Kale said as we settled on the grass in the field behind Roudey's to wait for Alex. "I don't like how he looks at you."

"Yeah? Well I'm not his biggest fan either, but he might be able to help us. Trust me, if I can tolerate being in the same room with him for a little while, so can you."

"Tell me why you don't like him."

"It's in the past." I shrugged and wanted to smack myself for the constricting feeling gnawing at my insides.

Kale stared. It was like he was looking through me. Peeking past my bullshit and seeing right into my head. Into my heart.

He started to stand, but I stopped him. "We used to date. He cheated on me."

"Date," he repeated. "The hand thing, right? He made you

feel special?"

It was times like this that I found it hard to look at Kale as someone dangerous and capable of murder. He was—I could see it sometimes when I looked in his eyes, but he was so much more. Something innocent. "At one time, yeah, he made me feel special. Then, one day, he didn't anymore."

Kale looked confused. "So then why did you stop me from touching him? He did something wrong, didn't he? He hurt you?"

I was the last person who should be explaining right and wrong to someone. "He did hurt me, but people sometimes hurt each other. It's part of life."

Kale nodded in confirmation. "And when they do bad things, they must be punished."

I groaned. "What they taught you at Denazen was wrong, Kale. There are different levels of wrong in the world. So many different levels."

"Why?"

"*Why*? Why what?"

"Why make it so confusing? There is right and there is wrong. Why does there need to be different…levels?"

My head was starting to spin. "Because that's the way it is! You don't treat a murderer and a shoplifter the same. You wouldn't condemn a cheater to the same punishment as, say, a rapist. Some wrongs are worse than others."

"That doesn't make sense," he hissed, fists clenched. "Wrong is wrong. You obey the rules or you get punished. Why does it need to be so confusing?"

"Because it's more complicated."

"That word again. Complicated. You use it too often."

I looked him in the eye. "It's *wrong* to go killing people. It's not for you—or Denazen—to decide who lives and who dies."

"Who decides then?"

I shrugged. "The government and lawmakers, but the point is, it's rare to punish crimes with death."

He seemed surprised. "So then how do they get punished?"

"Criminals go to trial, and a judge and jury hear the case. If guilty, they incarcerate them."

"Incarcerate?"

"You know. Locked up."

Understanding slipped across his face, followed by something else—something almost sad. "Now I understand."

I got the feeling he still didn't get it, but didn't have time to question him because Alex had arrived. From across the field, he swaggered closer, arms swinging casually at his sides. His eyes jumped from Kale to me, lips twisting into an angry sneer. "Am I interrupting something?"

I ignored the jealousy act and got to my feet. "Where are these people?"

"They aren't coming to us, we have to go to them."

"Where?"

Alex shrugged. "The location changes every day for safety reasons. Tonight, they're over in the old abandoned warehouse outside of town. We can take my car." Without waiting for a response, he turned and started off.

I hurried to catch up, Kale at my side. "Wait, the location of what exactly?"

He slowed his pace but didn't stop. Grinning at me from over his shoulder, he winked and said, "The party, of course."

• • •

From the outside, the warehouse looked empty. No crowds gathering out front. No flashing lights or pulse-pounding beats. Only eerie silence. When questioned about whether or not he had the right place, Alex only waved us forward and jumped from the car.

We made our way to the back, where we found two burly guys standing in front of a single metal door. Alex turned to me as we approached them. He was smiling like a guy who'd just stolen the last cookie. "Here's the catch." He inclined his head to the two men standing guard. "The guy on the right can tell if you're a Six or not. No genetic abnormality, no entry."

My mouth fell open and a chill raced down my spine. "You're telling me they'll only let me in if I have an ability?" This was an unexpected and potentially disastrous turn of events.

Alex relaxed and cracked his knuckles. Leaning in, he bared his teeth. "I know this is a totally foreign concept to you, but you don't have a choice." Without waiting for a response, he turned to the two men. "Howdy, boys."

The bouncers turned. "Shit," I whispered. Attempting to cover up the terror I knew was creeping across my face, I shoved past Alex. I had to get control of the situation before it was too late. If I didn't, there'd be some serious explaining to do. Standing between the two men, I smiled sweetly and placed my hands on my hips. This did two things. It accentuated my slim waist, and it also allowed me to hook my thumbs into the material of my T-shirt, stretching it *just a bit* tighter. I had to make this look *good* so no one would be suspicious. "So do they make you stand out here all alone *all* night?"

The older of the two pinched the bridge of his nose and closed his eyes, but the younger guard smiled back at me. Bingo. He leaned across the doorway, stretching out his arm and subtly flexing his muscle. "We gct an hour break halfway through the night."

I tilted my head toward the door. "An hour is plenty of time to get in some trouble. If you let me in, I'll wait for you. Bet we can find a nice quiet corner to get to know each other a little better."

His smile bloomed into an all-out grin as he pulled the door open, gesturing me, Alex, and Kale inside.

As we entered, Alex shook his head, a small grin on his lips. "You're the only non-Six girl I know who could flirt her way into a place like this."

I pushed through the door with Kale beside me. Once Alex tried to shoulder him away, but a single look from Kale and the subtle hint of removing his glove, had Alex trailing behind. I steered us to an empty table in the back corner of the room where there were fewer people. Kale was nervous about the crowd so I was hoping it would help him relax.

Thick, velvety swatches of onyx material covered the walls while strobe lights danced across them, skimming the edges before assaulting the ceiling in an array of rainbow color. Around the bottom layer of the room, several makeshift bars were set up, each manned by a beautiful and very well-endowed blonde. The upper level was a mass of bodies, all grinding and thrashing to the techno beat blaring from well-hidden speakers. The sound system—as well as the acoustics—were fantastic.

"So what is all this?" I asked, having to lean closer to Alex than I would have liked so he could hear me. I couldn't help being aware of his leg pressed firmly against mine. Somehow I'd ended up between him and Kale.

"This is where the Sixes go to party. They come from all over. If you thought the raves down by the river were wild, you ain't seen nothing yet."

I wanted to smack him. "I get that it's a party, you idiot. What I don't get is why it's Sixes only? And while we're at it—why are they called Sixes?"

"Because Stan Lee already has the patent on mutants?"

Alex snickered, leaning back. "There's a genetic abnormality that shows up in the sixth chromosome. Not incredibly original, but appropriate."

After searching the room for a moment, he tapped me on the shoulder and pointed to the upper level. I tilted my head skyward in time to see a small-framed girl in a blue leather bustier and really cute boots dump a large box over the edge. Like silver snow, a million pieces of metallic colored confetti rained down on the crowd. With a flick of the girl's wrist, the confetti stopped its descent and began swirling and fluttering above the dance floor, moving to the beat. It was beautiful.

A loud explosion tore my attention from the dancing confetti. A stocky shirtless boy stood by the entrance with his arms raised high above his head, sparks shooting from each of his fingertips, while a young girl who looked no more than twelve or so watched with a wide grin. Fluttering in the air above her head for a few seconds, the sparks twitched and jumped until they formed a single word. *Amber.*

In front of our table, a couple stopped long enough to kiss passionately. The girl looked familiar—I was sure she'd been in my English and Math classes last year. When their lips touched, the air hissed and sizzled, sending smoke curling skyward.

"Wow," was all I could say as they disappeared into the crowd. Alex grinned at me, a too-familiar expression I'd told myself I hadn't missed. Below his lips, Fred, the smiling yellow labret bead, seemed to wink. I shook my head to clear the stupidity. No way was I going *there* again. "So they're free to be themselves here."

"Exactly. No one has to hide."

"Isn't it a little dangerous? I mean with people like Dad and Denazen never far away, is it smart to have all these Sixes bunched up in one place together? What happens if you're, like, raided or something?"

"Raided? I think you need to lay off the TV, Dez." He snickered. "Besides, I told you, the location changes all the time. Plus, we're in no danger from the local PD—we have a few Sixes on the force."

"How do people know where it's going to be if the location is always changing? I'm guessing there's no mass email…"

He smiled. "Craigslist."

"Huh?"

"Each afternoon, someone posts an ad for something under the *lessons* section. When Sixes call the number listed in the ad, they're asked a question. If the answer given is right, they get another number to call.."

"So…it's like a scavenger hunt?"

Alex smiled. "Zactly."

"Couldn't anyone figure out the answer?"

He shook his head. "Nah. Not likely. It's usually something silly and unrelated. Something only one of us would know. The first time, you'd have to know someone to get the answer right. Something that happened at a previous party, or you might be given a name and asked what their four-one-one is."

"Four-one-one?"

"You know a Six's four-one-one and you know their gift. Their ability."

"Well, what about Denazen? You don't think they could find you without the ad?"

"You saw the outside of the building. Did you have any idea this was anything more than an old abandoned building?"

"Yeah, what about that?"

Alex shrugged. "A Six," he said with a wink. Glancing down at his watch, he sighed. "We have a little time till she gets here." Hand extended, he nodded to the dance floor. "Shall we?"

The room was loud. Surely I'd heard him wrong. "You did

not seriously ask me to dance with you."

He slid out from his chair and stood. The sleeve of his dark T-shirt rode up to reveal a tiny glimpse of the tattoo hiding beneath. The Chinese symbol for freedom. I remember asking him why freedom. He'd told me he liked the symbol. Another thing he'd lied to me about. "It's just a dance, what harm could it do?"

I thought about it. The music pumped and the air was electric. On the floor, bodies swayed and convulsed, lost to the beat. Would it hurt to have a few minutes of normalcy? I thought back to the way our bodies moved together. Even after all this time, the memory brought a flush to my skin and a rush of heat racing through my limbs. I slid over and stood, giving him a quick nod. "You're right, what would one little dance hurt?"

His grin widened. "Zactly."

"What do you say, Kale? Want to dance your first dance with me?"

Kale looked from me to the dance floor. It was packed, but I'd already scouted a small corner at the edge that was fairly empty. It'd be safe. He must have seen it too, because he smiled and stood. Out of the corner of my eye, I saw him grin at Alex, a totally guy smile that said *nah-nah-nah-nah-she-picked-me-not-you*. We left Alex sitting alone at the table with a sour expression on his face.

My fingers tangled with Kale's, and I led him to the edge of the dance floor. Leaning close, I whispered, "Don't take this the wrong way, but you know what dancing is, right?"

He didn't answer. A sly grin spread across his lips and he grabbed both my hands, tugging me close as the slow, rhythmic beats of a new song began. Pulling me in and spinning me out, Kale moved across the floor with skill and confidence. At about six feet tall, he was the perfect height for me. I didn't have to stand on my tiptoes, but still needed to look up a bit. The music pounded inside my brain, filling up every inch of space, and my eyes…well they focused on nothing other than Kale and the way he moved us around the small space.

His eyes sparkled and hair fluttered into his face, and at that moment, he looked like a normal boy. Fancy twirls and elegant dips, we moved across the floor. For a split second I panicked, sure we were about to collide with someone, but on second glance, I saw the crowd had moved back, forming a wide circle for us. They stood watching, some cheering, some clapping. Kale, taking advantage of the extra room, spun me wildly away from him, feet moving in some complex maneuver, before pulling me back in an extravagant display ending with a deep dip that left me dizzy and disoriented—but tingly.

Very tingly.

The crowd erupted in a chorus of hoots and shouts, and I couldn't wipe the smile from my face. I grabbed his hand and led him off to the side as the crowd reclaimed the dance floor. "That was amazing! Where did you learn to dance like that?"

His eyes stayed on mine, intense and unwavering. He wasn't frowning, but his expression was one of utmost seriousness. "Was that good?"

I squeezed his hand. "Good? That was…" Then, like someone dimmed the lights, everything drifted away. The music, the crowd, everything disappeared. The only thing that didn't fade, the only thing that remained behind, was Kale. The sharp curve of his cheek, the angular set of his jaw—complete with nervous twitch—all inches from me now. His lips, pressed in a thin line as he awaited my judgment, looked soft and inviting. How easy would it be to lean forward—just a few inches separated us.

I'd made the decision to go for it when a large hand clamped across my shoulder.

"Crap!" I jumped forward, almost knocking Kale backward into a large man with a mohawk.

"She's ready to see you now," Alex said, arms folded. He looked annoyed. Good. I'd mainly danced with Kale to piss him off, but now… Things felt different.

We followed Alex through the crowd and up the stairs leading to the second level. Past another bar and to the right, there was a single door. Alex knocked three times, then twisted the knob. It opened with an ominous creak.

"So Alex tells me you're looking for our help," a voice said from across the room. In the corner, seated on a cushy red recliner—the only thing in the room—sat a little old lady. Wrinkled and stooped and totally out of place, she appeared to be your typical grandma, complete with flowery housecoat and bluish hair. But the look in her eyes was far from typical. Something told me Granny could go a few rounds with Dad and not break a sweat.

The door closed behind me. "No, *technically,* we're looking for the Reaper."

The old woman's eyes narrowed. "Quite the tongue on you, child."

I smiled and took a bow. "I get that a lot."

"Dez—"

The woman held out her hand to stop him. "It's fine, Alex. This one amuses me."

At the other end of the room was a door with two beefy guys standing stone-faced in front of it. The old woman snapped her fingers twice and the guy on the right disappeared through the door. A few moments later, he reappeared with a plastic cup brimming with red liquid. She took the glass and gave him an offhanded wave as she lifted it to her lips. I had to hold back a giggle at the site of this bruiser scurrying to cater to this old woman. Obviously, she held some serious sway with these people.

"So what are you, like the Granny Don of the Six mafia?"

She cackled, mouth opening to reveal several missing teeth. "Something like that."

A few moments of silence ticked by. I decided to go for it.

"Since I don't know what my time limit here is, lemme get right to the point. My dad's the asshole in charge of Denazen. We've been told this Reaper dude is some kind of Yoda to you Sixes. My mom is being held at Denazen. Since this Reaper is the only one ever to get out of there alive, I need his help to get in, rescue her, and get out." There. Short, sweet, and to the point.

The old woman cackled. "Not asking for much, are you?"

"Hey, gotta dream big," I said.

She turned to Kale. "If you've managed to free yourself from Denazen's chains, why are you still here? Surely you know Cross won't give up on you?"

"Cross is relentless," Kale confirmed. Beside me, he squared his shoulders and took my hand. "But I am staying with Dez."

The guy who'd tumbled down the embankment, landing at my feet—the Six who'd tried to kill me— as more than that now. I didn't know when it happened, or *how*, but there it was. "I'm going to get my mom back and I'm not going to let him take Kale back there."

She was silent for a few moments, seemingly lost in thought. "I will help you," she responded finally. My joy was short-lived though.

"But of course, I need you to do something for me." What a shock.

There was a catch.

There's always a damn catch. "What do you want? Cause if you ask me to get you a horse's head, the deal's off."

"Denazen has been a thorn in the side of Sixes everywhere

for a very long time. As I'm sure you can deduce, we've been trying to find a way to take them out."

I hadn't *deduced* that, but sure, whatever. "Okay…"

"What we lack, however, is certain information."

"What kind of information?"

"There is a main database with the names of all the Sixes Denazen currently has in captivity. I need that information."

Speechless. There were no words I could think of to reply to a request like that. How the hell did this woman expect me to get into Denazen, much less get them to allow me to copy secret files? "Are you high?"

"You asked for our help. I have named my price." Clutching her cane, she rose. "There is no expiration on my offer. I feel this is a fair exchange. Get me the information we need, and I will help you find the Reaper so you may free your mother."

She paused at the door. "I will also offer you a bonus. If you get me the information I seek, I will get Kale the help he needs to control his gift."

10

"Wait!" I surged forward, but Alex grabbed my shoulders. "Let go of me, jackass!"

Alex waited for the door to close before releasing me. I crashed into the door and jerked the knob. Nothing. Locked.

"You don't want to push her, Dez. She's not the tolerant type."

I whirled on him, fists curled tight. "What the hell was that about? You bring me here so she can offer to trade information about this Reaper guy for something I have no hope of getting?"

Alex actually had the nerve to look hurt. "I didn't know what she was going to ask, I swear. Ginger is a hard-ass, but she's usually fair. A little strange—but fair. If she asked you to get it, she thinks you can. I don't believe she'd ask if she thought it was beyond you."

I sank down into the armchair. "How the hell am I going to do this?" I turned to Kale. "Any ideas?"

He wasn't looking at me. He was staring at the door Ginger

had disappeared through.

"Kale?"

"Do you think it's possible? I might be able to control it?"

We'd latched onto different parts of what Ginger said. Kale heard salvation. I turned to Alex. "Is it?"

"If Ginger says it is, then yes."

"Fantastic. An even bigger carrot."

"Let's go sit," Alex said. "Try to figure this out."

We wove our way back down the stairs and to the first floor. I couldn't help feeling a sting of jealousy when I glanced across the room. All these people living it up. Partying till dawn. A few days ago, that had been me. Blissful and ignorant and content.

We settled at the same table, which had remarkably remained empty despite the crowd. Alex nursed a beer, while Kale and I had soda, though mine sat untouched. Kale's was gone. Well, his first was gone. And the second. And the third. He was on soda number four now. He loved the bubbles.

My head thumped heavily onto the table. "This is impossible."

"Alex, baby!" an annoyingly high-pitched voice cooed.

I lifted my head and saw a tall, willowy redhead standing in front of our table.

"Hey Erica," Alex said with feigned enthusiasm.

She gave an eager wave and threw herself into the seat next to him. "So where have you been hiding yourself? I haven't seen you in forever!" She swiped the beer from his hand and took a long pull before setting it down on the table—not in front of Alex, but Kale.

"Yeah, well—"

She threw an arm over Alex's shoulder and gave Kale a smoldering look before turning to glare at me. "What's up with the man-hogging? Pick one." She inclined her head toward Kale. "You've got both ends of the spectrum here, sistah. What'll it be, day or night?"

I watched Alex cringe as she reached up to run a finger through his spiky, white-blond hair. Out of the corner of my eye, I saw Kale pick up Alex's beer. He took a sip and set it down. A moment later he picked it back up and downed the entire thing.

"I'm not—" I started.

"Not going to share?" She gave a mock pout. "You don't need both of them, do you? It wouldn't be fair to the rest of us girls if you held both these droolables hostage!"

Hostage…

Maybe *that* was the answer!

First, I needed to get rid of Little Miss Gropey. I snaked one arm around Kale's waist and the other, though it pained me to do it, I draped across Alex's shoulder. "Actually, I am being selfish, but I need 'em both."

A little disappointed, she gave me a knowing grin. "I'll bet!" She stood and leaned over the table, winking. She was about to leave, but hesitated, squinting at me. "You're Dez, right? Aren't you the girl who did Troy Beldom and Mickey Doon at the Deerfield party last week?"

Oops. I'd started the rumor the day after the party by telling bigmouth Markie Fray. Markie's mom was Dad's *secretary* at the *law firm*, and I knew the news would get back to him. It'd only taken forty-eight hours for him to bust through the door and lecture me about being the town train. Score one for me. I'd gotten a reaction.

With one last, longing look at Alex, Erica stumbled off in search of more promising prey. Alex pried my hand from his shoulder and glared. Disgusted, he said, "Seriously? Beldom and Doon?"

I bit down on my tongue and slipped both hands under my butt to keep from punching him. "Is there anyone here you trust?

Not like casually trust, either. I'm talking trust with your life."

He thought about it for a minute. "I'd bet my ass on Dax's loyalty."

"Is this Dax guy here now?"

Alex pointed to the door, where a tall, well-muscled man in his mid-twenties was entering. Cleanly shaven head and dressed in black from head to toe, he looked like the kind of guy you'd cross the street to avoid. "That's him."

I smiled, my devious little mind already working out the scheme. "Oh my God, he's perfect!"

"For what?" Kale asked, horrified.

"To kidnap me."

. . .

The phone rang five times before Dad bothered picking up. Obviously, he wasn't waiting by the phone with bated breath for his MIA teen daughter to call. I tried to ignore it, but the hurt stuck in my throat. Like trying to swallow stale bread. "Hello?"

"Dad!" I cried, but Dax took the phone from me. He stepped across the room as Alex threw a chair at the wall. I cried out, and Alex yelled for me to shut the hell up. I had a hard time not laughing.

Next to me, Kale picked up his own chair and copied Alex. He heaved it against the wall and turned to me, smiling. "That was fun!" he half whispered.

After Erica left, Kale had ordered another beer. I was pretty sure we were witnessing his first buzz. I fought a grin and tried to focus on my impending abduction.

"Keep quiet and listen to what I have to say, Cross," Dax hissed into the phone as he paced the other side of the room. We'd moved away from the party to one of the office rooms on the second level. Everything was coated in thick layers of dust. "Obviously, we have your kid."

Dax was silent for a moment—probably listening to Dad's colorful reply.

"This will not work," Kale whispered. "He doesn't care about anyone. He will agree and double-cross us."

We'd never gotten along, but up until I found out what he'd done to my mom, I would have disagreed with Kale. He was my dad after all. He wanted me safe. But now? Now I worried Kale might be right, but I didn't know what else to do. I had to get on Dad's good side. This was the only thing I could think of.

"He won't be able to," Alex said, leaning against the wall. "Dax would see it."

It hadn't occurred to me to ask about Dax's gift. "He sees the future?"

Alex shook his head. "When he hears someone's voice, he can see their true intentions play out in pictures inside his head."

I blushed. It's a good thing he hadn't been there when I'd been dancing with Kale.

"What I offer is a trade," I heard Dax saying. "I will exchange your daughter for two of the prisoners you have in your custody. Monica and Mona Fleet."

I raised an eyebrow in question at Alex. He leaned in and whispered, "They're Dax's twin nieces. They were taken three years ago from their schoolyard. They were only six years old at the time."

"Jesus…"

"Monica was a very brave little girl," Kale said, turning to watch Dax. I could tell the older man heard him because his shoulders stiffened and his pacing stopped. "She resisted Denazen's training. Mona begged her to do what they asked, but she wouldn't."

On the other side of the room, Dax was as still as a corpse—probably listening to my dad argue two wasn't a fair trade for one—but he was staring straight at Kale.

Kale turned away. "They separated them after that. I saw Mona several times, but never saw Monica again."

We waited while Dax made arrangements and finished the call. Obviously, they'd come to some agreement. When he hung up, Dax crept across the room with slow deliberation, brown eyes fixed on mine. I told myself his expression, a mix of pain and anger, wasn't meant for me, but I couldn't help feeling like it was.

"He'll trade Mona for you," he said evenly. Something in the sound of his voice made me shiver.

"Monica?" Alex asked.

"She had…an accident." Dax's fists tightened at his sides. "Cross said he was *sorry* for my loss."

Alex clasped his shoulder. "I'm sorry, man."

Dax waved him off, still glaring at me. "I have nothing against you, kid, but I'll be honest…" He took several steps closer, stopping only when his face was inches from mine. Breath smelling faintly of beer and stale cigarettes puffed across my face. "If I didn't know that bastard couldn't care less about you, if I couldn't see the truth of it in his voice—and yours—I'd kill you myself and mail you back to him in pieces."

Ouch.

"Back away," Kale said in a low growl from beside me. He made a move to tug off his right glove.

Dax didn't budge.

"Now." The glove was off, clenched between the fingers of his left hand. "If you threaten her again, I will kill you."

Dax stepped back and bowed his head. When he looked up again, the anger was gone. "I apologize, Kale." What about my apology? I was the one he'd threatened to chop up and Fed-

Ex home. His gaze bounced to Alex, then back to Kale, before turning to me with a small grin. "I don't envy you."

11

Three hours later, Dax and I sat on a bench inside Memorial Park. Dad was due with Mona any minute. Kale had wanted to come with us, but I made him wait with Alex, who'd flat-out refused to show himself. They were waiting farther down the path by the lake. We couldn't see them, but if things went wrong, they were within shouting distance.

I tugged at the hem of my red T-shirt, wishing Brandt had picked something ratty instead of one of my faves. It was pretty much ruined. Typical boy. No clue what *on-the-run* clothing was.

"Can I ask you a question?" Dax and I had called a truce. Sort of. I couldn't hold a grudge. Hell—who could blame the guy? Part of his family had been stolen and I was the closest thing to payback he could get. While I wasn't a fan of the slicing and dicing imagery, I understood. But we had a common enemy here and that's what we needed to focus on.

"Go for it," Dax said, leaning back. In the dark, the only part of him I could really see was his shaved head, which kind of glinted against the moonlight. He fidgeted with his keys, twirling them around his pointer finger.

"You said you knew Dad wasn't worried about me being safe."

An apologetic look crossed his face. He opened his mouth to speak, but I stopped him.

"No, it's okay," I lied. "I was never his favorite person. I just always thought it was because of my mother, which obviously it's not. But if he doesn't care, why *does* he want me back? He's making the trade, but I doubt it's to keep up appearances. It doesn't seem like it's something he'd need to do…"

Dax didn't answer right away. He looked down the path, then tilted his head to the sky. After a few minutes passed, he said, "I'm torn. You're a good person, I can tell. I want to tell you not to go back to him, but I need my nieces back."

He realized his mistake and squeezed his eyes closed for a second. "Niece," he corrected as his foot stomped against the ground.

"I know you have to do this to get the information for Ginger, but be careful. He intends to use you. You've been on the other side of enemy lines. You're a new source of information now. You might be able to make it work in your favor—I can see what you're planning to do—but I'm warning you. It might be harder than you think. If he were to find out who you really are…"

I opened my mouth, but Dax stopped me.

"I'm not going to say anything to anyone. Your secrets are your own. I just want you to know there's a good chance this won't go the way you're planning. For all you know, he has it all figured out. And if he doesn't, well, your father's not a man easily fooled. You may have to play that ace you've got tucked inside your sleeve. You can't hide yourself forever…"

Normally, if someone had said that to me, I'd tell them I'd

made a career out of fooling my dad, but I wasn't sure anymore. I was the one who'd been fooled all this time.

"Look alive." I nudged his arm and whispered, "Make it look real."

Seeing Dad walking down the path, Dax seized my arm, fingers digging into my skin, and hauled me from the bench. We stood in the path and waited while Dad and a tiny ghost of a girl approached. As they neared, I tried to keep my expression one of fear and pain. It wasn't easy.

Mona walked beside Dad like a zombie, eyes vacant, expression dead. Her measured steps tapping the ground matched his perfectly.

Clap. Thump. Clap. Thump. They stopped about five feet away, Mona staring ahead, straight through her uncle. There was nothing. No emotion, no recognition. Only empty brown eyes, partially obscured by a mop of mousy brown curls.

"What's wrong with her," Dax growled. He probably didn't mean to, but his fingers twitched, and I bit down on the inside of my cheek to keep from yelping.

"She's fine," Dad replied.

"Bullshit! Look at her. She's the walking dead."

"For the sake of my own safety, drugging her was a necessity for transportation. It will wear off in several hours."

I got the feeling the drugs *would* wear off in a few hours, but the damage Denazen had done to this little girl would never wash away. Rage burned. Had they drugged Kale, too? I could see it sometimes—that small, unmistakable hint of madness sparking behind his eyes. I remembered his words to Alex back at Roudey's. *"It hurts to be grabbed like that."*

How could I be the flesh and blood of such a monster?

"Send her over," Dax said, twisting my arm with such force that it brought tears to my eyes. He gave me a hard shake for good measure. "And I'll send this one over."

"Send Deznee first."

Dax laughed. "Of course. Because you'd never think of double-crossing me."

"Of course not. That's my daughter you have there. I would never risk her safety."

LIAR, I wanted to shout, but held my tongue.

"On the count of five, they both go." Dax compromised. Dad nodded in agreement, and Dax began to count. "1…"

I knew the whole thing was a setup but still, acid bubbled in the pit of my stomach.

"2…"

Dad's face remained impassive. "Everything will be all right, Deznee."

"3…"

The sound of his voice burned my ears.

"4…"

I tried to clear my mind. Brandt told me once I had an expressive face. It gave everything away. All my anger, my surprise, and, most of all, my worries about Kale had to be pushed from my mind.

"5."

With a slight shove, Dax released my arm while at the same time Dad leaned forward and whispered something in Mona's ear. She started walking. The distance we had to cover was short, but her steps were small, so I slowed my pace. When we crossed in the middle, she gave no acknowledgement of the situation or my presence and passed without a word.

Dad didn't put up any appearances. He wasn't standing on the other side with open arms welcoming me home safe. He stood rigid and expressionless, waiting in silence as though annoyed this was taking so long. Was it too much to ask for a little fake emotion? When I reached him, I turned to see Dax wrapping his arms around the little girl, who returned neither his embrace nor tears of joy.

He looked up and our eyes met. I cleared my mind, knowing he could see the truth behind my thoughts, not the words. "I'll kill you for what you did to me," I said quietly.

He chuckled, arms tightening around the child. "You'd have to find us first."

I gave him a smile that was all tooth. "Trust me, I will."

• • •

We rode home in silence. Dad hadn't said anything since we'd reached the car and he told me the door was unlocked. Now, as we drove down the main drag, I had to fight the urge to grab the wheel and veer us into a tree. Dad never wore his seatbelt.

I had to say something. There's no way he'd believe my silence, even if I did manage to pull off the trauma angle I was going to aim for.

"Were you worried about me? Even a little?"

His eyes never left the road. "Don't be foolish. Of course I was worried."

Silence.

"When—" I stopped myself in time—I'd almost said Kale. Using his first name definitely wouldn't portray enough fear. "When *he* knocked on the door the other night, I thought it was you. That you'd left your house key at the office again." I kept my eyes straight ahead, looking at the dashboard. "When I opened it, he surprised me and forced his way inside."

Dad didn't look convinced. "Why did you run off with him?"

Yeah. That would need a good explanation. Deep breath. "Seriously? I live to piss you off. I would've French-kissed Satan on your desk if I thought it'd irritate you. You obviously didn't want me near him, so I left with him."

"Then what happened?"

"He said he knew a friend of mine. We went to his house, but people showed up and tried to take him away. I didn't know what to think, one of them attacked me, so I ran with him again. We ended up at a downtown bar. He traded me to that guy for some cash and took off."

"So he's gone?"

"I'll find him. I helped him—he tricked me and then *sold* me to that Mr. Clean psycho."

"Did he hurt you?" His question was empty of emotion—clinical, like inquiring about a used car for sale.

"He—" This is where I had to really ham it up. "He made threats." I touched the side of my face where the man from Denazen had smacked me. The bruise had lightened, but was still there. "He roughed me up a little—nothing major—but the threats... The things he said he'd do if you didn't give in to his demands... He was going to rip me apart and mail me back to you piece by piece." At least part of it was the truth.

I squinted against a set of oncoming headlights—stupid high beams—as we turned into the driveway. Dad shut the engine off and turned to me. Time to put my bullshit skills to the test.

"I was so scared, Dad. I thought he was going to kill me."

I'd never been a cryer. Even as a child, skinned knees, loud noises, darkened rooms, nothing ever set me off. So when I decided to turn on the waterworks for a major impact, I was worried I wouldn't be able to pull it off.

It hadn't been the memory of the cold, dead look in Mona's eyes, or the expression on Dax's face when he overheard Kale talking about Monica. It wasn't even the thought of being in the same room with Alex after so long, hearing his voice or the memory of finding him with that girl.

It was Kale. The slightly haunted look in his eyes. The way his hair flopped over into his face. The way he'd tried to attack Alex and Dax—for me. Strange and damaged—possibly beyond repair—but there was still something about him that made me feel alive. More alive than any rave or cheap thrill I'd ever chased before.

I hurt for the things my dad had done to him.

I missed him.

The tears came with ease.

12

I must've taken after my mom, because Dad could sleep through a Powerman 5000 concert. On stage. Under Spider One's boot. It was a fact I'd exploited countless times to get in and out of the house in the middle of the night. But a pin could drop down the road, and I was wide awake.

Keeping my eyes closed, I shifted under the covers. The wind whistled through my open window but that hadn't been what I'd heard. Someone else was in my room. My first thought was Dad, but I tossed that idea out right away. I'd locked the door, and since it locked from the inside he couldn't get in from the hall.

Someone was breathing softly in the corner—probably near the window. Alex had snuck through countless times while we'd been together. But this wasn't him. It didn't *feel* like him.

And then I knew. There was no doubt in my mind who stood there. Kale.

A jolt of excitement coursed through my body. Alex used to tell me he'd sneak in and watch me sleep. I always knew he was there, though, and feigned sleep, loving the idea of his eyes on me. It gave me a thrill to know he was watching. Occasionally I'd let my bare leg slide from under the blanket, visible all the way to just below my danger zone.

This…this was different. I could feel Kale's eyes on me, his breathing a bit faster than normal. I imagined his hand skimming my bare leg from hip to knee, remembering what his lips had tasted like back at the hotel. The images had me fighting to keep my own breathing even as my pulse spiked.

Eyes still closed, I turned onto my back, managing to slide the comforter down until it was tangled between my feet. By the window, Kale shifted positions as well, moving closer. He made no sound, but I was aware of him all the same.

Arching my back, I turned on my side, toward the window. I feigned an itch, hooking the edge of my tank top over my finger as I rolled, causing it to ride up. Knowing his eyes were on me, knowing he was slowly moving forward, made me bolder. I stretched my right hand above my head, over the pillow, and brought my left hand up to brush my hair from my face.

Kale took another step. Now he was standing over me.

It took serious willpower to force myself to stay silent and keep my eyes closed. I didn't know what he'd do if he knew I was awake. I didn't want him to back away. Didn't want him to *look* away.

The chilly night air sent an icy jolt to my exposed skin. To my surprise—and unbelievable happiness—the end of the bed dipped as Kale sat down. A moment later, a touch, cottony light, traced a path from my toes, up my leg, and stopped right below the hem of my shorts.

I couldn't help it. I inhaled sharply and shimmied onto my back, somehow managing to keep my eyes closed. His fingers stayed there, resting on my exposed skin for a few moments before trailing upward, over the material. Palm down, he ran his hand up my torso and paused at the hem of my white tank top, now just below my heart. For an insanely drawn-out minute, I thought for sure his fingers would slip beneath, warmth enveloping me. I'd open my eyes then and test my limits.

But they didn't.

His hand lingered for a moment more before he pulled it back. "Dez?"

A little disappointed, I brought my hands up and rubbed my eyes. "Hmm?" When my vision cleared, he was standing again, inches away from me. "Kale?" I sat up, adjusting my top. "Are you all right?"

He backed away a bit and shook his head. "I've been thinking about what you said, about locking the bad people away."

"Okay..."

He was tired. His eyelids were drooping. "Did they know I'd do bad things? Is that why they kept me there?"

"Huh?" I didn't understand what he meant at first. When it hit me, I felt like someone had dropped a brick over my head. "Oh God, Kale, no." I slid back, leaned against the headboard, and motioned for him to sit next to me. He hesitated for a few moments before climbing across the bed.

"After you left, I talked to people, I read a—newspaper? I'm a horrible person. I deserve to be punished. Like I punished all those people. I *murdered* them. That's why Denazen kept me locked up—because I deserved it." He turned away, looking back at the window.

"That's not true."

"In the beginning, when they started my training, they'd go days without bringing me food if I didn't do what they told me. They only gave me a glass of water a day. They'd dump it out and tell me bad children had to lick it off the floor. By the time they brought food again, I could barely stand." He shook his head, lips twisted in anger. "Dax's niece will never be normal—*I'll* never be normal. They isolate us, break us down. They dig in our heads until they find what makes us tick, then they rip it out. Most crack. They just cease to be. All they are, are Denazen-made weapons. Others are weak. They become what Denazen shapes them to be. In exchange for their humanity, they get some semblance of freedom."

He took a deep breath. For a minute I didn't think he'd continue.

"I thought I was different, though—I had Sue. She told me I'd make it through as long as I held onto my humanity. As long as I remembered she loved me, they couldn't destroy that. But she was wrong." He looked up at me, eyes glistening, and shook his head. "When I turned ten, they made me kill for the first time. They were graphic—very detailed. They said they'd peel the flesh from Sue's body if I didn't do as I was told. By the time I was twelve, I accepted my life. Denazen owned me."

My mouth was dry. "No one owns you," I whispered.

"I knew it was wrong. Everything about Denazen—it was all wrong. But then, when you left earlier, I found out *I* was wrong. I'm as much to blame for the bad I've done as they are. I could have made the choice Monica did. I could have refused to let them use me. You said I was strong, but I'm not. I'm weak."

He reached down and ran his index finger from my thigh, right below the hem of my shorts, down to my knee. It left a trail of fire in its wake. "I don't deserve this."

For the second time in twenty-four hours, tears came easily. "Stop it," I whispered. I didn't know what *this* was, but the lump forming in my throat and the heat building in the pit of my stomach told me I needed to find out.

With his eyes on me, so sad, I couldn't take it. I sat up and climbed onto his lap, resting my forehead against his. Inhaling, I committed his scent to memory. Earthy. Like the woods after a long rain. My arms slipped across his shoulders, and my lips found his. The kiss was tentative at first—brief. I pulled away until I could see his face. I'd had a lot of guys look at me like I was a fun vacation on the beach, but the way Kale's ice-blue eyes devoured every inch of me, full of heat and hope, I felt like Christmas morning. Timeless and perfect.

It spurred me on. I leaned in again, but this time Kale met me halfway. His strong arms encircled my waist, dragging me closer. His mouth moved with mine and twice our teeth clinked, but it didn't matter. When Alex first kissed me, our teeth had banged together. It made my skin crawl. Kale's hands were everywhere— my neck, my face, under the back of my tank top—anywhere he could make skin-to-skin contact.

I drew his bottom lip in and nibbled. God, he tasted good. Like root beer and bubble gum and heat mixed with something unique. Something all Kale. His fingers clutched the sides of my face, sliding up to tangle in my hair. I broke our contact once again—despite his protests—and tugged off my tank top. He didn't waste time staring. Urging me close, we crashed into each other, collapsing in a heap.

When I finally drew away again, we were lying across the bed, our legs intertwined with each other.

"I don't deserve to feel like this." His voice cracked. The weight of his gaze shattered me. "Not after everything I've done."

"Come here," I whispered. When he managed a sitting position, I pulled his shirt up over his head and ran my hands down his neck and across his shoulders. I remembered what he said about his daily training schedule. The weights and the hours of martial arts. He was in amazing shape. My index finger trailed down the middle of his chest and I fought back a shiver.

With each touch, his breath quickened. I could feel the heartbeat hammering inside his chest as he clung to me, almost as if he was terrified I'd let go.

Kale's eyes were wide as he brought his hands from my face to my bare throat. His touch, like an electric current, slid down my neck and over my shoulders, then down each of my arms. I arched my back as he struggled to pull me closer, nails scraping bare skin in desperation. But I resisted with a sly smile—just to see what he'd do—and I wasn't disappointed.

"Please," he rasped as he pushed us down and turned me onto my back. "Please…"

I opened my mouth to tell him he didn't need to beg, that I wanted this as much as he did, but his actions stopped me. Lowering himself, he slid one arm under the hollow of my back, the other resting across my stomach. Reaching over, he grabbed my hand and laced his fingers with mine. As he nuzzled my stomach, a soft noise escaped his throat.

The wind outside picked up as Kale's breathing evened. I wrapped my arms around him and closed my eyes.

"I understand now, Dez," he whispered sleepily. "I understand the hand thing."

13

Before I opened my eyes the next morning, I knew Kale had gone. The room was quieter without his breathing. Colder.

I grabbed my tank top from the floor and pulled it over my head. The memory of last night brought a flush to my skin. I'd been prepared to go further—all the way, probably—but somehow, what happened between us was far more intimate than sex.

Gathering my things, I wandering to the bathroom in a daze. I showered, brushed my teeth, and dried my hair, all the while wearing a goofy grin and thinking about Kale. When I opened the bathroom door letting out the steam, the room cleared. And so did my head.

There was work to be done. Time to focus.

I found Dad downstairs at the kitchen table with his usual breakfast—a cup of coffee, a boysenberry scone, and *The New York Times*.

"Hey." I grabbed a mug from the cabinet. He glared at me in

silence as I poured the off-limits coffee into the cup. "Last night's bonding experience aside, I need to talk to you."

Eyebrows raised, he nodded for me to continue.

"I need to feel like I'm in control," I started. "Maybe I got that from you. What those bastards did to me, keeping me tied and locked in the dark, making all those threats, it made me feel *out* of control. I need to find some balance."

Dad put down the paper and leaned back, hands folded across the table. I could tell by the subtle twitch of his lip and the slight tilt of his head I had his attention. "What do you mean, balance?"

"I need to do something about it. These people are out there—God knows how many—and I can't help but wonder if that's all I'll think about from now on each time I close my eyes."

"What exactly do you propose?"

"Take me to Denazen. They filled my head with horrible lies that won't wipe away. You can fix it." I slammed the cup on the table, sending half of it sloshing over the edge. "I'm gonna go out on a limb here and say that one thing they told me was true. You're not a lawyer. I need to know the rest. I need to know the *truth*."

He was silent for a long time, eyes searching mine. I thought it all sounded pretty convincing, but it was hard to tell with Dad. The guy had invented the poker face. I'd started to think he'd seen through me when a slow smile spread across his lips.

"Go put your shoes on."

. . .

As we pulled into the parking lot, it occurred to me that I'd never been here. Dad had been working for Denazen for as long as I could remember, and not once, even back before we publicly despised each other, had I ever been to his office.

We exited the car in silence, walked up the stairs, and stopped inside the glass doors at the reception desk. The man on the other side raised an eyebrow at me while handing a clipboard and pen to Dad.

The lobby was bathed in bright white with pristine, cherry wood floors and matching trim. A set of elevators flanked both sides of the room. One set silver, the other white as snow.

Dad scribbled his name on the paper, looked at his watch, and pointed to the white elevator doors. "Let's go."

There were no buttons, only a thin strip on the wall that looked like a credit card swiper. Dad reached into the right side pocket of his jacket and pulled out a small card. With a swift pass through the swiper, the doors opened.

Without a word, we stepped inside. I waited several moments, and when nothing happened, I asked, "Well?"

"Patience."

Another minute ticked by before a loud, odd, vacuum-sounding swoosh filled the air. Another set of doors opened on the far wall of the elevator.

Dad pointed to them and stepped through. "This is the real elevator." Clearing his throat, he stepped inside and said, "Fourth Floor."

Amazed, I followed him in, and the doors closed with a *ping*. A moment later, the elevator jerked to life and we began to climb.

"The only way to operate this set of elevators is by using a security badge. Without it, the elevator doors won't even close. It won't take you any higher than your security card clearance allows."

After a short climb, we stepped out into a long, empty white hall and through a steel door. There was no one there as we made our way toward the single doorway at the other end of the hall. The silence made for an eerie stage and I wanted to fill it by asking questions—I had a million of them—but didn't want to come across as too eager. Once we got through the door, everything changed.

Our entry into the building felt surreal next to the bustle and activity now laid out in front of me. A long row of desks lined the entire outside of the room. It reminded me of the ASPCA charity call center setup from last year's fundraiser. At each one someone was on the phone, head down, furiously jotting notes onto paper. No one looked up as we entered.

In the middle of the room was a large reception area with a sign above that said *Reception/Check In*. Behind the desk, a chubby brunette with a wicked overbite flashed Dad a flirty smile. "Mornin', Mr. Cross."

Dad nodded and honored her with a rare smile. "Hannah."

"Is this a new acquisition?" She gave me an almost fearful once-over before turning back to him. No secret what *she* thought of Sixes.

Dad laughed. "No, this is my daughter, Deznee."

Hannah clucked her tongue in sympathy and nodded. "This is the poor dear that was assaulted by the Six, isn't it?"

"I wasn't assaulted," I snapped before remembering I was supposed to be on the nay side of the Six fence. "I mean, I held my own with the bastards."

She gave me a thin smile, one that said you-keep-telling-yourself-that. "Of course you did, dear."

"Please have a temporary level yellow pass made up for her. She'll be spending the day with us."

Hannah rubbed her plump fingers together and giggled. "How exciting this must be for you!"

I forced a smile and hoped it didn't look too fake. "It really is."

"This way," Dad said.

We left the room and turned right, coming to another set of elevators—these doors were green. Once inside, Dad said, "Fifth floor." After a moment, he added, "All the elevators in the building are color-coded for the different security levels. The first three floors are silver, for the *law firm*. The fourth floor, Denazen's real reception area, is white. All Denazen employees must pass through there before going anywhere in the building. The cafeteria is also on that floor. The fifth floor, where we're heading now, is green."

"What's on green?"

"There are ten levels here at Denazen," he said, adjusting his briefcase. "The fifth floor is where the new Sixes are brought in, received, and processed. It's also where security is located—and my office."

The elevator jerked to a stop and the doors opened to a short man wearing the same blue, pinstriped suit I'd seen the men at Curd's wearing. He smiled, chipmunk-like cheeks scrunching his beady brown eyes to thin slits.

"Mr. Cross, they've brought 104 back. Things were a complete success."

Dad nodded, and we stepped off the elevator. "Good. Make sure he's brought back to level eight."

"Eight, sir? Don't we usually house him on seven?"

"We did—until he incinerated the person who brought him dinner two nights ago. He stays on eight until further notice." Dad turned to me. "Follow and stay close."

Chipmunk Cheeks paid me no mind as we passed, turning away from Dad to bark orders at a man approaching us.

"Someone got incinerated?" I balked. "Seriously?"

We stopped in front of a door at the end of the hall. Dad pulled the card he'd used in the elevator out, and passed it through the swiper on the door. It opened and we stepped inside.

"Have a seat." He gestured across the room to a large mahogany desk. A cushy looking chair sat on either side.

"These *Sixes* are dangerous if left unchecked. But when trained and put to proper use, they can be quite handy. We bring them here, train the ones we can, and house them. In exchange for food, shelter, and protection, they work for us."

He was so full of crap! Food, shelter, and *protection*? More like starvation, cages, and torture. "So the ones you have here are employees?"

"Some, yes. They're given every comfort and convenience in exchange for their services. Due to the nature of our work, they live on site as they're on call twenty-four hours a day. Others, the dangerous ones we can't *rehabilitate*, are held here for their own good. That boy you helped escape was one of them."

Helped escape. Not that boy who *took you hostage*. Not that boy who *tried to kill you*. Even now, I could do no right. He loved rubbing it in.

Just you wait. Payback's a bitch, Daddy.

"What exactly is his deal?" I figured now was a good time to ask questions. "He touched someone and—" I shook my head, feigning fear. "He touched someone and they died. Shriveled up and turned to freaking dust!"

"98. His touch is devastating—as you had the unfortunate opportunity to witness. It brings instant death to anything organic. People, plants, any living thing. Destroyed with a simple brush of his skin."

"Except for you." He watched me with an odd kind of curiosity and hunger. It made my skin itch. It was the same look I'd seen on my high school English teacher, Mr. Parks, when he'd waved his winning lottery ticket at the class and skipped out.

"Why? Not that I'm not glad," I said, kicking back and

throwing my feet onto his desk. He glared at me but said nothing. "Why didn't I shrivel up?"

"That's a *very* good question."

· · ·

After some seriously uncomfortable probing—the verbal kind—Dad had taken me on a tour of the fifth and sixth floors. Training and Acquisition Research. I'd gotten to watch a young woman burn a hole through a concrete block by simply glaring at it, a man whose skin could turn to ice at will, and a small child transformed into a beautiful blue and gold parrot before my eyes. If I didn't know what was really going on here, this place would have impressed me. I asked about the other floors, but he said anything involving containment and *housing* was off limits, and that had been the end of *that* conversation.

We were standing in front of the elevator doors when Dad pulled out his security card. The doors opened and we stepped in. He was about to swipe the card when I reached out and snagged it from his hands.

"Wow, that's a really shitty picture, Dad," I said, gripping the card tight between my fingers. The plastic was cold, smooth, and slightly flexible. Slipping my other hand into my back pocket, I fingered the yellow security badge I'd gotten at the desk when we came in. A knifelike jabbing assaulted my temples. It only lasted a few seconds, but stole my breath nonetheless.

Dad didn't seem to notice. With a swift move, the card was back in his hand, through the swiper, and disappearing into the folds of his coat. I gave myself a mental pat on the back. Oh, yeah. I was smooth.

By the time we made it back to the fourth floor, it was almost two in the afternoon. Dad had something to *tend to*, so he deposited me in the cafeteria. I was about to hit the elevator when someone plopped into the seat beside me.

"Howdy!" said a cheerful voice.

I swiveled in my chair to see a guy about my age. He was looking at me with soulful eyes, a springy curl of his chestnut brown hair falling into his face. He extended his hand, smiling. "I'm Flip. Haven't seen you before. New?"

"Um, Hi."

"First day?" he asked, taking a bite from the thin end of a raw, unpeeled carrot.

"I'm actually here with my dad. Marshall Cross."

"You're Cross' kid?" He beamed. "Your Dad is amazing. Someone had a man-crush. "I take it you're a fan."

"Hells, yeah. Your Dad is a great man. He really looks out for us." He laughed. "I take it you're a Nix?"

"Nix?"

"It's what we on the inside call the non-Six folks."

Wow. Way original.

"You'll love it here," Flip continued. "Denazen is awesome."

"Seriously?" I couldn't hide the surprise in my voice. Thankfully, Flip was too oblivious to notice.

"Hells, yeah! We're like frickin' superheroes. Out there fighting the good fight. Making the world a safer place for mankind and all that." He leaned in closer. "We take out the bad guys and restore order. We're totally like X-Men or Justice League and shit!"

I wondered if someday Flip's diarrhea of the mouth would become fatal. "So they treat you okay?"

"Are you kidding? I was a runaway. Totally clueless about things. Denazen found me, gave me a home, and taught me all the good I could do with my gift. We, like, help the *government* sometimes."

Talk about frigging delusional.

"You're not, like, a prisoner or anything?"

That earned me a funny look. "Prisoner?"

"You can come and go as you please?"

"I don't see why not...but we don't. We stay here. It's safer." His expression turned thoughtful. "There's a lot of bad shit out there. Denazen's pissed off a lot of bad guys. Made a lot of enemies. On the outside, we're walking, talking target practice. In here, we're safe. They protect us."

"In exchange for your service," I said, trying to keep the sarcasm out of my voice. If I didn't know better—if I hadn't met Kale first—the crap Flip was selling might have been more believable. But I'd seen behind Denazen's mask. The truth was out. Now, if I had my way, I'd make sure everyone and their uncle knew. "And you're all cool with that?"

He frowned. "Most of us, yeah. There are always some uncooperative ones. Some of us can be pretty dangerous. If Sixes starts hurting people, they bring them in and try to reason with them."

Rehabilitate.

"And if they can't?"

"The police have jails, right? Same concept. Anyone with abilities that goes on mass killing sprees or whatever are criminals." He looked down at his watch. "Crap. I'm late for the weight room." He stood, giving me a wink. Flexing his arms, carrot hanging from the corner of his mouth, he said, "They help us get and stay ripped. I'm a total babe magnet now."

I smiled. "It was nice meeting you, Flip."

I watched him leave, breathing a sigh of relief. I wanted to get things moving.

With the coast finally clear, I stood and made my way to the elevator. What I planned to do was risky, but it was the only hope

I had of getting back into Dad's office alone.

They hadn't let me into that Six-only party because I was cute.

When I was seven, Uncle Mark took Brandt and me shopping right before Christmas. I saw a Barbie doll I absolutely *had* to have and begged him to buy it for me. He'd refused of course—money had been tight. When Uncle Mark went to check out, I snuck back. Grabbing the beautiful new doll, I clutched my old, raggy one, wishing she had the same beautiful, flowing white dress and shimmery crown sitting in a mass of golden hair. When I looked down, both dolls were identical and I threw up all over aisle eight.

As I got older, I figured out how it worked. I could mimic one object into another so long as I was still touching the original. As long as the general size was the same, it worked. I'd experimented and found that my limitations were almost nonexistent. If I had a tuna sandwich and wanted a cheeseburger, no problem. It tasted exactly like a cheeseburger. If I wanted beer, but had soda? No worries! Liquid fun was only a wish away.

You'd think with something as awesome as this, I'd be doing it like crazy, right? A teenager with the ability to basically get *what* she wanted *when* she wanted would go nuts. Other than the obvious *I should keep this to myself* opinion formed at an early age, the pain wasn't worth it. Each time I did it, my brains felt like they were being yanked out through my nose with a fishing hook. Size mattered a little. The bigger the object, the worse the pain. But when mimicking something as small as an ice cube caused you to blow projectile vomit and see stars, there better be a damned good reason for doing it.

Last year, Dad had a brand new, fifty-two-inch flat screen delivered to the house while he was at work. I'd come home, messing around with some guy I met at a rave, and we'd knocked it over. After I got him to leave, I'd gone to the garage, dragged in the cardboard box, and *voila!* New TV. The hardest part had been getting rid of the ruined remains of the original with a blinding headache and gut-wrenching nausea. It lasted an entire day.

I'd never told another living soul. What would I have said? Hi, my name is Dez and I'm some weird human wish factory? Wish in one hand...and it comes true in the other. Um, no. It came in handy in an emergency, but still, it was freaky. Then, when I heard about that kid who was dragged away at Sumrun and never heard from again, I kept my secret for a whole 'nother reason. I was scared as hell.

When Kale told me about my mom and what she could do, it'd been so hard not to smile. Even though I'd never met her, it made me feel less alone. Like mother, like daughter—sort of, anyway. I'd never even considered trying to mimic myself into someone else. I mean, what if I couldn't change back? And I couldn't even begin to imagine the pain that would come with something that big. It'd probably kill me.

Now, working my mojo here—essentially the equal of shooting up in a police station—I was taking an insane risk. Dad had locked Mom away because of what she could do. How would he react if he found out what *I* could do?

I swiped the card and said, "Fifth floor."

I don't know if somewhere in the back of my mind I'd expected it not to work, or maybe I thought sirens and flashing lights would go off, alerting the entire building, but when the doors closed and the elevator jerked to a start, I felt a tidal wave of relief.

I knew it was a long shot—there's no way it'd be this easy—but the best place to start looking for the information I needed was Dad's office. The new security card unlocked his door with no problem. I closed it behind me and dove for the filing cabinet.

After about twenty minutes of searching, I'd gone through

all the files in the small cabinet next to his desk. Business expense receipts. A few personnel files—ones marked for a raise. But there was nothing saying how many Sixes they had at Denazen, much less who they all were. The only things left were his desk drawers. As I started forward, reaching for the top drawer, a voice snapped from the doorway.

"What the hell are you doing?"

My blood ran cold. I looked up into Dad's furious face.

14

I climbed to my feet, brain working at warp speed to come up with some logical excuse.

For once, I had nothing.

He stepped inside and closed the door behind him. The snap of it made me jump. "Answer me. What are you doing? And how the hell did you get in here?" He stalked forward and for a second, I thought he might hit me.

"I—" I stumbled. It wasn't for show either. I was coming up totally blank. A first. Usually, I could sell ice to Eskimos. "I wanted to see if I could find any information on that Dax guy."

"How did you get through the security locks?"

I went to pull the badge from my pocket. It was there, the cool smooth plastic rubbed against the tips of my fingers. But I couldn't hand it to him. He'd see *his* security badge—not *mine*. My mimics didn't revert on their own and since I didn't have a copy of my original badge, I couldn't change it back. I gave him my best, sheepish smile. "Um, crap. I must have lost it."

"You lost it," he repeated.

Eyes down, I pretended to scan the floor. "I must have dropped it. Has to be in here somewhere."

He was quiet while I played it up, walking the length of the room in search of the security badge. Once, from the corner of my eye, I could swear I saw him smiling. He let me search for a few minutes before clearing his throat.

"Let's go. We're leaving."

. . .

In the car, the silence was more than eerie. It was heavy. Angry. I had to do something to diffuse the situation, otherwise I was never getting near that building again. Dad was still livid I'd been snooping. I'd never get Ginger the information she wanted unless I did some damage control. Fast. It had to be something drastic. World shattering. If I was going to weasel my way back into Denazen, I had to show the only card I had. My ace in the hole.

Unfortunately, it was the ace of spades.

"I want in," I blurted into the silence. "I want to work for Denazen."

Dad chuckled. "That's not possible."

"Why not?" I demanded. "Those people that took me, they're animals. They're planning to attack Denazen."

Out of the corner of my eye, I saw Dad's eyes widen. "What?"

"It was one of their threats. They're going to rise up and take you down. They think they're better than everyone else," I said, laying it on thick. "I *need* to be a part of this, Dad. I need to help stop them."

"Deznee, there's hardly anything *you* can do to help." Another Dad might have sounded sympathetic. Another Dad might have said the same thing, meaning it was too dangerous for his teenage daughter to get involved in. Not mine. His words were cold, harsh. They said there was nothing I could do to help because I was useless. Oh yeah? We'd see about that.

I inhaled and said a silent prayer, reaching for a pen from the console. Holding it tight, I grabbed the marker rolling on the floor at my feet. I'd dropped it two months ago when Dad had picked me up from school and never bothered to pick it back up. I pictured myself holding *two* markers, instead of one pen and a marker.

A few seconds later, Dad swore and jerked the wheel hard to the left. The car fishtailed, tires squealing, and for a moment I thought for sure we'd crash. Thankfully, after several nauseating moments, the car came to an abrupt stop.

Everything spun a little, and the throbbing in my head was starting to subside.

Dad stared at me not with shock or horror, but something else. Vindication? Barely contained excitement? Whatever it was, it was way creepy. He had to know it was a possibility, right? He'd screwed Mom and she was a Six. There'd be a fifty-fifty chance I'd be one, too.

"I think I could be useful in some way, Dad. Don't you think?" I turned, looking him in the eyes. Balling my fists, I repeated what I'd told him yesterday. "I *need* to make them pay."

. . .

Considering the shocking secret I'd confessed, I was surprised—but relieved—when Dad left me alone to go back to work. As soon as he'd made it down the street, I was out the door and headed through the woods into town.

My first stop, Roudey's, was a bust. Alex hadn't been seen

since he'd left last night to meet Kale and me. Thankfully, though, Roudey gave me his new address. Which was good since I hadn't realized he'd moved. But then again, that can happen when you avoid someone for over a year. After a short chat with Roudey and a promise to not be a stranger, I was on my way.

I headed down to the pizza place on Fourth. It was one of the only phones in the area I knew of outside. The rest were next to bathrooms and in lobbies. Way too easy to be overheard. Hello, paranoia.

Picking up the receiver, careful to avoid the wad of dried, pink gum stuck to the side, I dialed Brandt. "Hey." I said when he picked up. "It's me."

"Jesus, Dez. About frigging time," Brandt snapped. "I've been freaking!"

"I know, I know. Sorry. I'm back at the house. I mean, not this second, but Dad came and got me yesterday."

"Came and got you?"

"Long story," I said, leaning my head against the edge of the phone booth. There was still a slight hum in my head and my neck ached a little. "Did you find anything?"

On the other end of the line, something creaked—he was sitting on his bed. Brandt gave a heavy sigh. "Dez, this is some serious shit. They call them Sixes because their funky abilities? They come from an abnormality in the sixth chromosome. Some of these people? Seriously dangerous."

"Yeah, that information is old news. What about Denazen? Did you find out anything about the organization?"

"Oh, yeah, they've got their hooks into *everything*."

I swallowed. "What do you mean?"

"Well, I did some digging. I found connections to Denazen *everywhere*."

"Connections?"

"Does the name Martin Bondale sound familiar?"

"Yeah, kinda. Why? Who is he?"

"Remember that guy who was up for DA last year? The one who had that woman come forward claiming he'd banged her the entire summer? Everyone went nuts when she turned up dead?"

"Oh yeah," I said. "I remember. Everyone thought he did it, but he got elected anyway!"

"Uh-huh," Brandt said.

"Wait. You're saying Denazen had something to do with it?" As the son of a hardcore investigative reporter, Brandt always had a conspiracy theory or three ready to go. As much as I wanted this to be one of them, I knew better.

"He's just *one* on a list of city, town, and government officials who have links to these people."

"Are you crazy?" I whispered. Glancing over my shoulder, I made sure I was still alone. "When I said see what you could find out, I didn't mean dig like you're looking for China. These people are dangerous. They—"

"Dez, trust me when I tell you, I understand what kind of dangerous they are." A pause. Then, a second later, a metallic rattle. He was spinning the wheels on his skateboard.

"Okay, I gotta find Kale. Make sure he's okay."

"Whatever. Let me know if you need anything else. And be careful," Brandt urged. "Without me there to watch your back, you're just a helpless girl."

"Sure. And without me to watch *your* back, you're just a big, clueless guy." I smiled and went to hang up but stopped. Bringing the phone back to my ear, I said, "And no more digging!"

Alex's apartment was in the seedier part of town, un-affectionately dubbed The Fix. Even though The Fix was where most of the local drug deals went down, the cops tended to avoid the area altogether. They had no problem busting the dealers the moment they stepped onto school property or at the mall, but The Fix seemed to have a government all its own. It had its own rules and its own enforcers. Ones you didn't cross.

As I climbed the narrow steps leading to the third floor—the elevator didn't work—I tried to hold my nose. The hallway smelled like urine and unwashed bodies. I made a left at the top of the stairs and counted the doors. The apartment numbers were mostly missing, but when I came to Alex's, the numbers 342 had been filled in with black magic marker.

I raised my hand to knock as the door swung open.

"Dez?" Alex stumbled back. Obviously I hadn't been expected. "What the hell are you doing?" He reached out and dragged me into the apartment. "You shouldn't be here!"

"Please tell me you've seen Kale?" He'd been gone when I woke this morning—which made sense—but I didn't know where he went or how to find him.

"I'm here," came his voice from behind Alex. He stood in the hall, wearing a pair of Alex's black jeans and one of Brandt's long sleeved green T-shirts. He smiled at me, and I couldn't help but smile back as the panic drained away.

"You left. I didn't know where you'd gone."

He stepped past Alex, stopping only when his shoulder brushed mine. "I left when I heard your father get up."

From the corner of my eye, I could see Alex watching us, eyes narrow. "What is he talking about?"

Kale, apparently feeling helpful, answered for me. "I stayed with Dez last night. We took off our shirts."

I didn't have to see my face to know it turned a bright shade of red. Kale and I were going to discuss the appropriate level of sharing. *Soon.*

Alex folded his arms and shook his head. "First Beldom and Doon, now Rain Man here? Is there something I should know,

Dez?" He turned to Kale. "I thought you stayed here with me last night."

Kale shrugged and turned away from him. "I left when you fell asleep."

"There's no way you snuck out of here without me knowing it." Alex was jealous, I could see that—but he'd lost that right a long time ago.

"You sleep loud," Kale said to Alex, still smiling at me. "It was easy."

Alex looked like he wanted to lunge for Kale but maintained his distance. He turned to me, disgusted. "He seriously spent the night with you?"

"Not like you're thinking, but yes! And who the hell are you to care? Your college skank not giving you enough these days?"

Kale looked from me to Alex, face darkening. At his sides, fingers twitched. "You hurt her. She told me. Why do you care if she lets me kiss her? She holds *my* hand now, not yours!"

Alex let out a horrible laugh. "Aww, you poor shmuck. You got shafted, trust me. Haven't you heard? She lets other guys do a lot more than that."

I didn't think, only reacted. A lot like the day I found him groping the college bimbo in the back room of Roudey's. My fist shot out, nailing him right in the corner of the jaw. He took the blow like a trooper, but I could tell it stung. It better have, because my hand felt like it might fall off.

"If you're done being a dick, then I have some news."

And like flipping a switch, Alex turned serious. Kale spending the night, as well as my well-placed right hook, was forgotten.

"I start my new job tomorrow," I said with barely contained pride. It probably should've bothered me that I was putting myself in the hands of men who used people like me as puppets, but I was riding the high. I'd gotten myself in and managed to pull the wool over Dad's eyes. Again. That never failed to give me a warm, fuzzy feeling.

"New job?" It took all of about six seconds before Alex caught on. His eyes widened, and he flashed me a truly appreciating smile. Suddenly, I was his hero—heroine. "Excellent! How did you manage it?"

Yeah. This was going to be the hard part. I knew Alex would make a stink. Kale was liable to get downright volatile.

"I have something they need."

Kale watched me, suspicion replacing the anger he'd been directing at Alex.

Alex was just plain confused. "No offense, Dez, but what could you have that they could possibly need?"

There was a baseball across from me on the end table. I grabbed it and headed to the kitchen, where I'd seen an orange sitting on the counter next to Alex's car keys. With both items in hand, I headed back to the living room and stopped in front of them. Closing my eyes, orange in one hand, baseball in the other, I imagined taking a bite of the orange, citrusy juices dribbling down my chin. Pictured the unsmooth surface and thick skin simply waiting to be peeled away. It was definitely harder than usual—not that I did it often—but it did work. I knew not by the weight or texture change of the ball but by the sudden spike in pain and loss of gravity. Several seconds of black, and I was on the floor.

"Jesus!" Alex swore, sprinting forward.

Kale beat him to me. "Dez?"

I nodded, and inclined my head to our right. Two oranges had rolled to the corner of the room.

"You're—"

"A Six," Kale finished for him, sounding less surprised. He gathered me in his arms and helped me to the couch. Tilting my head up, he brushed the hair from my face. "You're bleeding. What happened?"

I swiped at the wetness under my nose. Blood. Well, that was new.

"I don't use it because it's too much of a strain on my body. It physically hurts to do it." No need to elaborate.

Alex snorted. "That looks like a little more than hurts. You're bleeding, for Christ sake."

"That's never happened before," I insisted. "I think it's because I've been doing it a lot more than usual."

About ten seconds later is when the piss really hit the fan.

"Are you out of your mind?" Alex bellowed.

Kale began pacing the floor like a wild animal, growling, "Not a chance!" He was flicking his fingers again. Pointer, middle, ring, pinky.

I waited a few minutes for them to get it out of their system—testosterone and all that. It took longer than I'd hoped, but eventually they'd settled for menacing glares and silent seething.

"How could you not tell me?" Alex asked after five minutes of heavy silence. He'd retreated to the corner of the room and was fisting a purple stress ball. After mashing it in his hand several times, he hummed it at the wall and threw himself onto the couch.

"Oh, because you shared *all* your secrets with me?" Frigging hypocrite! He looked away, guilty.

"I do not like this." Kale had stopped pacing and settled against the far wall by the door. Maybe he thought to block it in case I made a mad dash to Denazen or something. Who knew.

"The Six is out of the bag now. Dad already knows what I can do, so there's no turning back. I screwed up yesterday. Got caught snooping. I needed something drastic or I never would have been allowed back inside."

"This is beyond drastic, even for *you*," Alex grumbled. "Can't you run away? Why are you fighting so hard to get Ginger's help?"

"Because I *need* to find the Reaper. He's the only chance I have of getting my mom away from that place."

"We'll figure something out. Stay and I'll hide you. We can make it work."

Next to me, Kale stiffened. The way he'd said it, I wasn't sure if Alex meant me and him, or evading Denazen, but either way it was out of the question. "So *you're* going to help me spring Mom? I don't think so. And what about Kale?"

"It'll take some time, but we'll figure out a way to help your mom. I promise. As for him," Alex said, flicking his wrist in Kale's direction, "they'll stop looking eventually. How important could one Six be?"

"They put a lot into creating me," Kale said in an eerie, low voice. "They've never found anyone like me before. They will not give up. I am of dual use to them. It's not only my touch they use, but my blood."

Alex cringed. "Your blood?"

"I've been gone several days now. They'll be frantic to recapture me." He turned to me. "That man's niece, she wasn't drugged. She was injected with a serum made up in part with my blood. When injected into the bloodstream of any Six, it causes them to become vacant. Pliable. They're effortless to control. The blood is taken often and in small batches because the serum sours quickly."

"Then leave town. Seems like that'd be the best bet. For you, and for the rest of us."

"He can't just up and leave. Not unless I go with him."

Alex slammed his foot down. "What, now you're like his personal bodyguard with benefits?"

"He's lived his entire life inside Denazen. He doesn't know anything about the world we live in."

"Whatever," Alex mumbled. "Not like I can stop you."

"I can make this work, I know I can." I threw myself onto the sofa next to him.

"You think it hurts now to do what you did? Can you imagine how you're going to feel after an hour at Denazen? They're going to make you perform like a street corner monkey. It'll frigging kill you!"

"I can handle it," I insisted. Truthfully though, I hadn't thought about it that way. They would test me. Make me show them what I could do. How much could my body take before it broke?

"What if I asked you not to go?" Kale said from the other side of the room. He was glaring at Alex.

"It wouldn't matter. This is what has to be done." It's not like this was what I wanted. It was the only choice. "Unless either of you can think of a better idea. If so, lemme have it."

Silence.

Yeah, that's what I thought.

Kale shook his head. "That place destroys most people."

It irritated me that neither one of them seemed to have any faith in me. "Then it's a good thing I'm not most people."

15

Bleary-eyed, I glanced at the clock again. Two a.m. I hadn't specifically told Kale to come when I'd left him at Alex's, but I assumed he would. Hoped, anyway. While the memory of last night's kiss stayed fresh in my mind, I was nervous—scratch that, *terrified*—of the quickly approaching morning, and thought having Kale here would calm my nerves.

Right as I was about to surrender to the pull of blackness, a movement by the window caught my attention. He said nothing as he swung from the branch outside and in through the open window, landing with a soft thud on my beige carpet. Our eyes met and a thrill raced up my spine. Tonight, he wasted no time, crossing the distance between us in two long strides, his mouth covering mine before I had time to blink.

I'd worn a pair of flannel boxer shorts like every other night, but instead of my usual grungy tank top, I'd opted for a lacy black demi bra. There was no hesitation this time, no clinking teeth. There was no doubt in my mind that I'd been the guy's first kiss, but holy hell did he have a knack for it.

When we finally came up for air, he was smiling at me. It seemed to come easier to him now, smiling. It did funny things to my stomach. "Hi," he said.

I gave a soft laugh and snuggled close. "Hi back." We stayed like that for a long time, Kale tracing a path from my chin, down to my waist. Sometimes with a single finger, sometimes the back of his hand.

"Please don't go to that place," he said after a while had passed.

"We went through this before. I can't not go. It's a done deal. It's the only way now."

His face scrunched, lips twisting as if he'd just sucked on a lemon. "You have no idea what those people are capable of. You don't know what they do to people like us."

People like us. Sixes. I'd accepted the things I could do, never truly knowing. Never really understanding. The last few years had been all about the next party. The next big thrill. Anything that might make me feel alive—because I'd felt empty inside. Hollow. The rest of my time was spent searching for new and amusing ways to piss off Dad. And all the while, there were others out there, people like me—like my mom—struggling for freedom.

Alex was right. I could take Kale and run. But I couldn't live with myself for very long. Not knowing what Denazen was doing. Not knowing my mom was in there somewhere, being held against her will.

"Let's not talk anymore about Denazen," I took his hand. "Tell me about the dancing. How did you learn?"

"Something Sue showed me once when I was younger, an old film on the television," he said, voice thick and drowsy. "I was fascinated with it. The man, Fred, danced a lot. That's how I learned."

Old movie? Fred? "Fred Astaire? Is that who you mean? You're saying you learned to dance from watching a Fred Astaire movie?"

"That sounds right. I watched him twirl that woman across the dance floor, holding her close. He told her he loved her." He pulled away, looking down at me, those ice blue eyes intense. "I think I understand that now. I think I love you."

My stomach gave a tiny flutter. Alex. Alex had been the last person—the only person—to say he loved me. Hearing it from Kale, while sending tiny prickles of heat and excitement shooting through my veins, hurt. He couldn't love me. Not really. He couldn't know what love was. Not from watching a movie.

"I know you might think that's how you feel, but I'm not sure it's possible. Not yet. It's too soon. Plus, other than the fact that I'm the only girl you know, I'm also the only living thing you can touch. That's gotta mess with your head. I know you feel something for me, but I don't think you love me. Not really."

You'd expect a guy to get annoyed after a speech like that, but not Kale. He only shook his head, expression one of pure resolve. "I don't understand how things work out here. I don't understand people and why they do the things they do. I don't even think I have a clear understanding of right and wrong, but I'm not completely in the dark. I can tell the difference. I like Alex, even though something inside"—he thumped his chest twice—"tells me there's a reason I shouldn't. But thinking of him doing what you're about to do doesn't fill me with fear. It doesn't make me sick."

He leaned back, his lips twisting into a scowl. "When I think of you going to Denazen, my head feels funny. My chest hurts. It's almost like I can't breathe right. When I think of them doing to you any of the things they did to me, I want to scream." He reached out, tilting my face up so I was looking at him. "I don't feel that way about Alex. I never even felt that way about Sue. If I had the ability to touch anyone else in this world, I still don't believe I'd want it to be anyone but you."

"Kale, I—"

His hand clamped down over my mouth and his eyes went wide. Without a word, he darted off the bed and out the window in three fluid steps. Ninja. The guy was a ninja! I stumbled from the bed in time to see him race across the lawn, shirtless. Moments later, the doorknob jiggled, and Dad was yelling for me to let him in.

My fingers grabbed the first shirt they touched—the one Kale had been wearing—and I stumbled to the door. "What the heck is all the—" Unceremoniously shoved aside, Dad and two suit-wearing Denazen monkeys pushed their way into my room. "Um, is there a reason you're allowed to bring guys into my room, but I can't?"

"98 was spotted in the area a short time ago." He turned to me. "Haven't I told you not to lock that door?"

I narrowed my eyes and put my hands on my hips. "And haven't I told you I have no intention of leaving it open?" I gestured to the two men with him. "Seriously not going to change my policy if you're planning on dragging strange men through the house in the middle of the night."

"No one's been in here?" one of them asked.

"Actually I'm hiding the football team in my closet, so if you don't mind, I'd like to get back to it."

The man watched me, wide-eyed.

"As in, no, now get out of my room."

The other man stepped up to my closet and yanked open the door. Jesus, did he think I was serious? He bent forward, moving some of the hangers to the side in quick, jerky motions. Satisfied I was alone, they made their way to the door. Dad stopped at the edge and turned. "Get some sleep. Tomorrow's going to be a long day."

. . .

Morning came way too fast. After I'd gotten rid of Dad and his flunkies, it had been impossible to get back to sleep. I kept waiting for Kale to come back, but he never did. Probably just as well. Knowing Dad, he'd probably had the house watched.

I showered and dressed, dragging the comb through my hair as I made my way down the stairs. As usual, Dad sat at the table with his coffee and paper. I held my arms out and twirled. "Is this okay?" I had on my favorite black shark bite tank and a brand new pair of skinny jeans. On my arms were the black leather cuff bands I knew he hated.

Dad saw me and stood, clearing his throat. "I'm afraid there's been a slight change in today's plans. I'm sure you'll understand."

"Understand what?" I turned to the coffeepot and poured the rest of the off-limits liquid into my Mickey Mouse mug.

"You'll start at Denazen tomorrow. Today is going to be a bit hectic."

I flopped down into the seat he'd abandoned. "Oh? Why, wrestle in a new big bad?"

"They caught 98 last night," he said, watching me. "About a block away from here."

My mouth was dry. The Sahara had nothing on me at that moment. A test. Maybe it was a test. Maybe Dad wanted to see if what I'd said about wanting Kale to pay was true.

I waited too long. His brow furrowed and the right corner of his lip did that twitching thing. The dead giveaway he knew something wasn't right. "I would have thought you'd view this as good news, Deznee."

"No. I—" I shook my head. "It *is* good news. I can't believe he got that close. A block away? Do you think he was coming here?"

Dad folded the paper and set it down. "That would be my guess."

"I want to see him," I said, standing. "I want to look the bastard in the face."

"That won't be possible, Deznee. For everyone's safety, he will be contained on level nine until we can decide what to do with him."

"What's level nine?" I was proud. I managed to keep my voice even. For the most part.

"Transition and termination."

The stairwell of Alex's apartment, if possible, smelled worse than it had the other day. Pinching my nose in a vain attempt to block out the stench, I dashed up the stairs two at a time. I came to the second story landing and tripped over a man slumped across the floor. "Crap, I'm sorry." I bent down to check on him as he maneuvered onto his side and threw up, narrowly missing my shoes. "Okay then, enjoy the hangover."

Two minutes later I was at Alex's door, pounding like a crazy person. I had no idea what his days consisted of now, but it was only just after ten in the morning. That was like six a.m. to the Alex I'd known a year ago. Hopefully, I'd caught him before he headed off to Roudey's—or wherever the heck he spent his days now.

The door jerked open and there stood Alex, shirtless in black sweat pants that sat low on his hips. Hair tousled and hazel eyes bleary, there was no doubt he'd just woken up. His face wrinkled into a mask of annoyance until he actually took a good look at who was standing in the doorway. "Dez?"

I pushed him aside and stepped into the room. "Please tell me Kale's here."

"Déjà vu, Dez. Didn't we do this yesterday?" He wasn't happy.

"When was the last time you saw him?"

He shrugged and went over to the couch, sinking down. "I was out most of the night at a party downtown. I asked him if he wanted to come, but he said no. Got home a little after four, was a little buzzed, and crashed. Didn't look to see if he was on the couch. I agreed to let the dude crash here. I'm not playing babysitter."

"Dad said they got him. Late last night."

He gave a half shrug. "Those are the breaks, I guess."

I glared at him, fists tightening.

"Look, I'm sorry they got him, I really am, but for the most part, it's every man for himself when it comes to Denazen." He shrugged again.

I couldn't believe that. "You have to help me."

"Help you do *what*?"

I stared. "Get him out! They'll kill him. Dad pretty much said so! Come with me. Go undercover. With the two of us there, we'll find the information faster. Maybe we can get Kale and my mom out without the Reaper's help."

He took a step forward, taking my hands in his. "I know you were kinda attached to the guy, but you need to let it go."

I ripped my hands from his and backed up a few steps. Could he really be that cold? "Were you always such an asshole? I mean in all that time we were together, how did I not notice what a selfish prick you were?"

That hit a nerve. Alex covered the room in three steps and pushed me back against the door. "Denazen wiped out my entire family. They slaughtered my parents. My grandmother took me in, and when Denazen came for her, she gave her life so I could stay free." A hand on each side of my shoulders, he gave a rough shake. "Why the hell would I willingly walk into that place?"

"To help me," I said quietly.

For a minute, I thought he might scream. Face twisted and red, his lips curled into a silent snarl. After a moment though, he visibly relaxed. The pressure on my arms vanished, and he spun me toward the door. "Get the hell out."

. . .

The car ride to Denazen the next morning went by in a flash. Somewhere close to midnight the night before, I'd started getting seriously cold feet. Kale was locked up somewhere, Alex wouldn't help me, and Brandt, for whatever reason, wasn't picking up his cell. When I'd come up with the idea to infiltrate Denazen and find Ginger the information she needed in return for her help, I'd been filled with excitement. This was the ultimate rush, with the added bonus of screwing over Dad in the process. But after trying—and failing—to sleep last night, my stomach remained a mess of knots. I couldn't shake the look of raw anger in Alex's eyes when he told me to leave. The icy tone of his voice told me I was truly alone in this. If something went wrong, there'd be no one to go to for help. Was I really up for this? Sure, I could be resourceful, but these were the big dogs. I couldn't help feeling like I'd crawled way out of my league.

Dad whipped the car into his private parking spot and opened the door without a word. I followed him into the building and to the white elevator doors. Once they closed behind us and the real set opened, he began to speak.

"Before we proceed, I must make sure you understand. This

is not a joke, and it's not a game."

He stopped and it took me a moment to realize he was waiting for confirmation. I nodded.

"Denazen takes its training very seriously. You will be asked to do things you don't want to do. Things that will make you uncomfortable. All these things are for the greater good."

Greater good? Was he seriously trying to sell the *nobility* angle to me?

"There is no option to walk away. Once you start forward, there is no going back. Do you understand me?"

The elevator stopped, and I gave a nervous giggle as the doors opened. I guess that meant there'd be no going easy on the boss' daughter. "So it's a lot like the mob, then?"

He wasn't laughing.

I cleared my throat. "I understand this won't be easy, but it'll be worth it."

Another nod and he stepped out of the elevator. I followed. Dad signed in as Hannah watched, eyes glued to his every movement like he was the second coming. After Dad was done, she pushed the clipboard to me. Today, I had to sign, too. Without a word to Hannah—or me—he started to the next set of elevators.

"You will be spending the day on level six with our acquisitions interviewer, Mercy. She will interview you and explain things."

"Interview? I thought I already had the job?" Which is funny because I didn't know exactly what *job* I had. Technically, I'd said I wanted to work for Denazen. I never said what I wanted to do for them. Or if there'd be money involved.

"It's not the kind of interview you're thinking. All Denazen employees are interviewed on a monthly basis for the first year to ensure there are no—problems."

I didn't ask what kind of problems he meant. My imagination ran wild and the knot in my stomach got a little larger.

When the doors opened again, we were on level six. Off the elevator and into a room that looked a lot like the one on level five, neither of us said a word. A large marble island in the center manned by a tall black woman and a short white man was hard to miss.

"Good morning, Nika." Dad turned to the man. "Peter." He nodded to me. "This is Deznee, a new acquisition. I need for her to spend the day with Mercy."

Nika nodded, expression blank. She reached for the phone and turned away from us, speaking quietly into the receiver.

Peter, on the other hand, wasn't so dismissive. He stared, eyes wide and appraising, drifting between my chest and regions lower. Tongue darting in and out like a lizard, he licked his lips and leaned forward. "And what's your gift, little cutie?"

I gave him my most wicked smile. "Ass kicking. Want to see?"

He straightened up and turned to Dad with a chuckle. "This one's a ball of fire. Where'd you find her?"

"This one is off limits, Peter. Deznee is my daughter." Dad's voice came out stony and cold, but not in the way a protective father's should be. This was different. Oddly possessive. Like I was a shiny new toy he couldn't wait to take out for a test drive. One he didn't want to share.

Peter's face paled and his eyes became impossibly large. "Your daughter, sir?"

"That's what I said," Dad snapped. Peter took the hint and quickly turned away, busying himself with a stack of papers on the other side of the counter.

A few moments later, Nika hung up the phone and eyed me warily. "Mercy will be down shortly to collect her." She had a thick accent that I couldn't place. An odd mix between Australian and British. I wanted to ask where she was from, but I didn't think that would portray the right image. Cool and detached. That was what I'd need to survive this place.

I figured I should look at this like prison. Go in and project a badass attitude and maybe no one would screw with me. I glanced over to see Peter sneaking lecherous glances at me again when Dad wasn't looking.

Dad pulled me away from the desk and into the corner to wait for Mercy. "I have instructed Mercy to treat you no differently than any other acquisition. She will ask you the same questions and expect the same answers. You are to respond truthfully because she will know if you are lying."

He reached out, taking a firm grip on my upper arm. There'd be a bruise there tomorrow for sure. Out of habit, I almost jerked away, but thought twice. That probably wouldn't be accepted. Not here. I wasn't his daughter anymore—I couldn't get away with shooting my mouth off or flipping him the bird. He looked down at me, eyes full of anticipation. I was finally in a place he could control. He was eating this up. I could see it in his eyes.

"Denazen is an environment onto itself. To survive here, the key factor is *obedience*."

17

Mercy was a petite woman with dull green eyes and mousey brown hair. She wore it pulled into a severe bun that did nothing for the shape of her face. Her beige slacks were wrinkled and a bit too short, and her blue blouse was tucked too tightly, hugging snug in the shoulders. With most people, you can tell a lot about them from not only the clothes they wear, but *how* they wear them. If clothing was any indication, Mercy was tragic.

At first glance, everything about the woman screamed weak-willed, milk-toast. I bet myself a new pair of boots—black suede—that when she spoke, her voice would be wispy and soft. Her posture slightly slumped, she fidgeted with the pen in her hand—flicking the point in and out, in and out. I stuffed my hands into my pockets to keep from ripping the pen from her fingers and jabbing her with it. Then, when I thought it couldn't get any worse, she started chewing her bottom lip. I *hated* that.

Oh yeah. She'd be a pushover for sure. The kind girls like me were easily able to walk all over, chew up, and spit out.

"Sit down," she barked and pointed to a solitary chair in the corner of the room.

Holy hell, was I wrong.

On the other side, Mercy sat behind a long white desk and pulled a legal-sized notepad out of the drawer. "My name is Mercy Kline. I'm the acquisitions interviewer here at Denazen. I'll be asking you a series of questions. I advise you to answer them promptly and truthfully. We will—"

"What kind of questions?"

She looked up from her paper, eyes wide. "Excuse me?"

It wasn't that complicated a question. "What kind of questions will you be asking?" I repeated, slower. "And while we're at it, what am I gonna be doing here? Hunting down Sixes? Working in the cafeteria? No one's said, and I'd kinda like a clue."

The surprised look melted away, replaced by one of superiority. "Maybe Mr. Cross wasn't clear in his instructions." She leaned forward. Slamming one of the drawers closed, she said, "You are here to answer questions, not ask them. Do you understand?"

I nodded.

Placated, she continued. "Please state your full name."

"Deznee Kaye Cross."

"And your age, including date of birth."

"Seventeen. Born on February 1, 1994."

"Parents' names and ages?"

"Are you serious? You must know my—"

Mercy looked up from her paper. The weight of her stare hit me like a truck falling out of the sky. "Parents' names and ages?" she said again.

"My mom's name was Sueshanna. I really don't know her age." I managed to get the words out without flinching. Careful to phrase my answer generically, I omitted saying she was dead.

If it was true, and she could see a lie, she'd know right away it was crap. I hoped by avoiding the subject altogether, I could skate around it. "My dad's name is Marshall Cross and he's forty-five."

"Current relationship status?" Her voice cut like an arctic chill blowing through the room.

"If you mean me, then you're not my type. If you mean my dad, he's single, but I don't think you're his type either," I said with a small smile. Mercy didn't find it amusing. A small blue vein in her forehead started throbbing like crazy.

Of course, seeing how much it annoyed her only pushed me further. "Actually, come to think of it, I don't think he has a type. I've never seen him with a woman. Mercy, I hate to break it to you, but there's a very real possibility my dad is gay."

"Deznee—"

"Dez," I corrected. Dad was the only one who called me Deznee. I *hated* it.

"Deznee," she repeated. "Your father warned me about you. I'm sure he also told you I would not be going easy on you because of your familial ties."

"What'd he say?"

She blinked, not understanding.

"You said he warned you about me. What'd he say?"

Her smile turned into a toothy grin. "He said you were a disrespectful little cur in need of serious and harsh disciplinary action and that we shouldn't hold back."

"Ouch."

"Moving on." She bent her head over the desk again. "Current relationship status?"

"Single."

"Sexual orientation?"

I almost asked her if she was hitting on me, but after the previous display, I thought twice. "Straight."

"Heterosexual."

"Huh?"

"The correct answer is heterosexual."

I didn't say anything, though a ton of things came to mind.

"Allergies?"

Stupidity. Country music. Liars. Also, possibly shellfish. "None I'm aware of."

"How many sexual partners have you had?"

I gave her a look of mock indignation. "And what makes you think I'm not a virgin?"

She tilted her head up and, I swear, rolled her eyes.

"One," I answered, annoyed. This crap had nothing to do with anything and it was none of her business.

She looked up again, glaring as if she didn't believe me.

"Aren't you the human lie detector?" It came out a little defensive.

"Oh, I know you're telling the truth, I'm simply surprised."

I raised my eyebrows, but said nothing.

"The way your father made it sound, you were a regular Jezebel."

"Jezebel? No one says that anymore. The word you're looking for is whore. Or skank. Hoochie works, too." I told myself it was her purpose to bring me down a few pegs, to find a crack in my armor, but it still bothered me that Dad told her I was a tramp.

I shrugged it off and played it cool. I refused to give her the satisfaction of seeing it get to me. "I'm a tease more than anything else. It's a huge thrill to get a guy all wound up then douse him with a nice cold helping of I'm-not-ready, ya know what I mean?" I leaned back and gave her a once over. "Well, maybe *you* don't know what I mean."

"Name?"

"Didn't we go over this one already? Deznee—"

"The boy."

Crap. Would they know his name? I didn't have a choice—I had to answer—and she'd know if I lied. "Alex," I said, hoping she wouldn't ask for his last name,—even though I knew better.

"Alex, what?"

I'd officially lost my sense of humor about all this. "Mojourn." It took every ounce of self-control I had—and then some—not to snap at her.

She made some notes on her sheet. "And the others? What are their names?"

"I told you, there was only one."

"How many others were you semi-intimate with?"

"Semi-intimate? What the hell is *that* supposed to mean?"

"It means, give me the names of the ones you've…messed around with."

"You can't be serious."

She straightened in her chair. Tapping the pen against the edge of her desk, she asked, "Is there a problem, Deznee?"

"Actually, there is, *Mercy*." I stood. "I can't possibly remember all their names, and honestly, I don't see what it has to do with anything. Is being a Six catching? Are you afraid I gave them some disease?"

"Fine," she said calmly. "Then give me the names of the last three."

I sighed. "Joe Lakes, Max Demore, and—" Crap! Now what? No way I could answer truthfully without seriously incriminating myself and blowing my whole *I-need-revenge* cover story, and there was no way I could lie.

Then it hit me. I didn't need to lie. Technically, I didn't know Kale's *real* name.

"I don't know the third guy's name."

She studied me. Her eyes on mine, unwavering, made me

want to squirm in my seat. It had been a long time since an adult's glare did that. "How far did it go?"

"Excuse me?"

"With this unnamed boy, how far did you go?"

Taking a deep breath, I said, "With all due respect, what does this have to do with my working here?"

"How far did it go?" she repeated, voice even.

Fists balled tight, I stood. "How far? We were in my bed," I said in a low, throaty purr. "His hands were everywhere—tugging at my clothes, pulling my hair. It gave me such a thrill to know my dad was right down the hall. I—"

Mercy stood. "Let's take a break from the questions." She walked to the front of her desk and leaned back. "Let's go over some things about Denazen."

"Okay."

"You see, here at Denazen *everything* about your life is our business. Due to the highly…sensitive nature of this job, it is a requirement for us to know our employees. Inside and out. That requires difficult as well as uncomfortable questions. Another thing you should know—and pay attention, because this is important and it applies to you—Denazen has a zero-tolerance policy."

"What's that supposed to mean?"

Her lip twitched. If I hadn't been staring I would have missed it. "It means we don't suffer attitude-ridden little shits such as yourself."

I could be a bit impulsive—okay, I could be *a lot* impulsive—but I hadn't let anyone talk to me like that since kindergarten and I wasn't about to start a new trend. "Screw this." I stalked to the door and jerked up on the handle.

Nothing happened.

I pulled again, jiggling the latch. Still nothing. "What the hell?"

Mercy cleared her throat. I turned to see her holding up a small silver key, a wicked and very satisfied smile on her face. "You will return to your seat and answer the previous question without the theatrics. How far did you go with the last boy?"

My mind wanted me to think this wasn't happening. I jerked up on the handle one last time before giving up. Of course this was happening. Dad locked my mom away in this pit. Why the hell would *I* be exempt?

"So you're saying I'm a prisoner now?" I took my seat and met her determined gaze with one of my own. Show no fear.

"Not at all."

I raised my eyebrows and then looked back at the door.

"I know how this must look to you, Deznee. Understand, if anyone else had tried what you just did…" She reached down and held up a small black box with several ominous red buttons. Pointing to the floor, she said, "They'd be writhing on the floor in incoherent agony."

On the floor, barely noticeable, thin strips of wire were woven between the ceramic tile.

"I thought Dad said no special treatment." I swallowed and hooked my feet behind the back of the chair legs so they didn't touch the ground.

She stood, smoothing out her unsalvageable pants. Her posture seemed to relax a bit. "Yes, well, Marshall sometimes takes things a bit far when it comes to his work."

I looked back at the door again. "You don't say?"

"Shall we continue? Your father doesn't need to know about this."

I sighed, and because I couldn't see any other way around it, carefully told her all about the nameless guy.

18

Dad dropped me off at home and, thankfully, had to head back to the office. As soon as his car was out of sight, I headed to the warehouse. It was a long shot, but I had to do something. Ginger had been clear—her help for the list—but with Kale caught and Alex unwilling to get involved, I was hoping she'd make an exception. Throw me some backup, give me a hint—anything. There was nowhere else to turn. Of course when I got there, the warehouse was empty. There was one last chance. Craigslist. Maybe it wasn't too late to find tonight's party.

Using the last of my cash, I took the bus back across town. The corner of the seat was sticky and I had to lean to my right to avoid a very questionable stain. Oh, and the man across from me? He smelled like old cheese.

The woman next to me was on her cell phone having a heated argument with someone named Hank. Every once in a while, she'd fling her hands into the air, cursing. It was annoying, but saved me the trouble of asking her—or the cheese man—

what time it was. Her watch read 9:45. To make matters worse, I'd apparently gotten on a bus with the one driver in the county who believed in going the speed limit and hitting every stop even though there were only three of us on the bus. He dropped me off in the town square, and by the time I hiked through the woods and made it home, it was almost 11:30. Only half an hour left till they pulled the ad.

Booting up my ancient computer took forever. Pulling out the questionable bag of licorice from my top drawer, I pulled up Craigslist and went to work. Finding the right ad proved harder than I thought. Apparently, there were a lot of weird ads. When midnight came, I'd called four possible numbers—an advertisement for Belly Dancing lessons, one for learning the proper way to wash a dog, a man claiming to teach hamsters *amazing* tricks, and a woman stating that you too can gain ultimate revenge for a broken heart.

Okay. That last one was probably more self-interest than anything else.

Several very colorful responses and an hour later, I'd given up.

I called Brandt again—still no answer—so I left a not-so-friendly voice mail. This was getting ridiculous. He hadn't blown me off since we were in sixth grade and I'd kissed his best friend, David Fenrig.

Sleep came, but it wasn't restful. I spent the night plagued by nightmares. Well, *one* nightmare. A mega mash of freaky, block-of-ice-in-your-stomach weirdness, creepy enough to curl Clive Barker's toes.

I was back at the field party—the one on the night I'd met Kale. We were dancing. He was shirtless, wearing only a pair of faded blue jeans and what looked like a dog collar on his neck. Not bad. The view certainly had promise.

Things were going well. We were swaying to a thumping beat, dangerously close. Kale wrapped his arms around my waist. He leaned in, about to kiss me, but suddenly jerked backward. When I looked over his shoulder, through the crowd of bodies grinding and twisting on the makeshift dance floor, I saw Dad, a long leash in his hands. Another jerk of the leash, and the distance between Kale and me widened.

"You should have let him go," someone said from behind me. "You could have prevented all this."

I tore my eyes away from Dad and turned to see Brandt, dressed in his favorite pair of worn jeans and Milford Ink T-shirt, standing with arms folded. His hair was wild and looked wrong. Darker in spots. The expression on his face made my stomach turn over. The angry set of his jaw, coupled with the strange, almost scary spark in his eyes. Vacant, yet somehow full of rage.

Even in the dark, I could see there was something wrong. But it wasn't only his expression... There was a wide range of things that sent goose bumps skittering across my arms. His skin seemed a bit too pale, his eyes too dull. Even the way he was standing, tilted to the left and hunched, screamed wrong. His board was nowhere in sight. That alone felt jarring.

"You could have prevented all of this," he repeated, the venom in his voice unmistakable this time. I'd heard that tone before, but never, ever directed at me. He pulled the neckline of his T-shirt down to reveal an ugly red- and bluish-tinged gash along the length of his throat. It was covered in blackened, dried bits of blood and crawling with maggots. I gasped and stumbled back, resisting the urge to vomit.

I tried searching the crowd for Kale, but something tipped me backward, sending me to the ground. Before I knew what hit me, I was being dragged through the mud. When I looked up, there was Dad, another leash in his hands. This one attached to the collar on*my* neck.

Frantic, I searched for someone—anyone—I could turn to for help. Alex stood in the corner, arms clasped behind his back, wearing a look of apathy. Ginger sat next to him in a dark blue armchair. She wore a silver sequined dress and an elaborately decorated tiara on her head, and was sipping what looked like fruit punch out of a small plastic cup.

Dad hauled me to my feet as I screamed, "Alex! Do something, please!"

Alex ignored me.

I struggled against Dad's grasp, but it was useless. Suddenly, he seemed to have the strength of ten men. "Ginger!"

Ginger laughed, fruit punch dripping down her chin.

Dad had me by the throat now, our eyes locked. "You should have let this go, Deznee." He turned and nodded to the crowd.

I followed his gaze and saw Kale walking through the crowd, arms spread wide. As his fingers brushed them, one by one my friends shriveled and crumbled before my eyes. They turned to dust and fell to the ground. It only took moments. I blinked once and it was over. Thumping beats bounced eerily over the party-turned-graveyard.

Kale approached slowly, his leash still in Dad's hand. He stopped in front of me, saying nothing.

"Kale?"

He placed a hand on either side of my neck, slowly trailing them down my back to the middle of my ass. He'd killed my friends. Dad stood over us, watching. Alex was here, eyes cold and unwavering.

It didn't matter. Kale—his touch—his face now inches from mine—that was all there was. I was addicted.

"You should have let this go," he whispered as he leaned in, brushing his lips to mine.

Electric at first, so much like our first kiss—but it quickly changed. From my toes to my chin, everything started to sting and itch. I pulled away from Kale, who smiled sweetly at me. Looking down at my hands, my pulse spiked. Right before my eyes, my skin began to pale—then gray, finally shriveling like a grape left out in the sun. I watched as my hands crumbled, starting at the tips of my fingers and working down to my wrists. Next were my arms. Around my face, my hair fell to the ground, tiny tufts of dust rising as chunks of it impacted the grass.

Then there was nothing.

I woke up drenched in a cold sweat and gasping for air. I'd barely caught my breath when a loud knock came from the other side of my door. Dad's voice, cold and sharp, called, "We leave in twenty minutes."

• • •

"Tell me about your gift," the bulky man asked as he entered the room. No hello-how-are-you. No, hi-my-name-is. These people were obsessed.

"What do you want to know about it?" I asked, leaning back against the far wall. The first thing I'd done when I walked in the room was check out the floor. No metal wires.

"You can start by telling me what it is."

"I, uh, can change things."

"Define change things."

"I can mimic things. Change one thing to another, as long as the size is relatively the same and I'm touching both objects."

The man looked around for a moment, before digging into his pocket. He handed me a pencil and a ballpoint pen. "Demonstrate."

I took them from him. Yet another reason I'd never told

anyone. Being asked to perform on command like a monkey dancing for change on the corner pissed me off. Squeezing both writing utensils between my fingers, I closed my eyes. The pain was instant and fierce, sending stabbing prickles down my neck and into my shoulders. When I opened my eyes, I had two pens— and a slowly fading headache. He took them from me, scribbling a line on the back of his hand with each one. "It's solid. It actually writes."

I shrugged. "Of course it writes."

"So if you were to say, change a plum to a nectarine, it would taste like a nectarine?"

I nodded.

He seemed fascinated. "We have a shifter who works for us, but her shifts are nothing more than illusions. Tricks to fool the mind. And she can only change herself. Nothing foreign." He set the pens. down "What about people?"

"People?"

"Can you change into another person?"

I shifted uncomfortably from foot to foot. Suddenly, the room got a whole hell of a lot smaller. I couldn't even imagine what a mimic like that would do to my body. Fry my brain? Liquefy my internal organs? "I've never tried it." Despite my best efforts, my voice shook because I knew what was coming next.

Folding his arms impatiently across his chest, the man said, "Well, no time like the present."

"I really don't think—"

He tapped his watch. "I'm not getting any younger. Let's go."

Crap. Shaking slightly, I took his hand. It was clammy and I had to resist the urge to gag. Closing my eyes, I focused on his bulbous nose and chubby cheeks. The pain came fast. Shooting needles up and down my spine. I tried to swallow, but it felt like my throat was swollen. Trying to take a deep breath, I panicked when I realized I couldn't feel my ribs. After an agonizing few moments, I collapsed, gasping for air. "I can't."

Squeezing my hand harder, he hissed, "Try again."

Talk about performance anxiety. I closed my eyes and tried to focus. In the pit of my stomach, something snapped. A few seconds passed. The hair on the back of my neck tingled. Something wasn't right. I tried to take a step away from him, but my feet felt weird. Heavy and too big. When I managed a glance down at my hands, I gasped. So did the man. Sausage-like fingers attached to wrinkled, mocha-skinned hands instead of the pale, long fingers I was so used to.

He released me and I sank to the ground. Coughing, I wiped the back of my hand across my mouth. When I brought it away, it was streaked with red. *Don't let him see you panic!* I rubbed my hand over the soft material of my tank to hide the evidence.

He was eyeing me like a hungry lion would an elk. In order to unmimic something, I had to be touching both items. Technically there wasn't a *me* to touch anymore—something I should have thought of *before* I'd tried this. Would it even work? The thought of being stuck in this guy's body made me sicker than the actual mimic. And that was saying a lot. I closed my eyes and prayed to God that my insides—which *technically* I was touching cause they were inside—were still my own.

The edges of the room began to water. Ears popping, I had to force the air painfully in and out of my lungs to keep from passing out. The pain, if possible, was worse than before. On a scale of one to ten, it was peaking at about *fifty*. When my vision cleared, I saw the edges of my small, pale hands braced against the cool tile floor. Had I done internal damage? What if I'd broken something? Poked a hole in a vital organ or caused a hemorrhage in my brain? Oh, God. What if I hadn't been able to change completely back? External things that used to be his could now be mine… Extra appendages… I squeezed my legs together and let out a sigh of relief. No leftover man-bits.

"Hmmm," the man said, circling. "Side effects?" He leaned in a bit closer, studying me. His breath smelled like Cheetos.

"I'm tired, and a little hungry," I said casually. No way was I going to tell him I felt like I'd been dropkicked from a plane then rolled through a pile of searing glass. Two days here and I could already see how things worked. Kale was right. They dug deep in your brain, looking for the soft spots.

"We'll have to run more tests," he said, but not to me. He was flitting through the room, opening cabinets and talking to himself. I didn't like how excited he sounded.

"Tests? What kind of tests?"

He started as though he'd forgotten about me. "Physical tests. Reaction times, stimulus responses, things like that. We'll also need to see what your limits are. I'd like to do that on a day you haven't—*mimicked,* is it?—something large."

He was being vague and that scared me, but I didn't question it. Over the next several hours, the man, who finally introduced himself as Rick, assaulted me with a million and ten questions. With each answer, he grew more and more excited.

By four o'clock I was haggard and ready to fall over. The effects from mimicking my entire body hadn't gone away. The headache was finally bearable, but the dull, aching pain in my muscles and joints was making me want to puke.

Rick, mercifully out of questions, smiled. "I just want to get your blood pressure. Then I'll hand you over to your father."

"Perfect timing, Rick." Dad was leaning against the wall, arms folded, watching. It reminded me a little of when I was a kid and used to ride the carousel at the county fair. With each round, I'd look to see him watching with a wide smile on his face. Exactly like he was now. Only the smile was different. Or maybe it wasn't. Maybe I'd seen what I wanted.

"I heard you did very well today, Deznee," Dad said as Rick slapped the cuff on my upper arm.

"Piece of cake," I forced a smile. "So, what's the deal? I still don't know what I'll be doing here. Want to give me a hint?"

Dad's grin got impossibly larger. Loaded with dark, unspoken promises. "All in good time."

"Amazing," Rick breathed from across the room. "One twenty over eighty. Perfection!" He unwrapped the cuff and beamed at me. "You *are* a find, my dear."

He turned away to jot down some notes and Dad stepped forward. "I have a reward for you."

The way he said it was patronizing and insulting, and I wanted to deck him, but curiosity won. "Reward?"

"I expected you to give Rick a hard time, making this an unpleasant day for all involved, but you behaved exceptionally."

"Maybe before we head home you could let me crash on the couch in your office and we'll call it even?" I was having a hard time keeping my eyes open.

"If you'd rather rest than take a tour of the holding cells, that's fine too…"

He had my attention and he knew it. "The holding cells?"

"I thought it would be a nice treat to take you up and show you that boy behind bars. Locked up where he can't hurt you." He put his arm across my shoulders, leading me out of the room. "Maybe this will give you some peace of mind."

Seeing Kale in his old element—locked up like an animal— would only make the nightmares worse.

19

When we stepped off the elevator and onto floor nine—the furthest I'd been—I felt it right away. The air was different. You couldn't classify the other floors as laid back, but compared to the atmosphere on number nine, the rest were a damn party. In the middle of the room sat the same round desk as the lower floors, this one manned by an unhappy-looking man in a white coat and matching gloves. He ignored our entrance, speaking to a man at a desk on the far side of the room. I only caught bits and pieces of their conversation, but words like incineration, disposal, and cleanup were the gist of it. After that, I tuned them out.

As we made our way across the room, my footsteps clapped loudly against the floor. I looked down and saw it was concrete, with brownish stains scattered everywhere.

"It's easier to clean," Dad said when he caught me looking. "It gets a little messy up here at times."

Messy? I swallowed the bile rising in my throat as I followed him through the remainder of the room, picturing someone of the casual way he used to tap the fish bowl in the living room. The girl inside was younger than me—thirteen maybe. Fourteen tops. Large green eyes, glazed and lifeless, stared ahead. Her thin lips parted slightly, and at the right-hand corner, a small trail of pinkish liquid leaked down her chin. She sat on a cot in the corner with her hands folded neatly in her lap. On the floor by her feet was a weathered looking blanket and headless blue teddy bear. She wore a pair of ratty, stained sweat pants and a nondescript, oversized white T-shirt.

"Why is she up here?" It took all my focus, but I managed to control the rage in my voice. Kale had been here his entire life. Was this his life at that age?

"101 has been with us for a few years. Her mother was killed in an accident, leaving her alone and penniless. We found her and took her in. About a week ago, she snapped and attacked a doctor here."

"How did that little thing attack anyone?" Unless the kid was sporting a mouthful of needle-like teeth and poisonous spit, I didn't see it. She couldn't weigh more than eighty pounds soaking wet with two bricks in her hand.

"101 has the ability to stop your heart. That *little thing* killed three people before we were able to sedate her." He pulled down the chart hanging next to the door.

"Why?"

"Why what?"

"Why did she do it? She must've had a reason." I knew I was hopping on thin ice, but couldn't help it. Something had to make that poor girl snap. Maybe she'd spent an hour with Mercy…

"Nothing made her do it. Sixes snap sometimes. It happens."

I should've kept my mouth closed, but couldn't. "Do they? Is that what's gonna happen to me? Am I going to end up in one of these cages with a number instead of a name, *Dad*? The hosing it down to wash away blood and bits from the latest *termination*. By the time we made it to the other side and out another door, I was ready to puke.

"The ninth floor is sort of our problem-solving department. When Sixes get out of control, they come here while we determine the best course of action."

"Best course of action?"

"This job isn't glamorous, Deznee. And it's not always pretty. I have to make some tough choices from time to time. Some of those include deciding if a Six is salvageable or needs to be put down."

Put down.

Like an animal.

I bit my tongue and tried not to scream. A foul, coppery taste flooded my mouth as Dad continued talking.

"I know it may sound harsh to you, but what we do here is for the good of the community. Communities everywhere."

We kept walking. Dad pulled out his security card and swiped it, allowing us access to a small white room with a simple desk and a single red door on the far side.

"Afternoon, Yancy. I'm taking Deznee here on a tour of the cells. We won't be long."

Yancy nodded and unlocked the door. I could feel his eyes on me as we passed. When I looked back, he caught my eye for a second and then looked away. Maybe not everyone at Denazen took as much pride in their work as Dad.

We entered the room—though it wasn't actually a room, more like a wide, unbelievably long hallway. Lining both sides were glass enclosures.

Cages, actually.

We started down the row, stopping at the first occupied one. "This is 101," he said, knocking the glass twice. It reminded me next time I flip you off or come home buzzed from a party?"

He turned away from 101—I wondered what her name had been—and shot me a superior grin. "As long as you keep yourself out of trouble, you have nothing to worry about." He held my gaze for a minute—which felt like an hour—before moving on.

At the next cage he said, "Here we have 119. He's what we call a charmer."

I guessed he didn't mean ladies man. "Charmer?"

"There are many different variations of his ability on record, dating back as far as the early eighteen hundreds." There was a hint of fascination in Dad's voice. "His caress can make a victim fall under his control. We believe his kind are the inspiration behind stories of Incubi."

I watched him through the dirty glass. The man on the other side had a handsome face with an expression similar to 101's. He wore a pair of the same light gray sweat pants and simple white shirt. His brown eyes, though not quite as vacant as the young girl's, stared straight ahead, unseeing. "So why's he up here?"

"119's situation is a bit different from 101's. He's only been with us several weeks, all of which have been spent here, on level nine. We brought him in after the local police three towns over picked him up. They found him running a brothel."

"So he was a pimp? That's a big deal to Denazen?"

"It is when your girls are virtual zombies. They suspected him of kidnapping and drugging the girls."

"But it wasn't drugs, it was his gift."

"Correct."

We moved past several empty cages and came to the next occupant.

"We picked 121 up about a week ago. I believe she went to your school?"

I looked through the glass, horrified to see my fellow senior-to-be classmate and sometimes rival, Kat Hans, wearing the same dead stare as the others—broken and blank. Her auburn hair, normally kept so meticulously styled, hung limp, and her previously perfect complexion was dull and gray. We'd had our differences, but seeing her like that made me furious. Since third grade Kat had talked of becoming a vet. I was betting that dream died the moment Denazen laid eyes on her.

"That's Kat Hans! She went missing last week."

"She's been here with us." He turned away from Kat, disgusted. "Kat has been working with us for quite some time. Her father, Dean Hans, is one of our record keepers on level five." Dad tapped the side of his head. "He has a photographic memory." Dad glanced back at Kat. "His daughter's gift is a bit like 119's, only less dangerous and highly controllable. She can temporarily paralyze you with the touch of her fingers if she chooses."

"And lemme guess, she tried to paralyze someone she shouldn't have?"

Dad shook his head. "Not quite. You see, we allowed 121 to work with us because of her age and connections. As you know, Dax Fleet, the man who ransomed you, is among those trying to hamper Denazen and ruin all the good we do. We thought to use 121 to infiltrate and tear them down from the inside out. However, as it turned out, she was a spy for them—not us."

My throat went dry. "A spy? How does something like that even get past you?"

Dad laughed. The sound sent icy needles of panic poking up and down my spine. "It doesn't. We knew from the start but thought we could still use her to our advantage. When it became obvious nothing substantial would come of it, we brought her here."

"Wow."

"And that's where you come in."

I'm sure my face must have paled at that point. "Me?" I choked. "You can't possibly think—"

He laughed again. "That you're a spy? Of course not. You're smarter than that, Deznee. You're a survivor. I think you know how badly that would end, am I correct?"

I couldn't help the shiver that shot down my back. His eyes gleamed with a mix of amusement and something else—anger? I couldn't tell. But worse than the look in his eyes was his voice. Icy and sharp, it held the hint of a challenge. Did he know? Could that be the reason he brought me up here? To show me what would happen? I nodded, not trusting myself to speak. Nothing says *guilty* like a shaky voice.

"I'd like to get you up to speed so you can take over the task we set 121 with. I want you to infiltrate the rogue Sixes. There is a woman, Ginger Midlen. She's resourceful and has been impossible to find. She's organizing these people. Getting them riled up. We need to take care of her before the problem escalates."

This had to be a joke. Somewhere in the background, Ashton Kutcher would jump out and I'd realize I was being punk'd. Or maybe that other old guy, what was his name—Jamie Kennedy?

"And moving on, we saved the best for last," Dad said. He moved past several cages, stopping at the very last one. "You see? He's locked up tight."

On the other side of the glass, Kale sat on the floor against the far wall. His knees pulled up against his chest, he kept his head down. Like the others, he wore the regulation sweat pants and white T-shirt. It took a moment, but I realized it was the same clothing he wore the night we'd met.

"Hello, Ken," Dad said as a man wearing the same leotard suit as the men who chased Kale through the woods, appeared behind us. He set down a black small case and dug into his front pocket, pulling out a security badge with a red stripe across the front. "Is it harvesting time already?"

The man nodded and swiped the card through the reader next to Kale's door.

"You don't mind if we watch, do you? I'm giving Deznee here a small tour."

Ken gave a noncommittal shrug and retrieved his case before slipping into Kale's cell.

"Harvesting time?" I asked, watching as the door whooshed closed behind the man. Kale still hadn't looked up.

"The board voted to put him down, but we have a dilemma. 98 is a truly rare individual. His gift, of course, is highly dangerous, but he also has a latent ability we need. Something in the chemical makeup of his blood renders Sixes sedate and pliable. Unlike modern drugs that have nasty side effects and render the subject ultimately useless for a time, 98's blood obliterates any and all violent tendencies and makes them completely obedient."

"98 is an interesting case." Dad continued. "The boy's been with us since infancy. He was raised by another one of our residents and has worked for Denazen his entire life."

"I thought you said he wasn't an employee."

Dad shook his head. "He used to be. He was given military-grade combat training and continuous physical conditioning. We used him in the most important missions. But after an unprovoked attack and his escape—and of course his *abduction* of you—many of us feel 98 is unsalvageable at this point. Something snapped and now he's broken."

Like a toy.

"You're keeping him alive so you can bleed him dry?" I tried—and failed—not to let the horror in my voice come through.

Dad shrugged as though he hadn't noticed my reaction. "We've been trying to reproduce it synthetically, but we've had no luck. We've increased the harvesting schedule from one time a day to four, in case something happens and we need to terminate sooner. Unfortunately, this will only help for a short time. After several days, the chemical in his blood goes dormant and can no longer be used in the serum. We're trying to perfect a way to store it, but so far we've been unsuccessful."

I turned back to the glass and watched Ken haul Kale to his feet. Kale looked up, noticing us for the first time. Our eyes locked and the bottom dropped out from beneath me. He was too pale, with bluish bruises under both eyes and across his left cheek. He was having a hard time standing on his own—twice, Ken had to prop him up against the wall to keep him from sinking to the ground.

"He looks horrible," I whispered. It was the least damaging thing I could think of to say. Dad was watching me. No way he didn't notice my reaction.

"He put up a bit of a fight the first day back. I'm afraid some of our employees were forced to be quite rough. He's doing much better, though. Almost standing on his own."

Rage bubbled in the pit of my stomach. I needed to get him out of here.

Dad nodded to the corner of the cell. Along the wall several glasses were lined up like soldiers marching off to war, all filled with thick yellow liquid. Orange juice. "So far, he's been refusing to eat or drink."

Inside the cage, Ken was putting his equipment back in the case. On his way out, he stopped to pick up one of the full glasses of juice and handed it to Kale. He took it and turned back to me.

"Can he hear us out here?"

Dad shook his head and stepped to meet Ken as he exited

the cell.

Kale came forward as I glanced over my shoulder at Dad. He spoke to Ken in hushed tones, ignoring me. "Drink it," I mouthed. To my relief, he brought the glass to his lips and downed the entire thing. I kept my face turned away from Dad, stuffing my hands deep into my pockets to keep from placing them on the glass. "I'm sorry."

Kale's expression stayed neutral, but his eyes conveyed a longing that matched my own. If I could only touch him, even for a minute...

"Are you ready to head back?" I jumped as Dad's hand clamped down on my shoulder.

CRASH

Kale had thrown the empty glass at the front window of the cage—directly where Dad's head was. Tiny droplets of juice dripped down the uncracked glass and pooled on the floor.

He backed into the corner of the cell, eyes never leaving Dad's, and wearing a bone-chilling sneer.

20

We got home sometime after 7:30 that night. Dad had gone back to Denazen to *take care of some things*, so I was left alone. For the first time as far back as I could remember, all I wanted to do was curl up and cry.

I wandered the living room, picking up small mementos from a life that had never existed. A tiny porcelain kitten statue, a blue glass rose. All lies. I came to the vase. That stinking, ugly vase. I picked it up, turning it over as Kale had done the night we'd met and gave it a good shake.

This should have plants in it, right?

I ran my index finger along the rim of it once before heaving it at the wall. It shattered—much like Kale's glass—pieces exploding every which way. They fell, tiny plinks and clinks as they hit the hardwood and bounced across the floor.

The rest of the rooms went pretty much the same. A heavy fog had settled over my head and no matter what I tried, it wouldn't go away. I smashed things, ripped things—nothing helped. I tried calling Brandt again. No answer. I emailed. No response. At this point, I was getting worried. It could have been that he was blowing me off because he'd kept digging. I saw it in his eyes at the Graveyard. He'd never been able to resist a challenge, and since the guy couldn't lie to me, he was avoiding. The logic was flawed and didn't seem right, but it made me feel slightly better.

I found my way into the kitchen and fixed my favorite sandwich—turkey, tomato, and peanut butter—but after closer inspection, found it unappetizing. I took a bite regardless, but the bread tasted stale and crumbly, and the turkey smelled bad even though it was fresh. I spit the mouthful into my open palm, almost gagging. My stomach rumbled in hungry protest, but I dumped the remainder of the sandwich in the trash on the way up to my room.

Television—nothing on. Radio—all the songs sucked. Computer—all the usual chat rooms were empty. I entertained the idea of sneaking out to find some action—a few choice calls and I'd undoubtedly have the 411 on a party going down somewhere along the strip—but I didn't have the energy.

Instead, I kicked off my shoes and crawled under the covers. All the mimicking I did earlier had caught up with me again, and even though my head buzzed—annoyance over Brandt, disgust for my father, and fear for Kale—sleep came easier than I thought it would.

• • •

I woke sometime later to a soft but noticeable clinking sound. Sitting up, I surveyed the room. It was the second night of the full moon—the brightest of the three—and the floor of my bedroom was illuminated by silvery light shining through the window.

The window.

That's where the noise had been coming from. I slid off the bed, opened the window, and peered over the edge. Alex.

"What are you doing here?"

"Can I come up?"

I shrugged and backed away as he started to climb.

He slid through the open window and gave me a quick once-over, frowning. I was suddenly glad I never changed into my pajamas. "You just get home? I looked up and down the strip for you."

"Been here all night," I said falling back onto the bed. "Why were you looking for me anyway? Didn't we say all we needed to say last time we saw each other? Remember? You told me to get the hell out?"

"I was worried about you. Wanted to make sure you were okay."

"Next time, use the phone. Or email. Hell, use a carrier pigeon."

"I don't have your number anymore. Or your email. And I don't own any pigeons."

"My email's the same it's always been."

"Oh."

Silence.

"Well?" I snuck a look over at the clock on my nightstand. Only midnight. I must have dozed off because the last time I'd looked at the clock, it'd been 11:20.

"Well what?" he asked, irritated.

"You said you wanted to see if I was all right." I twirled once. "Obviously, I'm all right."

"God," he hissed through clenched teeth. "You're so irritating!"

"Thank you," I said, pointing to the window. "Would it be ironic if I told you to get the hell out now?"

Alex sighed. "Look, I'm sorry about the other night. Denazen kinda freaks me out. I—"

I wasn't interested in a patented half-hearted Alex Mojourn apology. "No big, okay? You gotta look out for you. I get it."

He was quiet for a minute, subtly surveying the room. "You haven't changed much in here, huh?"

The walls were still the same shade of royal blue they'd been when I was seven. Some of the furniture had been upgraded, but everything was still positioned in the same general place. If you pulled the bed away from the wall, you'd even see the small heart carved into the back of the headboard with both our names running through it. A thousand times after that night at Roudey's I'd pulled out the bed, kitchen knife in hand, ready to gouge the reminder from existence. Each time I stopped, unable to go through with it.

"There something else you want? I mean, besides admiring my décor?"

He fidgeted and looked at the floor. Fred wobbled a bit. "I need to tell you something."

Whatever he had to say was making him nervous. It was worth a few more minutes of my time. I sat back on the bed to enjoy it while he continued to squirm.

"I knew who you were."

I figured he'd finally give me some bullshit—and long overdue—apology for what he'd done. Closure. I should have known better. "Huh?"

He shifted from foot to foot. "I knew who you were. Right from the start. I knew you were Marshall Cross' daughter."

All the air drained from the room. It was the ultimate sucker punch. My mouth opened, then closed again. Words. I'd forgotten all of them. He used me? Was *that* what he was saying? It had all been a lie?

"I figured getting close to you might lead us to information about your father—and Denazen."

He stopped to gage my reaction. What he saw on my face must have worried him, because he rushed on, starting to pace.

"It wasn't long, though, before I realized you really had no clue about Denazen or what your father did. You were just an innocent kid caught in the middle of something you had no idea about."

At that moment, he was worse than my dad. Worse because I'd had so much faith in him. In us. To find out it'd all been bullshit was devastating. "How long?"

He held up his hands in surrender. "We'd only been dating like six months by the time I put it all together."

"What about the rest of the time?" I advanced on him. My head was spinning—he'd used me, to get to my dad of all people! "We were together over a year."

"I know, I'm sorry. Ginger and the others—they told me to break it off once we were sure you were a dead end. I couldn't though. I fell in—"

I lost it. My fist connected with the corner of his jaw in a satisfying, although painful, thud. "Don't you *dare* stand here and tell me you *fell in love* with me."

"Don't want to hear it?" Reaching up, he rubbed his chin, expression darkening. "Too damn bad. I fell in love with you. Nothing we ever had was fake."

I went to hit him again, but he knew me. Expected it. He caught my hand and deflected it and I stumbled to the side. Deep breath. "You're a prick. It wasn't enough for you to rip me apart once, you had to come and try to do it again?"

"If I remember correctly, *you* came to me this time. I had no intention of looking for you."

I didn't answer. We stood there in the moonlight, locked together in a stare-down. After a few minutes he spoke again, his voice low. "I'll do it."

"Do what?" I snapped.

"Denazen. I'll do it. I'll help you."

Priceless. Come in, gouge out my heart, then try to suck up? Such a typical Alex Mojourn move. "Why? Why change your mind? If this has anything to do with guilt—"

"Guilt has nothing to do with it. I can't sleep knowing you're in this alone."

I laughed. "All of a sudden you care about me? I don't need you to be my knight in shining armor. You're an epic fail when it comes to that, so do me a favor and scram."

"Jesus," he swore. "I'm really trying here, Dez."

"Well, don't! Who asked you to?" I pushed him hard toward the window.

He stumbled, recovered, and pushed me back. "You think you know everything, but you don't," he growled. "That night— at Roudey's—that girl was a Six."

I groaned. The last thing I needed was the gory details. Next he'd tell me her bra size and that she liked moonlit walks along the beach. "And why the hell would you think I care? It's old news. History. Moving on now. If you think that makes it okay, then whatever."

"She was doing me a favor."

"A favor?" And the funny kept coming. If this had been anyone other than me, I might have found the whole thing laughably ironic. But because I was the star of this little tragedy? Yeah. Not so much. "Letting you grope her while you sucked the lips off her face? That's one hell of a favor."

"It was a setup—I set you up. I *wanted* you to see us together."

A setup? What the hell did that mean? "You never struck me as the ball-less type. Why not break up with me if you'd gotten bored?"

"I told you, the others wanted me to call things off with you. When I didn't, they were annoyed, but oh well. They got over it. As time went on, though, they started talking about using you for more than information. They wanted to use you to get at your father. I didn't want you involved in anything to do with Denazen. I told them that."

"You're trying to say you broke my heart for my own good?"

"It was the only thing I could think of to wipe you out of my life. I knew you'd never forgive me." He squeezed his eyes shut and shook his head. "It killed me—the look on your face. The pain in your eyes. I did what I had to do to keep you out of it. If I'd had any idea you were a Six..."

"You're lying," I said, even though deep down in the pit of my stomach, I kind of believed him. Our relationship had been intense—or maybe it had only seemed that way to me because he'd been my first love—but I didn't want to believe it had *all* been a lie. If this was true, it didn't make up for things, but it gave me some small peace of mind at least.

He closed the distance between us and took my face between his hands. "I'm sorry."

I'm sorry.

The last of my resolve crumbled. All the anger drained away, leaving the gaping, empty wound he'd left behind. I'd waited so long to hear the words. I stretched on my toes, crushing my lips to his. He responded, equally eager. The way he nipped at my top lip, his rough stubble scratching against my cheek and chin—all the familiar sensations my mind associated with him—all exploding from the locked box I'd kept them hidden in for so long.

He pulled away long enough to drag the shirt over his head, before backing us up to the bed. We tumbled to the mattress, a tangle of limbs and greedy, clutching hands. "I missed you," he mumbled into my mouth. Fingers tugged at the edge of my shirt, inching it upwards.

The kiss was euphoric—a haze of buzz-worthy bliss mingled with fond memories that brought a flush to my cheeks and lit a fire in my chest. This...this was familiar. This was...

Wrong.

He managed to tug my shirt over my head as I pushed him away. The shock of the cool air against my skin was enough to make me lose my train of thought and pull back. Distance. I needed distance.

"Stop," I panted, scooting back across the bed.

Breathing hard, he closed his eyes and took several deep breaths. After a few minutes, his breathing slowed—as did mine—and he opened his eyes, watching me. "What's wrong?"

"I can't do this," I said. "Not now. Not with you."

"Not with—"

"Kale," I said, remembering the night he'd been recaptured—and the night before. How his touch—so gentle, yet somehow so primal—had burned him into my heart, mind, and soul.

The day Alex broke my heart, I thought he'd broken me, too. I didn't date after that. Not really. Nothing serious and nothing exclusive. I saw who I wanted, when I wanted, with no commitment. I hadn't slept around, but I'd sure as hell fooled around. A lot. Not once had I ever felt guilty. There was no reason to. No one had ever made me think twice about the choices I'd made. Monogamy wasn't for me. Not anymore. Not until Kale.

Alex jumped up, fuming. "Are you serious? You're telling me you're with *him*?"

"I'm not *with* him," I said, reaching for my shirt. Or was I? I pulled it over my head, tugging it into place, and stood. "It's complicated."

"Oh? How so? I still love you." He reached for my arm. "I know you still have feelings for me."

"Maybe I do," I admitted, ducking out of his reach. Part of me screamed that this is what I'd wanted for so long—him—but another part of me laughed. He deserved this. To be hurt. By me. Fair turn and all. I'd dreamed about giving it back to him. The slap of rejection. Now that I was in the position to get what I wanted, I wasn't into it. Hurting him like that didn't hold the appeal it used to. "But that doesn't change much."

He pulled on his own shirt and hissed, "Of course it does!"

I shook my head. "No. No, it doesn't. You messed up. It doesn't matter what your reasons were, you killed *us*. You could have told me the truth. You made the choice not to. You picked your path and now you have to live with it." Tears filled my eyes, threatening to overflow. "I do still feel something for you. I don't know if it'll ever go away and I'm sorry for that, but I also feel something for Kale. Something strong. I don't know what it is yet, but I have to find out."

He looked like he wanted to argue but kept quiet. "I should go. It'd probably be catastrophic if your father found me here."

I nodded. "Probably."

He raised his hand and pointed at my desk. A pen flew into the air, hovering for a moment, before diving at the pad of paper sitting on my nightstand. After several seconds of scribbling, the pen fell lifeless to the floor. "That's my cell number. Call me in the morning and we'll meet up to talk about the Denazen thing. I meant it. I want to help get your mother"—he swallowed and made a bitter face—"and Kale out of there."

I nodded and followed him to the window. Swinging his legs over the edge, he eased himself down to the branch closest to the house. After dropping to the ground, he paused to look back at me. "I'm not gonna let this go, Dez. I know I screwed up, but I'm gonna fix it. Kale or no Kale, you belong with me."

Then he was gone. Swallowed by the shadows.

21

The next morning I woke with my sheets tangled like spaghetti around my legs. My shoulders ached, my neck was sore, and I had a knot the size of a grapefruit in my back. Restless sleep. I'd awoken almost every hour, on the hour, having the same freaky nightmare as the night before, but with a couple of variations. Sometimes Kale kissed me with Alex looking on. Sometimes Alex intervened, shoving Kale into the crowd. Those were hard to watch because Alex always ended up dead. Sometimes, they both did.

I'd overslept—it was nearly ten—but I wasn't worried. Dad had told me to stay home today since all the mimicking I'd done had worn me down. My head still buzzed and my stomach felt off, but all in all, it wasn't as bad as I thought it'd be. Dressed and showered, I made my way downstairs, thrilled I'd be avoiding what was becoming an unwelcomed and twisted morning ritual. Coffee with Dad. He'd have left for sure by now.

As expected, when I entered the kitchen he wasn't in his

usual spot—but he *was* still home.

Not good.

Dad was across the room pacing, his cell phone tucked tight under his chin as he jotted down notes on a piece of paper. Whatever that call was, it was important. I knew the look on his face. It was the look he wore when things weren't going well with his *clients*.

I poured myself a bowl of cereal while trying to eavesdrop on the conversation. This proved impossible because Dad's end was nearly nonexistent. He mumbled simple, scant replies to the person on the other end, like *yes, sure, no,* and *absolutely*. Nothing that might give me any clue as to who was on the other end or what the subject matter was. He usually left the house by eight without fail, so something big had to be going on. At that moment, super dog hearing would have been more useful than mimicking.

Fifteen minutes later, he joined me at the table, cell phone out of sight.

"Surprised to see you still here," I said through a mouthful of Rice Krispies. For once, the thought of coffee kind of turned my stomach. "Taking the day off?" It was a joke. Dad never took a day off.

"I've been on the phone with Mark most of the morning."

"Really?" I put the spoon down.

"When did you last speak to Brandt?"

The unusual-for-June humidity vanished, replaced by a creeping, icy cold. I swallowed a lump of cereal in my mouth that suddenly tasted like cardboard and did my best not to choke. "I tried calling him all day yesterday. He's pissed about something, so he's been blowing me off."

"He's gone."

"Gone?"

Dad hesitated and turned away. If he couldn't—wouldn't look me in the eye—then this was bad.

"What does gone mean?" I pressed.

"Dead."

I dropped my spoon. It splashed down, sending droplets of milk and cereal raining over the edge of the bowl. The icy air turned thin. There wasn't enough oxygen to fill my lungs. Or maybe there was plenty of air. It was possible I'd stopped breathing. My fingers clutched the edge of the table for support because the floor was suddenly moving like the tilt-a-whirl at the local fair. Sick. I was going to puke.

Dad continued to speak, oblivious to my distress. "The police think it might be connected to a story Mark's working on. They found his body in the driveway behind Cairn's car this morning."

I opened my mouth to say something—at least I think I did—but nothing happened. For the second time in twenty-four hours, I'd forgotten how to speak.

Frowning, Dad rose from the table. His lips were moving. Something about Brandt's clothing and his blood. I couldn't hear him though. Not really. I was vaguely aware as he grabbed his keys and locked the door behind him on the way to the garage. My mind only half registered the roar of the engine and the mechanical thumping of the garage door as it opened, then closed. Not twenty seconds later, I sprang from my seat, into my black hoodie, and out the door.

For awhile, I ran blindly through the woods. It was humid and rainy, and my hair stuck to my face as I went. Autopilot kicked in, but it didn't take long to realize where I was heading.

Brandt's.

Brandt had lived next door my whole life. Granted, next door was separated by four acres of dense woods and a shallow stream, but still, he was never far away. I could see the flashing blue and red lights before I even broke the edge of the woods. People — police, neighbors, passing cars — were clumping in front of the house. Uncle Mark was silent. Watching the door while aunt Cairn stared blankly at the street, where two men were loading a large, long black thing into the back of the ambulance. I imagined the black bag containing trash, sand, even rocks — anything but my cousin.

With the most soul-crushing scream I'd ever heard, Uncle Mark lunged forward and threw himself at the gurney. "I need to see him. My boy. This is my fault!"

I couldn't watch another minute.

I tore back through the woods and after awhile found myself on the strip. I had a million acquaintances I could call. *Friends* of mine. *Friends* of Brandt's. But only one would understand what was going on. Only one wouldn't have me committed if I told him what I thought really happened to my cousin.

I rounded the corner and took off in the general direction of Roudey's.

Pushing open the back door, I slipped inside. I was drenched, and with each step, my sneakers squeaked and spit. My face was wet — it might have been tears or it might have been the rain — and I knew my eyes were red and puffy. There was no question I'd been crying when I came into the main room. All the ambient chatter died away.

Tommy, eagle-eyed as usual, saw me first. He rushed to my side. "Dez, baby, you okay?"

I never got the chance to answer. Alex pushed Tommy aside and dragged me into the back room before I could blink. "What happened? What's wrong?" He peeled back the soggy layer of hair from my face. "Are you hurt?"

I opened my mouth to talk, but the only things that came out were long, drawn-out sobs. He had his keys in hand and ushered us out the door before I knew what was happening, which was fine. My brain had officially stopped working.

. . .

An hour later I finally calmed down enough to speak. And think. I told Alex everything, including the fact I believed my dad had something to do with Brandt's death. Alex wasn't surprised.

"He was digging," I whispered. My throat was sore and my eyes were raw and the fading headache from all the mimicking was back in force. "To find shit on Denazen. I told him to stop, but really, I was the reason he started. I asked him to do it and I should have known better. Should have known he'd take it too far. I got him killed."

I remembered what Dad said the police thought. A connection to a story Uncle Mark was working on. Jesus. He was really going to let his own brother think himself responsible for the death of his son? I didn't know why it surprised me. It was another notch in the belt of heartless that was Dad.

Alex was in my face in an instant. "*You* had nothing to do with it. Do you understand me? This was all Cross."

I stared at him. "Brandt was his nephew. His brother's son. How could he—"

"That's the kind of people Denazen are. Family means nothing to them. We have to do this now."

"Do what?"

"Bring me in. There's no way you're going back in there by yourself."

"We haven't even talked about how we're going to *get* you in. And even if we do manage it, who says you're going to even see me, let alone be allowed to get anywhere near me. It's pointless to rush."

"We'll figure something out," he said, leaning back.

"This is hopeless. It's all so—I'm numb."

One minute I was sitting next to him on the couch, the next his arms were around me and I was in his lap kissing him. It was seamless. Not happening one second, then happening another. I knew I should pull away, but didn't. Greedy hands were everywhere, unable to get enough. Feeling. I had some feeling now. I slid my hands under the front of his thin T-shirt, fingers skimming the skin. He was more defined than I remembered. Harder.

I pulled the shirt up, but it caught on his neck. I struggled with it for a moment before he intervened, knocking my hands aside. With a low growl, he tore it off and threw it across the room. Broad shoulders. Hungry hazel eyes. Yes. That's right. It was all coming back. They changed from brown to hazel depending on his mood. Pale skin, flawless except for the rough, discolored patch on his right shoulder—the lone reminder of a dirt bike accident when he was fourteen. This was the Alex I remembered. Sharper and more vivid than the one from last night.

Every nerve ending in my body alive and urging me on, I pushed for a thrill of sensation that would deaden the pain. It worked, so I chased it further. I'd chase it all the way if that's what I needed to do to stay whole. Because I wasn't anymore. I'd lost Brandt. I'd lost Kale. I'd lost Mom.

Leaning into him, I tangled my fingers through his blond hair and pulled him closer. The scent of cigarettes mixed with mint Tic-Tacs surrounded me. Something in the back of my mind chastised me for letting him take advantage of my pain, but my body didn't care. I needed this. Needed to feel. I'd shot him down last night—somewhere in the back of my mind I remembered this, but I'd officially shut down. Now wasn't the time to *think*. It was the time to *act*.

His fingers lingered on the button of my jeans, waiting for me to protest.

My body wouldn't let me.

My soul, however, was screaming *stop*! Flashing neon signs and warning bells—it was pulling up on the emergency brake—repeatedly—but that brake was temporarily out of order.

Expertly, he flicked the button open and drew down the zipper.

Kale. I wanted to think of Kale.

Alex slid his hands under the material of my jeans, gripping my bare hips with an almost painful force. I shivered at his touch. Kale's fingers were warm, soft. Alex's were calloused and hard. Like ice. It was a jolt to the system.

Kale. At that moment, I'd do anything to keep my mind off him. Like Brandt, he was beyond my reach. I was beginning to think he might be beyond my reach forever, and that hurt more than I could stand.

I'd kidded myself into thinking I could do this. Kale and Denazen. I'd sworn off relationships when I ended things with Alex—and with good reason. You could have a good time, no strings attached. Without the strings, nothing could come back and choke you later when it didn't work out. What if I couldn't get Kale away from Denazen? Chances were good that if I failed, it would be due to exposure. They'd have Kale, and they'd have me. They'd still have Mom.

Alex's hands were now at the hem of my shirt, tugging upward. I almost stopped him.

Someone like me had no hope of going head to head with someone like my dad. Sure, I'd done it a million times—when I'd thought he was nothing more than a simple, arrogant lawyer. But after seeing what Denazen could do—what Dad *would* do—my second guesses had turned to the sick gum of denial stuck to the bottom of a desk. Sure, you could peel it off and force it into your mouth, but what good did that do? The flavor was lost.

Kale was lost.

My shirt now on the couch next to his, Alex nibbled a trail from the underside of my chin, down to my shoulder.

My mom was lost.

Alex hooked his fingers through one of the belt loops of my damp jeans, peeling them down. I rose onto my knees, letting him slide them farther. When they'd gone as far as they could, I leaned to the side and kicked them off.

Brandt was lost.

Taking my bra strap between his teeth, he tugged it down.

I'd lost hope.

Warm lips traced a path from my neck to my shoulder.

I'd lost myself.

No.

I wasn't a quitter! I reigned as Queen of the Stubborn. If it was a lost cause, then all the better. I loved proving people wrong—especially myself. I thrived on it.

Finally, reality began to ooze back, and I pulled away. Sure, kissing Alex felt good. Best of all, it *felt*. But it wasn't what I wanted. Not deep down. When I'd told him no last night, I'd been torn. He'd been right—I still had very real feelings for him— but it wasn't enough. Maybe it was because of what happened between us, and maybe it wasn't.

Kale was unlike anyone I'd ever met before. He made me feel happy. Alive. His simplistic way of looking at things, along with fierce enthusiasm for life, was something I couldn't see myself living without. Regardless of the damage Denazen had done to him, and the past Alex and I had, I knew who I wanted.

What I wanted.

I wanted the strings.

"I'm sorry," I said as I pushed him away. I didn't need to explain further. I could see it in his eyes. He understood. He wasn't happy, but he didn't yell.

He backed away, grabbing his shirt, and climbed to his feet. Something was off about his smile. Something that scared me. "We'll see."

• • •

The phone rang fourteen times before he picked it up. An all-time record as far as I knew. Dad was a strict third ring person.

"Marshall Cross."

"Dad, it's me."

A pause. He'd probably looked at the caller ID. "Deznee? Where are you?"

"I'm in town. I need you to meet me at The Blueberry Bean."

"I'm working at the moment. It will have to wait."

"It can't wait—and it *is* work. I'll meet you there in twenty minutes." I hung up. I could almost smell the steam that had to be billowing from Dad's ears. It made me smile. Warm fuzzies all the way.

"We set?" Alex asked, holding his hand out for the phone. I gave it back, and he stuffed it into his back pocket.

"I think so. You ready? It won't take him long to get there."

"I just gotta hit the john." He held out the keys. "Go start the car, I'll meet you down there."

• • •

As promised, twenty minutes later I sat under one of the large umbrella tables outside The Blueberry Bean, our local haven for coffee addicts. The rain still fell, but the umbrella would be large enough that we didn't get wet—not that it mattered. My clothes were still damp from this morning.

I glanced casually down at my wrist—there was no watch. "What took you so long?"

"I'm not amused by this, Deznee." Dad approached, cup in hand and filled with what I'd bet was black coffee with a double shot of espresso. Dark sunglasses and a deep brown trench despite the warmth in the air made him look like something from a secret agent movie. Another time, I would have mocked him. His buttons were so easily pushed when it came to wardrobe. I never understood it.

"Well, that's good, Dad. I didn't mean for it to be amusing." I smiled and leaned back, trying to pull off nonchalant. After the day I'd had so far, it took conscious effort. "So I took some initiative today."

He pulled out the seat across from me and sat down. "Oh?"

I crooked my finger at Alex, standing right inside the coffee shop. I'd been a little surprised when Alex still insisted on helping me after last night, and then again this afternoon. The old Alex had been selfish. When things didn't go his way, he packed up his toys and went home.

He stepped around the corner and out the front door. Without a word, he pulled out the chair between mine and Dad's and flipped it backwards. Straddling it, he said, "Hello again, Mr. Cross."

Face impassive, Dad said, "Mr. Mojourn. What an unpleasant surprise."

Alex smiled and leaned forward against the back of the chair. "Likewise, sir."

While we'd been dating, Dad and Alex had never been what you'd consider close. In fact, Dad had threatened to cut specific parts from Alex's anatomy and mount them on the living room wall on several occasions.

"*Anyway*," I said to Dad. "Alex is a Six and he's looking for work."

Alex flicked a long finger at the saltshaker from across the table. It rocked forward, and teetered on the edge for a moment before tumbling over the side.

I could tell Dad wasn't the least bit impressed. Maybe Kale was right. Alex's gift was a dime a dozen. "I'm fully aware of Mr. Mojourn's status. A telekinetic. How rare," Dad said, voice dripping with sarcasm.

"Wait—fully aware? You *knew* he was a Six?"

Dad sighed. "Of course. It's my *job* to know."

"What, do you guys like dump something into the water every night before bed? Is everyone in this town a freak?"

"This area has the highest concentration of Sixes in the United States. We're not sure why, but let's just say it's no coincidence that Denazen's main office is located in Parkview."

"Damn right, I'm useful," Alex piped up. "I'm resourceful and crafty and, best of all, my moral compass doesn't point north."

"Is that so?" Dad sounded a bit intrigued. I even thought I saw a small grin.

"It is," Alex confirmed.

Dad looked from Alex to me then back again. "And my daughter?"

Alex shrugged. "What about her?"

"What are your intentions?"

"Buddy, if you're asking if I plan on dating your daughter again, that'd be a big, resounding hell no. Way too high maintenance for me."

. . .

I drove with Dad back to Denazen, and Alex followed in his own car.

"You pissed about Alex?" No sense beating between the bushes. He'd been fairly quiet since we left the coffee house, and as usual, I couldn't read his expression.

"To tell you the truth, Deznee, I'm proud of you. You seem to be approaching this job with a new sense of responsibility and a level of maturity I didn't think possible of you."

Ouch.

"I'm recommending you start your field work within the next few days. I want you out there tracking down information on these underground Sixes as soon as possible. Something tells me our best way to find them is through you—and possibly Alex."

"Alex? As in you're going to, like what, team us up or something?"

"Would that be an issue?"

Score! Could my luck get any better? I swallowed a grin and forced a frown. "Well, I'll be honest, it's not my idea of a party. He's not my favorite person."

"You two seem pretty chummy."

"Um, hello? Trying to impress you by signing a new guy here. I have a feeling me walking up to him and sending his nuts up his throat wouldn't exactly win him over to the idea of Denazen."

Dad laughed. He actually chuckled. I'd never heard him laugh before. If I didn't loathe him so much, the sound would have made me smile. He flipped on the blinker and veered into the Denazen parking lot.

"I think this is going to work out very well for everyone."

22

They didn't let me see Alex again the rest of that day. Or the next. Dad assured me he was fine and making progress with the good people at Denazen.

I stood in front of the mirror, trying to decide if I should pull my hair back or leave it down. Brandt always loved it down. Said it made me look wild and that suited me. In the end, I went with what Brandt would have wanted.

After all, this was his day.

I smoothed my skirt and took one last look before grabbing the small, green wrapped package I'd been hoarding for months. Tucking it into my pocket, I went downstairs. Dad was waiting for me by the door, wearing one of the same suits he wore on a regular basis to work and looking at his watch. We were only a little late.

The ride to the funeral home was too short, while at the same time too long. The atmosphere in the car was cold and uncomfortable, so I was eager to get out. Yet I was in no rush to arrive at our destination. My dead best friend. A depressing room. And lots of crying people—most of whom had known very little, if not nothing, about him—all gathered in one place. Not good times.

I'd asked how Alex was doing the night before, but all Dad would tell me was they'd insisted he stay at Denazen during his training and I would get to see him tomorrow. I asked if he could be present for the funeral. Dad said no.

So I was on my own, stuck in the front row of the church next to Aunt Cairn. The woman looked downright scary. With no makeup, she looked ten times older than I knew she was. Lips pursed in a thin line, her eyes stared straight ahead, trained on the mahogany casket set at the front of the church next to the altar. Father Kapshaw's lips were moving—I'd catch a word here and there about tragedy—but honestly, I wasn't paying attention.

I focused on Dad, who sat in the front row next to Uncle Mark. Unlike his wife, Mark cried openly, clutching his brother's hand for support and mumbling apologies to his dead son. It made me sick. Twice I had to bite down to keep from jumping up and screaming, *it was his fault—not yours!*

The funeral home had been a bustle of activity. Friends and neighbors all dropping by to pay their respects and look in on the family. People I knew Brandt hadn't seen in years surfaced from out of nowhere to mourn his passing. Boys he'd gone to high school with, girls who'd been madly in love with him, people he barely knew—all claiming to be his best friends. It made me want to scream. They all stood in the corner, trying to one-up each other in barely contained whispers.

"I talked to Brandt the night before it happened! He sounded like he was freaked about something!" This from Manny Fallow, a guy Brandt never liked and who he'd gone out of his way to avoid every single day since the fourth grade. The guy always smelled

like mothballs.

"We had a date this coming Friday. We were so into each other." This from Gina Barnes, an old junior high girlfriend he hadn't spoken to in years. Into each other? Brandt had said just a month ago what a skank Gina had turned into. He wouldn't have touched her with a forty-foot pole.

"We were getting an apartment together next month. He already put down his half of the deposit," remarked Victor Jensen, a fellow employee of the skate shop where Brandt worked. I knew for a fact that he and Victor had thrown down two weeks ago after Brandt found him stealing cash from the register.

It was all too much.

Thankfully, the church service and actual burial were family only. And since our family now only consisted of me, Dad, Uncle Mark, and Aunt Cairn, the church stayed pretty empty. Well, my mom was still a member of the family, but how can you count someone you weren't supposed to know about?

Father Kapshaw finished his sermon and blessed the casket as six men filed out from behind the altar to lift it. I had to bite down hard to keep from lashing out as they passed. All six men wore the same cookie-cutter blue suit. Dad was a bastard.

We filed into the aisle as they passed, one by one, and followed them to the hearse. On the way out into the parking lot, I saw a guy standing off to the side. He wore simple black jeans and a brown button-down shirt. I remembered seeing him at the funeral home, but he hadn't stood with the others from school. He'd stayed at the edge of the room, speaking to no one, eyes sad. He said nothing to us as we passed, only watched as the six men from Denazen loaded Brandt into the back of the creepy black car for the trip to his final destination.

As we drove away, I looked back. The guy was gone.

...

The sun finally peeked out from behind the clouds as Father Kapshaw gave another longer speech about the tragedy of losing someone so young and full of life. He droned on and on about Brandt's charity within the community and his gentle, soft-spoken kindness.

Under me, the metal folding chair slowly sank into the mud. Above my head, a large, buzzing fly circled continuously. Next to me, Aunt Cairn began to hum.

"The peaceful soul of Brandt Cross will be with us forever. He will be remembered as a charitable soul who always had a kind word for all he—"

I wanted to jump up and call bullshit. I wanted to pull off my shoe and throw it at Father Kapshaw's head. At that moment, I would have given the world's supply of mint chocolate chip to see it imbedded in his pompous face. Hell, I would have settled for flipping them off and storming away. But as I told myself before, this was Brandt's day. The last thing I was going to allow was some bogus speech that said nothing about who he'd *really* been. Instead of making a scene, I stood, interrupting the Father's fluffy speech with one of my own. One Brandt would have truly appreciated.

"Brandt was a lot of things, but a soft-spoken, charitable soul with a kind word for all isn't one of them." I balled my fingers, nails digging into my palms as I fought to keep my tone even. The sting kept me focused. "Brandt was a foul-mouthed pothead who loved his signed Tony Hawk skateboard above anything else. He hated crowds and loved sushi. Brandt believed in animal rights, hell, he never even killed a bug, and hated war. He was loyal and stubborn, and *none* of you knew him at all." Unable to control it any longer, my voice broke and I turned away, leaving them to their fake sermon and empty words. I didn't look back.

I didn't wander far—just out of sight and across to a large white marble mausoleum. I needed some air, and sitting there with that bunch of posers was choking the life out of me.

"That was awesome," a voice said beside me.

I jumped, skimming along the smooth marble wall.

"Sorry," the guy said. "I didn't mean to freak you out."

"I saw you at the funeral home. And outside the church."

"Yeah."

When he didn't offer anything more, I pressed. "Okay, so who are you?"

"I'm Sheltie. Friend of Brandt's. I'm sorry we never got the chance to meet. He talked about you all the time."

Sheltie. The name didn't ring any bells, but he looked a little familiar. Like a face I'd passed in the halls at school or someone in the background at parties. With a head of thick, sandy brown hair and shoulders any linebacker would have envied, he was kind of cute. Not my type—but cute. He was rolling something in his left hand. A small, circular black thing with a red stripe down the middle. Horrified, I realized what it was. "Is that—"

He held it out, nodding. Rolling his thumb over the once-smooth surface, he said, "One of the wheels off Brandt's board."

I went to take it from him, but he jerked it away. "What the hell are you doing with it?" I demanded.

He hesitated for a moment before sighing. "Board broke a few days ago. I fix 'em."

"Why did you bring it here?"

He snorted. "Did you even know Brandt? He slept with that damn board. I thought a piece of it should be here, ya know?"

Why hadn't I thought of that? It was true and thoughtful. I felt like a bad best friend for not coming up with it on my own. Glancing back to the crowd, I said, "I didn't see you. How did you hear what I said?"

He shrugged, tapping the side of his head. "Killer hearing." He pulled out a small envelope from his back pocket and held it out. "Brandt asked me to give this to you."

"What is it?"

Another shrug. "I didn't open it."

I took it but didn't look inside. Instead, I stuffed it into my jacket pocket. It slid in, right next to the small box wrapped in green paper. "Why would he give you something to pass along to me?"

He sank down along the wall and settled in the grass. Rolling the wheel along the edge of the mausoleum, he said, "He didn't like what you were doing with that Kale guy. It worried him. Said he knew you'd never back down."

What would Brandt have said if he'd seen me almost give it all up two days ago at Alex's apartment? "He told you about that?"

"We were pretty tight." He picked up a blade of grass and twirled it between his thumb and index finger. "I know he loved you."

"I loved him, too." Guilt gnawed at my insides. "It's my fault. I asked him to do me a favor."

"Probably," he said. He didn't say it in an accusing way, just matter-of-fact. Still, it hit like a brick to the face. He reminded me a lot of Brandt. His in-your-face answers were blunt but not cruel.

"My dad had something to do with his death. I know it." I don't know why I said it—Sheltie was a total stranger—but something about him was comforting. I trusted him...which was pretty stupid considering the amount of betrayal bouncing around my world.

"I agree." He got to his feet. "There's one other thing. Something he asked me to tell you. He said you'd be wondering, and he knew how you hated unanswered questions."

"Okay…"

"Brandt was a Six. He told me he tried to tell you a few days ago…" He shrugged. "But too late, I guess."

I couldn't be mad at him for keeping it from me. I'd done exactly the same thing. And now I wouldn't get the chance to make it right. "Are you a Six?"

He gave me a sly smile. "I still say you should get the hell out of Dodge."

I froze. "What?"

Silence.

"What did you say?"

He tried to play it cool, but failed. There was a look of horror in his eyes.

"You said, *I still say you should get the hell out of Dodge.*"

"So?"

"That's what Brandt said to me the last time I saw him."

"I told you, we thought a lot alike." Sheltie stood, brushing the dirt from his faded black jeans. He pocketed the skateboard wheel and took several steps back.

"You can't *still* say something to someone you've never met before."

He shrugged. "I just did."

With nothing further to say, Sheltie turned on his heel and strode away without looking back. I got to my feet to follow, but Dad's voice stopped me.

"Deznee?"

I stepped out from around the Mausoleum. "Here, Dad."

"It's over. Everyone is leaving." He stepped forward and looked over my shoulder—like he expected to see someone hiding there. "I'll be in the car."

I nodded and watched him go. Once he and everyone else

was out of sight, I made my way back to the burial site.

The wind had picked up, knocking some of the flower arrangements to the ground. The top of the tent whipped back and forth, snapping like mad in the breeze. I bent down and pulled a white rose from one of the arrangements.

"What the hell were you thinking?" I asked the silent brown box. "Why would you do something so stupid? I told you to back off…"

Of course, I got no reply.

If wishes were horses…well, then I'd probably get trampled.

I stood there for a few moments more, just watching the wind whip the fake green grass-like cover at the base of the casket back and forth. I pulled the small green wrapped box from my pocket and brought it to my lips. Tickets to XtreamScream, our local version of the X games. Now he'd never go.

I dropped it into the open grave along with the single white rose.

"Happy Birthday, Brandt."

23

On the way back to the car, I overheard Dad and one of the men who'd carried the casket from the church talking. Dad spoke much louder than normal, so I could only guess he wanted me to hear. They'd made the decision to terminate Kale. Tainted, Dad said to the man. Ruined. They planned to bleed him dry and be done with it. Apparently, a suitable synthetic substitute for his blood had finally been found. They didn't need him anymore.

I had to act fast, but had no idea what I could do. There was no way for me to get past security and up to the ninth floor where he was being held.

"I have a few things to take care of at work," Dad said on our way back to the house. "I'm dropping you home to change. A car will be by in forty minutes to take you to Denazen. Mercy will be waiting to do another round of questioning. A car will return you home after she's finished."

"More questions?"

Dad nodded. "Yes. Tomorrow, you head into the field."

• • •

"How have you been, Dez?"

Today, dressed in an unflattering, tailored pantsuit the exact same revolting shade as pea soup, Mercy sat across from me sipping tea from a small china cup. "Have you found the rules here at Denazen hard to follow?"

I shrugged. "I've never been a stickler for the rules."

"So I've heard." She nodded and gave me a knowing grin. "You think you have it all figured out then?"

"I'm sure I have plenty to learn."

"I have a list of specific questions here, as requested by your father."

I tried not to look concerned, but obviously I failed.

"Does that worry you?"

"Should it?"

"Possibly."

I leaned back, trying to relax, and gave her my best go-for-it smile. "Let's find out."

"This morning you were at your cousin's funeral," she said without emotion. "When did you last see him?"

They knew. "A few days ago."

"And where did you see him?"

Crapcrapcrap. "The Graveyard."

"Graveyard? What were you doing in the cemetery?"

"Not the cemetery, the Graveyard. It's a place we all go to party."

Mercy nodded and jotted something down on a piece of paper. "And what did you talk about?"

I swallowed. "Not much."

Mercy set her pen down and sighed. She stood from her chair and stepped around to the front of the desk. "Let's take a break from the questions for a minute, shall we? Let me explain a little about how my gift works." She leaned forward and placed a clipboard in my hands. She set the paper she had been writing on onto the clipboard and tilted it up a hair.

I looked down at the clipboard and bit back a gasp.

Keep this tilted up. The camera cannot see it that way. We're going to end this session early. Meet me in the B section of the parking lot. I'm one of Ginger's people. When I ask you to read, say the following: My name is Dez and I'm a seventeen-year-old honor student.

God forbid Ginger tell me she had people on the inside. Cause, ya know, I couldn't have used the help or anything.

"I can tell if you're lying about something," she continued. "I've written a sentence for you, please read it out loud."

I hesitated for a moment before complying. "My name is Dez, and I'm a seventeen-year-old honor student."

She smiled. "See? A lie. Your aura spiked black—it does that when you lie. I can see it." She watched me for a moment, all smiles. "I can also tell when you're hiding something."

· · ·

I stood in lot B where Mercy told me to meet her. She told the clerk on level four when she escorted me to the elevator that she'd called and arranged my transportation to arrive early. I still didn't know what to think, or if I should really trust her. This could easily be a trick or some kind of test, but since I was running out of time, I decided to give it a shot.

Mercy didn't keep me waiting long.

"I have clearance for level nine where they're keeping your friend. He's scheduled for one last questioning this afternoon. This will be your only chance to get him before he's destroyed."

"Whoa there, lady. Slow down." I eyed her, feeling nothing but suspicion. Just 'cause she'd said she was with Ginger didn't make it true. I could name drop, too. "How do I know this isn't some huge setup? Not like you guys here at Denazen are known for playing it straight. I go along with this and, boom, next thing I know my new address is one of those nifty glass boxes."

"You're going to have to trust me. There's not a lot of time. Your father knows why you're really here. He knows about you and 98."

"Kale," I snapped. "His name is Kale, not 98." It was stupid, and in the face of this revelation, ridiculous to harp on a name, but it annoyed me. "And how the hell does he know anything?"

Mercy laughed. A dark, grating sound that came from deep in the pit of her stomach. "Your father has spies everywhere."

"Someone *told* him? Who?" The only ones who knew what I was doing were Ginger and her people, and Kale. Could Ginger have a double agent in her ranks?

She shook her head. "I don't know. But it doesn't matter. He's on to you, so we have to move fast."

I folded my arms, eyes narrowing. "If you're one of Ginger's people, why can't you get her the list?"

"She didn't ask me."

Seriously? I wanted to scream. These people were enough to make my head implode.

She held out her hand. "There's no more time. Hurry!"

"Hurry and what? Hold your hand? Sorry, didn't we go over this the other day? You're not my type."

"Mimic, you idiot!"

Oh. "OH!" I could be a bit slow at times. "Wait. That's not gonna work. Don't you have a car coming to bring me home? If Dad knows what's going on, he's gonna be keeping a close eye on what I'm doing and where I'm supposed to be."

"I'll go in your place."

I stared at her. "Um, no offense or anything, but other than the fact I'd never be caught dead wearing that, you're a little too tall, and a lot too old."

"I mean, we switch places," she rolled her eyes and looked over her shoulder. "You be me, go in and get 9—I mean, *Kale*. And I'll be you and take the ride."

"You mean mimic us both?" My brain screamed *No way*, and I shook my head. Rick. Ripping insides. Blood. No. Not again. "There's no way… It'll kill me."

She grabbed me by the shoulders and shook. "This is your one chance. If you don't go in there and get him, he's dead."

She was right. This was my one shot. But mimic two people? One had been nearly impossible. What were the odds on two? I had to try, though. For Kale. And if it worked, if I survived it, maybe I wouldn't need the Reaper to get Mom out. Maybe I could do it on my own.

I grabbed both her hands and closed my eyes, concentrating on what I wanted. The pain surged and a scream built. This time, though, there was no holding it back. Clammy hands clamped over my mouth as tears trailed down my cheeks.

And then it hit me. Like a jet falling out of the sky…and then passing through me. It felt like being ripped in half. Slowly. Cell by cell.

"Deznee? Dez, get up."

I opened my eyes and saw—me. Mercy. Mercy *as* me. Wow. Someone needed to get some sun. I let her help me to my feet, clinging to her arm for support. The pain in my head buzzed, almost drowning out her words, and the ground felt like it was tilting sideways, determined to flip me over. "I guess I lied. I would be caught dead in something like this." The cheap material made my legs itchy, and the blazer was stuffy and too confining.

Mercy snorted and pulled away, tugging at the bottom of my shorts. "You? How do you think I feel? These shorts are downright indecent! I look like a harlot."

Managing to stay upright on my own was a chore, but I managed. I snorted. "Are you high? I've got killer legs and a great ass. I'd be an idiot not to flaunt 'em."

A black sedan pulled into the lot. "Showtime." She slipped me her security badge. "All you need to do is go up to the ninth floor and tell them you're taking 98 for questioning. Bring him back to my office. Then make an excuse and take him outside."

Make an excuse? Like it'd be that easy? "Then what?"

"Then I suggest you both run like hell. It won't be long before they realize I'm not where I should be. Well, you're not where I should be." She stepped up to the car as it pulled along the curb. "Is there anything I should know?"

"Stay up in my room. I don't know when Dad will be home but if he does get there before me, ignore him and lock the door. Flip him off if he tries to barge in, whatever."

Mercy looked mortified. It weirded me out to see the expression coming from my own face. I didn't *do* mortified. "Flip him off?"

"There's a key taped to the underside of the front porch. Have a nice trip." I waved and pushed her to the car. She slid in and closed the door. As soon as the car left the lot, I slowly started back to the building—miraculously without collapsing. I didn't know how long I had, so wasting time wasn't an option, but moving faster than just above a crawl was impossible. The mimic had sapped all my energy. The only thing keeping me from passing out was the thought of Kale. If I didn't keep it together, he'd be lost.

Pulse pounding in my ears, I strolled past the first floor desk clerk and to the white elevator doors. Once inside, I swiped

Mercy's card and told the elevator to take me to level nine. I'd half been expecting sirens and flashing lights. Blaring alarms and gates crashing down from the ceiling to trap me in the car. Maybe even those laser beams you see in the movies—the ones to keep jewel thieves away. But when the car began its ascent without incident, I breathed a heavy sigh of relief. So far so good.

As the doors opened to the red walls and concrete floor of level nine, I did my best impersonation of the uptight, stick-up-her-ass Mercy.

"Morning, Mercy," a small-framed woman said from behind the main desk. I nodded and made my way around the corner and down the hall. Thank God I'd been here with Dad or I'd be screwed. Someone probably would've noticed if Mercy asked directions.

"Who's getting questioned today, Merc?" the guard at the end of the hall asked. He turned his key to open the door, giving her a flirtatious smile. Maybe Mercy wasn't as frigid as I thought. I winked and returned the smile. He seemed surprised—but happy. "One last round for 98 before curtain time," I said. The man raised an eyebrow, but waved me ahead. Crap. I needed to think like Mercy. Talk like her. Think long-winded and boring.

"I'll send Jim up with a suit to bring him down. You can meet him in your office."

"That's fine. I'll wait here and go down with them. I'd like the extra time to—observe him."

Apparently, it was the right thing to say. I started down the hall full of glass cages while the guard picked up the phone to call for someone. Everyone sat exactly as they had been the other day. Like they never moved. All in the same place, with the same expressions on their faces. Even the blankets on their cots looked undisturbed.

All except Kale.

Wedged in the corner of his cell, he stared straight ahead. When I stepped in front of the glass, he didn't blink and I worried he might be drugged. I was about to say something to let him know it was me, but he spoke.

"I told you everything I had to tell. More questions won't change that."

At the far end of the hallway, a man in one of the moon-man suits came through the door. So much for giving Kale a heads up. "There are always more questions to ask, 98," I said as the man approached.

"Level five?"

"Yes. My office, please."

The man opened the door and hauled Kale up. His color seemed a little better than last time I'd seen him, but he still wobbled on his feet. A little bit further and with any luck we'd be clear.

Back at Mercy's office, the man deposited Kale in the chair and handed me a tazer. "In case he makes a lunge for you."

I nodded a silent thanks and waited for the door to close behind him. I knew there were cameras in Mercy's office, so I couldn't just rush forward and tell Kale what was going on. I could have written a note, like Mercy had done with me, but anyone watching might get suspicious.

"You are aware they're going to terminate you, correct?" I asked. If anyone was watching—and I'd bet my favorite Mudd boots they were—they had to see Mercy doing her thing.

Kale didn't answer.

"Why did you run away?"

Silence.

What would Mercy do? She'd try to get some kind of reaction and build on it. "Did they tell you about the girl? Deznee, is it?"

That got a reaction. His head snapped to attention and his

eyes narrowed. "What about her?"

"She wouldn't do well here at Denazen, don't you agree?"

Kale's face paled. "What?"

"You don't look well, 98. I think you would benefit from a breath of fresh air." Were they really going to let Mercy take Kale outside? Without supervision?

"What about Dez?"

"Let's go for a walk."

He stood, the muscles in his jaw twitching. Fingers flicking, he took a step closer. "What happened to Dez?"

I glanced nervously at the camera in the corner of the room. Kale looked ready to lunge. My mimics seemed to be on a molecular level. If Kale attacked me while I was Mercy, would it kill me? It wasn't a chance I could take. Grabbing the phone, I gave him my—Mercy's—*don't even think about it* glare. I pressed the button on the phone that said main desk—five.

A gruff voice answered. "Yes?"

"This is Mercy. I'd like to take 98 outside."

The voice on the other end hesitated. "Is that wise?"

"I feel we'll get more out of him that way. He's been on the outside once already. He knows what freedom tastes like. A little crumb won't hurt."

"Would you like us to bring you a suit?"

"That won't be necessary." I winked at Kale. "He's going to behave if he wants me to tell him about the girl."

"Your funeral. Come out whenever you're ready."

I hung up the phone. "Now, let's set some rules. I'm going to do you a favor by taking you outside into the nice, fresh air. Think of it as one last parting gift. You're going to return that favor by behaving. You're going to go along peacefully and touch no one. If you behave and answer all my questions, Deznee will remain unharmed."

Kale's face fell. His fingers froze mid-flick. "You have her? She's here?"

"She's here and unharmed. For now. But understand, if anything happens to me, or another member of the staff while outside the building—if we fail to return—well, I think you know all the ways we can make your friend uncomfortable." I hated to torture him like this, but it was the only thing I could think of to make him cooperate.

He stood, clasping his hands harmlessly in front of him. The hate in his eyes sent shivers up and down my spine. I had to remind myself—repeatedly—the look was meant for Mercy, not me. "Understood."

I opened the door and gestured for him to move ahead. My heart raced, and I had to focus on every step—left—right—left—right—to be sure I didn't trip. The blood pounded in my ears, and I had to fight back a smile. The rush was unlike anything I'd ever felt. Bungee jumping from the Westend Bridge right outside of town, bumper sledding down the highway at sixty mph, even breaking into the school and making out on the principal's desk, they all paled next to this. Next to the thrill of being with Kale, nothing had ever jolted my system like this.

I led him past the desk and to the elevator.

Inside and down to the first floor.

Off the elevator and out the front door.

It was all too easy.

The moment we stepped out of the building and into the sunshine, it started. A tiny voice in the back of my head that told me something wasn't quite right. Like I was missing something— something huge—but I couldn't place it.

I nodded to a set of picnic tables to our left. "You can sit." A quick peek over my shoulder at the building and I could see the first floor desk clerk watching us.

"Listen to me very carefully," I said taking a seat across from him. "We're going to sit here and chat for a few minutes, then we're going to stroll across the lot and to the back of the building to where the gardens are. After that, we're going to hop the fence and book like hell."

Kale blinked several times. "You're bleeding," he said, understanding.

I cringed and swept my thumb under my nose. Crap. Had anyone else noticed? "It's me."

"You're bleeding," he repeated, reaching forward.

I jerked my hand back and swiped it under my nose. Sure enough, my hand came away with a thin streak of red. Shaking my head, I said, "I'm Mercy. If anyone sees you touch her they're gonna put two and two together pretty damn fast."

He pulled his hand back, smile fading. "Are you all right?"

"You're the one locked up in hell and you're asking if *I'm* okay?"

"You're the one—"

It felt like there was an army of men with jackhammers digging through my skull and I could probably sleep for a month, but having Kale in front of me somehow made it okay. "Bleeding. Yeah, I know. I'm fine."

His lip twitched and he frowned. "They know everything. She questioned me as soon as I got back. I didn't answer, but that was enough of a confirmation for them. They asked me if you knew about your mother. I'm sorry."

I shook my head. "It's okay. There's nothing you could have done. Believe it or not, Mercy's on our side. She set it up. We switched places. She's at my house waiting for us."

"On our side?"

I nodded. Kale wasn't convinced, but I could hardly blame him. The idea that someone at Denazen might want to help us had to be unreal to him after everything he'd been through at their hands.

"Okay, get up slowly, try to look sad or something, and let's walk to the garden."

We both stood and began to walk, each step bringing us closer to freedom. Everything was going great—until we rounded the corner and saw the two guards standing there, waiting.

"Afternoon, Mercy," the taller of the two said. The other pulled out a tazer. In his other hand he held a large white blanket.

"Afternoon," I said lightly, hoping they didn't expect me to call them by name. Denazen didn't believe in nametags. It was really inconvenient.

"I'm afraid we've been ordered to take 98 back inside."

"We'll be done in a few minutes." I tried to sound casual but failed.

"It can't wait," the short one chimed in. "Move aside so we can subdue him."

I turned to Kale, who backed away. The fence—and the forest—were only ten feet beyond the two guards. Ten feet. That's all that separated Kale and freedom. Now that he'd had a taste of the outside, Kale wasn't going to let a small thing like ten feet stand in his way.

No matter what.

I blinked, and Kale charged.

24

The tall guard, the outspoken one, proved himself a chicken by diving off the path and out of Kale's way. Smart considering the alternative, but so damn spineless. The smaller one, not so much. He spread his legs apart and fired the tazer—thankfully with crappy aim. When that didn't work, he threw the gun to the ground and charged to meet Kale.

I found it hard to believe these men were sent out to bring him inside without knowing the consequences of skin-to-skin contact. And yet, the obvious aside, this moron charged Kale like a bull would a toreador, arms outstretched and fingers reaching for his throat. They collided mid-way.

Arms up, the man delivered a well-executed high kick aimed for Kale's head. Kale dodged it with ease, spinning around to the man's back. If I'd blinked, I would have missed it. The man whirled and tried again, but this time, instead of dodging the blow, Kale caught the man's foot inches before it collided with the side of his face. Out of what I could only guess was stupidity, the man's hand shot out, clamping onto Kale's neck. There was a single twitch of his fingers as he exhaled sharply, released his hold on Kale, and fell to his knees. His skin grayed and cracked, hair dulling and falling to the floor in dusty clumps. A scream died on his lips as, within a matter of moments, he became nothing more than a pile of dust scattering in the breeze.

Kale didn't waste any time. He grabbed my wrist and we took off over the fence.

Free.

. . .

When we were sure they weren't following anymore, I stopped to mimic back. It took longer than it had with Rick and was ten times more painful, but it felt good to be me again. It felt even better to be in my own clothing. That suit had been restricting, hideous, and itchy as hell.

"I can't believe the risk you took," Kale said as we made our way through the woods. "You could have been hurt."

"Probably not." I remembered what Mercy said right before she got in the car and tried to ignore it.

"Your father knows why you're really here. He knows about you and 98."

"I'm guessing Dad wanted a shot at using me like he had Kat Hans—the first one they sent in to dig up information on the Sixes. I don't think he would have hurt me. At least not so early in the game."

Kale stopped short and wrenched me along with him. I cringed at the sharp movement, doing my best not to cry out. "Do not think like that. Never underestimate them. The things they do… The things they could have done—" He swallowed. The slight protrusion of his Adam's apple bobbed just a bit. "If it should happen in the future, you leave me there. Do not do that again."

"It's fine though. We're out and everyone's—" A lump formed in my throat and my blood went icy. "Alex. I left Alex in there."

"Alex? What's he doing at Denazen?"

"I convinced him to help me get you and my mom out," I groaned. "I got you out and forgot about him. How could I have left him there! Now God knows what's going to happen to him."

"We'll get him out. And Sue."

Sue. Mom. "Did you see her? While you were there, did you see her?"

He shook his head, and we began walking again. "They kept me in lockup the entire time. Other than the men who came in daily to draw my blood, I saw no one other than you and Cross the other day." The disappointment must have been all over my face because he said, "She's fine though, don't worry. Sue knows how to handle herself. She knows how it works."

We were in the bushes beyond the house. Dad specifically said he'd be out of contact until after five. It wouldn't be long though before Denazen sent someone to the house to search for us. We had to get in and get out. Hopefully, Mercy was okay.

Mercy had used the keys I told her about under the front porch to get into the house, so Kale and I had to go in through my window. Not easy considering my limbs felt like stretched out rubber bands. When we swung inside, the room was empty.

"Mercy?" I stepped into the room, grabbing a stapler on the way to the door. Not the best weapon, but the only one I had on hand. Slowly, I turned the knob and peeked around the corner. Empty. Creeping across the landing, I bent over the railing. Nothing.

"She must have left for some reason," I said, coming back

into the room. "Maybe someone from Denazen showed up."

"Get what you need and let's go. We shouldn't stay here long."

Kale was right, of course. Staying here was a bad idea. I scooped up an old backpack. Stuffing anything I could get my hands on inside, I moved through the room. When I got to the corner, I noticed my address book sitting sideway across the top of my desk. I didn't remember pulling it from my nightstand drawer.

It wasn't until I came to the side of the bed that I froze. On my pillow a small folded note lay underneath a red flash drive.

Dez –

The mimic wore off and I didn't want to take any chances, so I left. I won't be going back to Denazen. They'll figure out eventually I assisted you. I hope all is well, and you and 98 Kale made it out okay. On this drive, you'll find two things. First is the list of names you were searching for. While still working at Denazen, there was no way I could pull those files without arousing suspicion. Since I won't be going back, it doesn't matter anymore. Also on this drive is a bit of information that might help you get a step closer to your mother. It's not much, but it might help. Good luck.

— Mercy

"Jackpot!" I squealed, waving the flash drive up and down.

Kale eyed the small red piece of plastic between my fingers and squinted. "How will that do anything?"

"It's a flash drive." When his only answer was a blank stare, I continued. "It holds information from a computer."

He took the drive from me, giving it a hard shake. When nothing came out, he proceeded to tap it against the edge of the windowsill. "How do we get the information out?"

I rescued the drive before he could smash it to bits. "We have to plug it into a computer." My own machine sat in the corner but that was a bad idea. The damn thing would take forever to boot and there was no telling how much time we had. Everyone I knew had a computer. It was only a matter of finding someone at home. "Come on, let's get out of here."

The fact that it was later in the evening worked against us. Most of my friends had hit the strip already. But I refused to give up. We could have gone straight to Ginger and handed over the drive, but I wanted to know what was on it. Never play your cards without at least checking out the hand.

After about two hours of searching, we ended up at the Rinaldis' place. They'd been vacationing on the Jersey shore every summer for the past four years. Last year, they'd paid Brandt to watch their dog and house-sit. As far as I knew, they hadn't asked anyone else for this year since the dog had died.

I led Kale up the walkway to the back of the house and under the porch. There, taped to the bottom of the top step, was the key to the basement door.

When we entered the house, we went room to room in search of a computer. We finally found one in the last room we searched. I felt like I'd walked into another dimension. A shrine. The shelves were lined with collectibles and the walls covered with posters.

"What kind of place is this?" Kale whispered, eyes wide, as he followed me through the door.

"The Rinaldis' son is twelve. I guess he's a Pokémon fan." I said over my shoulder as I made a beeline for the computer. While the machine booted, I sank into the chair. When the monitor came alive, an annoying little yellow dude—Peekaboo or something—hopped across the screen, babbling incoherent chatter in a squeaky voice. I bit back a joke and slipped the drive into the USB slot.

After a moment, the file popped open and a list of names scrolled down the screen. I skimmed through—there had to be at least a hundred. The title at the top of the document read, *Residents*. A list of all the Sixes Denazen had on site.

Score!

Skimming the document, I was shocked to know so many of the names. Some were people in the community that had gone missing over the last few years, others were classmates and neighbors.

I scanned the room, finally finding the printer wedged underneath the desk. Flipping the power switch and clicking print, I waited for the pages. Kale was quiet beside me. "Are you okay?"

"Okay?"

"Did they hurt you?"

Kale fingered the yellowing bruise on the side of his face and shook his head. "They can't hurt me," he said. "But when Mercy told me they had you…"

"It wasn't Mercy, it was me."

"I didn't know that at the time. I believed. All I could think about was what they'd do to you."

I swiveled the chair around and took his hands in mine. "I'm fine. You're fine."

"We're both fine," he said, planting a quick kiss on my cheek.

I nodded. "We are. And once I get Alex and my mom out of there, we can put this whole mess behind us. Maybe after we get settled, I can take you to see a real movie. None of that dancing stuff. A movie at an IMAX theater. One with lots of explosives. Guys love seeing things blow up, right?"

The printer stopped. I leaned back, Kale's hand still in mine, and picked up the sheets. Skimming them, I smiled. Perfect. One last thing to do.

Opening the browser, I pulled up Craigslist. Searching the ads, I was relieved to find there weren't many new weird ones. In fact, there were only two. One for lessons on how to raise cattle and the other claiming to teach llama training.

"Are these people supposed to be home soon?"

I folded the list and stuffed it in my back pocket. Grabbing a pen from the other end of the desk, I wrote both numbers on the back of my hand. "Nope, why?"

"'Cause someone's here."

I went to the window and cursed. The Rinaldis had obviously replaced Brandt. I grabbed Kale's hand. "Hurry, we need to leave."

• • •

We hit the pay phone in front of the Blueberry Bean, leaning in close as people skirted around us on the busy sidewalk. The first ad—the one about cattle raising—remarkably turned out to be legit. As I dialed the second, I said a silent prayer.

"I'm calling about your Craigslist ad. The one about llama training?"

"How many llamas do you own?"

"Um, two?" I replied. I had no clue what the magic number was.

A long pause on the other end. Not good. "I'm sorry. That's too many."

"This is Dez Cross," I said quietly into the receiver. *Pleaseplease please* let this be the right ad. Then, for good measure I added, "I have the information Ginger wanted."

The man on the other end hesitated for a moment. It seemed to take forever, but finally he gave me an address and hung up.

"We're in," I said, turning to Kale. "Let's see what we have here and then we'll head over and see Ginger."

Hanging out in front of the Bean was a bad idea. Too public. So I tugged Kale's shirt and nodded to the side of the building. Once we were in the shadows, I pulled the pages from my pocket. There were only three sheets of names, the rest of the bulk was something else. An email. From my dad to someone named Vincent.

> The party is the perfect setup. Crowded and loud, we should have no problems. My sources have confirmed that both targets will be present. I also expect to handle a small problem that has recently come to light. I've discovered the instigator of our recent rash of disobedience. I will deal with it.

Party?
Underneath it was Vincent's reply, dated two days ago.

> This is very good news—and on top of your other surprise, too. I must congratulate you. I've been told Supremacy is now fully operational. You have my go-ahead on the party, Cross. I think this will work. Who will you send?

Next page. Another email.

> Thank you. I am very pleased about Supremacy. I was beginning to lose hope. As for the party, I have the perfect group. I'm thinking about sending Alex Mojourn along with Sueshanna Odell. I understand it would be Alex's first

assignment, but he knows this crowd and I feel it could work to the advantage of our goal to send someone familiar. I have someone hunting down the party's location as we speak.

"Oh my God," I breathed.

"What's wrong?" Kale jumped to his feet, head swiveling from side to side.

"The file." I waved the papers. "It has information on where Mom's going to be. Alex too!"

"Where?" Kale sounded hopeful.

I flipped to the next page—the last one.

Then it's settled. The day after this Sumrun, we should have two new Sixes in our stable and the problems with insubordination should be quelled.

25

The bouncer outside the party winked as we went inside. The same guy I'd promised to wait for the first time we'd come here. Good to know he wasn't holding any grudges.

Without Alex, I didn't know where to find Ginger. After about twenty minutes of searching, though, I spotted Dax in the corner talking to a tall, thin blonde. We moved along the outside edge of the room—it was less crowded and made Kale feel better—on our way to Dax.

He saw us approaching and parted ways with the blonde, greeting us with a friendly smile and wave. "Nice to see you two again. And in one piece."

"Same," I said, smiling. "How's Mona doing?"

He sighed. "She's stopped screaming at night, and sometimes we think we can see a small spark of recognition in her eyes." He shook his head. "But she's not much better than when you last saw her. She doesn't speak except to call out for her sister."

"I'm sorry."

"We still have hope, though. In time, she might come out of it."

I nodded, but didn't say anything. Why dash his hope with my negativity?

"Any idea where Alex has been? I haven't seen him for days," Dax asked.

"Alex is at Denazen."

Dax dropped his drink to the floor. The plastic cup bounced, sending droplets of blue liquid everywhere. "What?"

I reached into my pocket and pulled out the flash drive. "Do you know where I can find Ginger? This has the information she wanted. If what's on here is accurate, we can save my mom and Alex."

Dax wasted no time. He started for the stairs and motioned for us to follow. It looked like the building had been a department store in its day—we found Ginger at the other end of the building in what had once been the receiving room, surrounded by seven shirtless men holding trays full of fruit punch.

"Must be nice to be the queen," I whispered.

Kale leaned closer. "Why are they all shirtless?"

Ginger apparently had ears like a dog, because she heard us. Turning to Kale, she winked, taking a sip from her punch. "It's a benefit of being the *queen*." She waved the men off and beckoned us closer. "I hear you've found my information?"

We'd only spoken to Dax, who'd never left our side. How she knew why we were here was beyond me. "And then some." I stepped closer and handed her the drive.

Greedy, wrinkled fingers shook just a bit as they snatched the red plastic from my hands. She examined the drive before handing it to one of the men standing behind her chair. After she whispered something in his ear, he left.

"And?" I said when Ginger made no move to speak. "What

about our information? The Reaper?"

"Do you think you still need him? You have the information needed to save your mother and Alex."

I wanted to ask her how she knew what information I had. She hadn't looked at the drive, but I was too pissed. I opened my mouth and closed it again. She was right—sort of. I knew Mom was going to be at Sumrun from the email on the flash, but a lot could still go wrong. I wanted a backup, just in case. Plus, I'd busted my ass to get what she'd asked for. I took a huge risk and gave up the secret I'd been hoarding for years. Even if I didn't need him anymore, fair was fair. Plus, I was way curious.

I stood straighter and folded my arms. Expression fierce and chin out, I said, "A deal's a deal."

Ginger considered this for a moment before pointing to Kale. I glanced at him, then back to her. "What about him?"

"You wanted to know who the Reaper was." She flicked her wrist at him. "Here he is."

Kale looked over his shoulder. There was no one there. "What is she talking about?"

Red. All I saw was red. "You manipulative, wrinkled old bitch! You played me! There is no Reaper, is there?"

Knuckles white as they clutched her cane, Ginger stood. The men flanking her all took two steps back. "I did nothing of the sort, child, and I suggest you watch that tongue of yours. Show some respect." She hobbled around the room, plastic cup still in hand. "Do you know what my gift is?"

"No," I snapped. "And I can't say I really give a damn right now."

"I'm a visionary. I can see a person's path when I look in their eyes."

"You only met me a few days ago, yet you're insinuating I'm the Reaper? Sue told me about him when I was twelve. How can that be?" Kale asked.

"I met you years before you showed up at my party."

"That's crap," I spat.

Kale turned to me and frowned. He was frustrated. "This is very confusing."

I took his hand and squeezed. Turning to Ginger, I said, "Some people get off on messing with others."

Ginger narrowed her eyes at us. "I was there when Kale was born."

"Don't listen to her Kale, this is all b.s."

"I looked into those blue eyes and saw the one person who would one day have a shot at saving us from Cross. I started the rumor of the Reaper years ago to give our kind hope."

She had his attention. The Reaper forgotten, he focused on Ginger. "You know me? If you were present when I came into this world, tell me. Tell me who I am. Tell me who my mother is."

Ginger's expression softened. "Felecia. Your mother's name was Felecia."

Kale's face fell. "Was?"

Silently, Ginger nodded and looked away.

"I thought you said no one had ever escaped Denazen before? How did you know Kale's mother if *he* was going to be the first to escape?"

"Stupid child," Ginger hissed. "He was not born in Denazen. He came into this life at a hospital in the city."

"How did I end up at Denazen? What happened to my mother?"

"Wait," I interrupted. "If Kale was born in a hospital and you were there and saw him, didn't you know what would happen?" Rage filled my head and made my blood pump faster. "You knew he'd end up at Denazen and you did nothing?"

Ginger's brows furrowed in anger, then settled in what I

supposed was regret. "There was nothing to be done. These things can't be changed. Things happened as they were meant to happen so he would one day become the Reaper. Every event in people's lives shape their future. You *cannot* change these things."

Kale didn't seem to care that she'd done nothing to help him. His only concern was for his mother. "Why were you with my mother when I was born?"

"I was there the moment she herself came into being. It seemed no less fitting I be with her when she brought her own child into the world."

The sharp, stubborn chin. The ice blue eyes. I hadn't noticed before. It all came together. "Felecia was your daughter."

Ginger nodded. "From the first moment I looked into her eyes, I knew what would become of her." She stomped her cane into the ground. "Do you think it's easy raising a child, each day looking into her eyes and seeing the black future she had before her? Do you think it was simple for me to stand by and watch the events that would bring upon her end unfold, day after day, unable to stop it?"

"But why not try? There had to be something you could have done. Send her away? Warn her?"

"These things are not to be toyed with," the old woman snapped. "Each person's future is tied to a thousand others. Change simply one thing and you have chaos. Everything is thrown out of balance and horrible things happen."

"You let her die?" Kale asked. His face was neutral but I could hear the agony in his voice. In my hand, his fingers twitched like he was trying to flick them, but I held tight.

"An ancestor of ours, the first known visionary, learned this lesson the hard way. Newly married and with child, she and her husband Winston were the picture of happiness. They had their own home, a baby on the way, and a bright future ahead of them. Our ancestor, Miranda, being a visionary, had access to information that told her otherwise. She saw she would lose her beloved husband at an early age to a horrific stable fire."

"She intervened."

"She stopped him from going to the barn that night. She thanked God for her gift because it had enabled her to save her husband. But her thanks did not last. Soon after their child was born, Miranda regretted what she'd done."

"Why would she regret saving the one she loved?" Kale asked.

Ginger's expression softened. "Because, Kale, Winston was destined to die in that fire. If Miranda had never interfered with his destiny, then Denazen would never have been formed."

"What?" Kale and I gasped in unison.

"It happens, but it's rare that the offspring of a Six, even with only one parent, is born without the genetic chromosome defect. As you can probably guess, Miranda's child grew to be a Six. Narrow-minded and foolish, Winston was unable to handle the truth. He branded the child—and its mother—evil, and drove them away. He started the organization that would become the Denazen we know today. Because of Miranda Kale's selfishness, we live in fear, hiding from the repercussions of her mistake."

"Miranda *Kale*?"

"I named you, child. I found it fitting that you, destined to free us from our chains, bear the name of its instigator."

"What about your daughter, was she like me? This Felecia?"

Ginger shook her head. "The opposite of you. You take life, and she gave it."

Kale's fingers tightened in mine. "Will we be able to save Sue?"

"I don't know. I've never met the woman."

I stepped forward and placed my face inches from hers. "You've met me. Do we save my mom or not?"

Silence.

"You owe me," I growled. "You sent me into Denazen to get you this damn list in exchange for something I had all along."

"You were never in any danger. I knew you would return with the list. That is why I asked. You were meant to get it for me."

"That's not the point." I was yelling now, making no attempt to keep my voice down. It's not like anyone could hear me over the thumping beats of the party below.

"I am not a fortune-teller," Ginger said. Her face reverted back to its usual, stony set. "Do you see a crystal ball? Am I wearing a turban? The information I am privy to is not for others."

"So that's it then? You get what you want and I get nothing out of it?"

"You will always have sanctuary among us. A place to go and food to eat. An offer like that, for *you*, Deznee Cross, is a generous one. I have sent word. Misha Vaugn has redacted your ban of the hotel. You may stay there when needed."

"Wow. Thanks," I said sarcastically and turned away. I wasn't getting anywhere else with her. Time to cut my losses and focus on the important stuff. Mom. Ginger was right. I didn't need the Reaper, I had the information needed to make it happen.

We were nearly to the outside edge of the room when Ginger called out. "One more thing."

Something told me not to stop, but I did it anyway.

"I'm sorry for everything."

I didn't answer, only continued on my way. I didn't ask, but something told me she wasn't apologizing for lying to me.

It was almost midnight when we left the party. Kale and I were both tired and hungry, and as much as it bugged me, the only place we could think to go was Misha's.

The money Brandt had given me was basically gone—a bus trip was out of the question since I had nothing on hand to make spare cash with. And besides that, the idea of mimicking anything after the last few days turned the air in my lungs to ice.I It looked like we were hoofing it across town. We were only four blocks from the hotel when I heard someone yelling my name.

"Dez, helooo? Are you deaf, girl?" A car pulled up alongside and Curd hopped out. Looking sleek in black leather pants and a crisp black button down.

"Curd!" I threw my arms around his shoulders. "Are you okay?"

He pulled away, glaring at me. "No thanks to you. Not cool to split on me like that right as I crashed."

"Crashed?"

"I went up to get you and your boy a soda and voom! Last thing I remember was pulling a cold one from the fridge, enjoying my buzz. One too many uppers that morning, I guess. I passed out cold. But to leave me facedown on the floor? Not cool."

He didn't know what had happened. Part of me felt grateful. "I'm sorry. I got a call and we had to book."

"Whatever." Curd gave me a once-over and frowned. "What are you doing over here? There's a red square rave in the field outside Fallow Farm. Heading home to change?" In my wrinkled hoodie and dirty jeans, I must have looked like a walking disaster. Definitely not how Curd was used to seeing me.

"No party for me tonight. It's been a long few days. I'm heading to a friend's to crash."

"Aww. I told Fin Meyers you were gonna be there. You were asking about him so I figured—"

"Who is Fin Meyers?" Kale asked. From the way he snatched my hand and squeezed, I got the impression he was jealous. He was *definitely* more normal than he realized. I gave his hand a reassuring squeeze in return.

"*When* did I ask you about that jerk?"

He looked at me as though I'd shown up wearing last year's jeans. "Um, this afternoon? When you called me? Wouldn't let me get a word in edgewise? We discussed Sumrun invites, or do you not remember that either?" He shook his head. "I gotta say, with your drool scale, it surprised me you wanted to be bothered with a walking disease like Fin, but to each her own. I heard you were into some weird shit."

Kale's brow furrowed. "When did you have time—?"

I shook my head. "I didn't." To Curd, I said, "I haven't spoken to you since the day we showed up at your place."

A wave of nausea washed over me.

Mercy.

That's why my address book had been open on the desk. I hadn't pulled one over on Denazen—they'd pulled one over on me. The list, the emails, Kale's escape, it had all been a setup.

Curd's voice echoed through my haze. "You're looking a little pale, Dez. Everything all right?"

I couldn't answer right away. If I opened my mouth, I'd scream my head off.

"Dez?" Something slipped over my shoulder. Kale's arm. "What's wrong?"

I remembered the emails on the flash drive. Of course. They'd need someone to get the party's location. Who better than *me*. Sumrun was one of our town's biggest secrets. They could ask Alex, but he'd tell them he didn't know. Mercy had my voice and my address book. I'd practically handed her the location on a golden platter. "You told me where the party was being held this year when we spoke on the phone earlier, didn't you?"

He nodded and leaned forward. "I thought you gave up all that"—he put his fingers to his lips and inhaled deeply—"stuff."

"It's been a really long day. Refresh my memory?"

Curd sighed. "The old Shop Rite warehouse by the docks."

"Oh, right." Think. Think fast. I contemplated telling Curd that something big was going down, but decided against it. What good would it do? Nothing I said would make him consider changing locations this late in the game, and as far as I could tell, Curd knew nothing about Sixes. He'd write me off as crazy or, better yet, stoned, and walk away laughing.

I needed this party to happen—but on my terms, not theirs. "Hey, I know the party's in a few days, but I came up with a killer idea and I forgot to mention it earlier."

"I'm all ears, baby."

"Let's make it a costume rave this year."

"I dunno. I mean I *love* the idea, but ya think we can get the news out this late in the game?"

"Totally! Do a mass email. People will spread the word!"

"That's a serious idea." He reached into his pocket and pulled out a pack of Marlboros. "Hey, where you two headed? I can give you a lift before I hit the square."

"That would be great, thanks."

· · ·

Even though Ginger said we had use of the hotel whenever we needed it, I half expected to be turned away at the door. To my surprise, though, we were escorted up to the third floor and deposited in a single room with two queen-size beds. Ten minutes later, after Kale finished checking under the beds and in the closet, a knock came from the hallway. When we opened the door, no one was there, but a cart full of assorted food sat unattended.

"What is this soft white stuff?" Kale asked, sitting across from me. We'd jammed the food cart between us and pigged out. I couldn't remember the last time I'd eaten so much. I was ready to pop.

"*That* is a fried cheese stick. Pretty much in its own revered food group. It's only earthly equal is the chocolate food group." I leaned across the table and pushed a small dish of still-warm marinara sauce at him. "Dip it in there and you'll think you've died and gone to heaven."

He did as instructed, and I watched his lips curled into a deliriously happy smile. A small moan came from deep inside his throat as he chewed his fried cheese. The sound—as well as the smile—gave me goose bumps.

I reached for my glass of water at the same time Kale reached for his. Our fingers brushed. It was enough to make him forget the cheese stick.

He was on his feet, around the cart, and next to me on the bed before I had a chance to blink. Gesturing to the empty cart of food he said, "They've fed us and locked us in. Can I kiss you again?"

"They haven't locked us in, Kale. We're guests here, not prisoners."

"They locked us in last time we were here. We were *not* guests."

"Things were a little different last time. And they didn't lock us in, they requested we stay in our room. They didn't know if we could be trusted." I slid down the bed and made my way to the door. "See?" I opened it and stepped into the hallway. Kale followed.

He looked up one end and then down the other. "Now they trust us?"

I shrugged. "We got them the information they wanted, so I guess so."

"How far will they allow us to go?"

"How far? We can go wherever we want. I mean not into other people's rooms, obviously, but we could leave if we wanted."

Kale slid past me and went for the stairs. I made sure I had the room key, closed the door, and followed him. He didn't stop till he hit the lobby. The desk clerk offered him a friendly smile, then turned back to her newspaper.

Kale watched her suspiciously, taking small, tentative steps backward. She ignored him.

"What are you doing?" I asked, trying not to laugh.

But Kale was serious. He put his hand on the door handle and the desk clerk glanced up from her paper to give him a truly confused look. Staring at her, Kale pushed open the door and stepped outside.

Nothing happened.

He stayed there, on the other side of the thick glass door, for a few minutes before coming back inside. The bell above chimed, and the desk clerk looked up again. "Did you guys... need something?"

Kale didn't answer. Instead, he pushed back out the door, this time taking several steps away from the building.

I rolled my eyes. "Sorry. This is all a little new to him." I opened the door and pulled a very stunned-looking Kale back inside. "Can we go to sleep now?"

The whole way back to our room—it took a few minutes because he still wouldn't get into the elevator—Kale remained silent. We reached the room, and I pulled out the key. Kale leaned forward, arms wrapping around my waist. His cheek skimmed up my neck and across the side of my face as we walked inside. "Is this okay?" he whispered, voice a bit hoarse.

"Um," I swallowed, fighting for control of my voice. "Sure."

He drew away and pulled off his shirt, then without missing a beat, mine was gone as well. Large hands spun my body to face his and lips met my own as the fire started to build.

"I can see it in your eyes," he breathed between kisses. "You still don't believe this."

"Hmm?" A mumble was about all I could manage. I wanted less talking and more kissing.

He pulled away and laced his fingers through mine, holding them out in front of me. "This."

I sighed. It was a shame to ruin such a perfect toe-curling kiss, but he seemed determined. "It's not that I don't believe you. I'm being"—I tried to think of the right word— "cautious."

He frowned. "Cautious?"

Obviously not the right word. "I know this is all really hard for you to understand but—"

"You keep assuming I don't know anything at all. Because I've never seen a DBD, had a cheese stick, or had someone who makes me happy, you think I can't figure out how I feel."

"DVD."

"What?"

"It's a DVD, not a DBD. Digital Video Disc."

He glared at me. "I'm not simple. I know Alex hurt you. I know about things in your life changing you. I know about being cautious."

"You asked me if I was afraid of you."

He pulled further away and I could see a hint of fear in his eyes. "Yes."

"I said I was, sort of."

"You did."

"That's what I mean by cautious. I'm afraid of you because I have to be careful."

His expression twisted and he looked as though I'd hit him. "I would never hurt you. I can't—"

"That's not what I mean. I'm afraid of the way you make me feel. I'm the first person you've ever been able to touch. The way you feel about me isn't going to last. Eventually you're going to want something else. Someone else…"

"You're the only person who *can* touch me, Dez."

"For now. Remember, Ginger said you can learn to control it. Eventually, you'll be able to live a normal life. You'll be able to be just like everyone else. You're going to want to date other people."

"You're not hearing me." He pulled me closer. "You're the only one who can touch me. Someday I might be able to touch other people without turning them into a dusty husk, but that won't change the fact that you'll still be the only one who can *touch* me."

He pulled my hand up to his chest and placed it over his heart. "I don't know how you feel, or understand exactly what you mean by date other people, but if it's this"—he squeezed my hand to his chest—"then you're wrong."

Then he kissed me. Not a gentle peck or a tentative pull of the lips. A scorching, soul-wrenching hammer that pounded a heart-stopping rhythm from my toes to the tips of my fingers. Alive. Like his other kisses, it was the strongest high I'd ever had. A thrill I intended to ride all the way to the end this time.

I backed us up against the wall. "How I feel? You want to know?" I ran my hands over his face and tangled them into his messy hair. "This is unlike anything else. I've bungeed off buildings, I've skateboarded off roofs. I've even gone train surfing. Nothing comes close to the high I feel when I'm with you. You've been through horrible things, and yet you're one of the kindest, truest people I've ever met. At first I thought it was because you were safe. I could feel something for you because you couldn't hurt me. Not the way Alex did. But it's more than that. It's *you*. Who you are. The way you are. Everything from your smile to the way you always say exactly what's on your mind. Your soul, Kale."

I took a deep, shaky breath. "It terrifies me to say it, but I think I might be falling in l—"

"I love you," he said. His arms encircled me, fingers digging into my lower back. They slipped down, sliding inside the back of my jeans. His words came in thick, hot rasps that tickled the side of my face as he kissed a trail from my chin to my ear, and back again. "Just you. Only you. *Always you*."

I pulled him away from the wall and backed toward the bed. He followed, never breaking contact. Like me, the room, the entire world would vanish if he let go. We reached the bed and I turned, breaking the kiss. He strained forward, eager to reconnect, but I resisted. I took a step back and made a show of slowly unbuttoning my jeans. Kale stopped fighting me and froze. He stared, eyes trained on my hands as I slid my jeans down to the floor. When I kicked them away, he reached forward to grip my hips. A small sigh of contentment escaped his lips as he made contact again, pulling me closer.

I let him pull me on top of him before grabbing both his wrists and pinning them to his sides. Planting tiny kisses all the way from his neck to his belly button, I smiled. The Reaper. *My* Reaper. I flipped my hair aside and raised my head to watch him. "How does this feel? Tell me."

The muscles in his arms tightened and his legs went ridged. "It's amazing," he gasped as I resumed my kisses, dropping below his navel. Unbuttoning his jeans, I pushed them down a few inches and paused above the waistband of his boxers for a moment before tugging them down, along with his jeans. As my fingers brushed his hip, he jumped, sucking in a sharp breath. "Oh God…"

With each shocked gasp and shallow, gasping breath, Kale brought me higher. There was no ceiling with him. Happiness stretched on forever. Every moment I spent with him seemed to find me someplace new—feeling something new. I hadn't loved Alex. I'd cared about him, yes, but I hadn't loved him. Not once in all our time together had I ever felt like this. Free. Euphoric. Content.

Reluctantly, I pulled away. The subject of protection was silly considering his life before me, but I still felt like it was something we both needed to get out. "Um, you've never—I mean obviously this is the first time…"

He trailed a finger across my bare shoulder. "Of course not." Frowning, he added, "You have, though."

It was the last thing he'd want to hear, but I didn't want there to be any lies between us. "This is kind of awkward... I mean, Alex and I..."

I tried to draw away, but he stopped me. "That was your past. I am your future. There's no more Alex?"

"No more. I know what I want. I just wanted you to know that we'd—I mean I'm on pills because I've already... So I can't..." God. I felt like an idiot.

Kale didn't seem to notice. He smiled and pulled me close again. When he kissed me, everything else melted away. Our underwear and Kale's jeans joined mine on the hotel floor. I settled on top of him, inching down slowly as I watched his face. "No," I said when he closed his eyes. "Look at me, please."

Ice blue eyes burned as he grabbed my face and pulled me to him. "Please..." he pleaded. "I need to..."

"It's okay," I whispered, my own voice thick. "Go ahead."

Before I knew what happened, Kale was above me, strands of black hair falling forward. I reached up and pushed them away—I wanted to see his face—no, I *needed* to see his face. His eyes never left mine. With anyone else, in any other circumstance, that type of scrutiny would have made me squirm, regardless of my self-confidence. With Kale it was different. He wasn't staring at me, he *saw*. More clearly than anyone else ever had. It was like a drug and I needed more. I'd always need more—and that still scared me a little. Kale was truly the one fix I'd never get enough of. My nirvana.

"This can't be real," he hissed. "I don't deserve—"

"You do," I insisted. Tears gathered in the corners of my eyes as I silenced further protests with a fierce kiss. Every cell in my body was ready to explode. No outside world. No Denazen. No Dad. Only Kale and me.

"For me," he said. It came out as a cross between a choked growl and a whimper. It was shocked, and it was possessive. Full of pain, and laced with joy. "You were made for *me*."

For a brief moment time stood still, then raced forward. The world exploded.

And there was peace.

27

We lay low at Misha's the entire next day. Kale was fascinated with TV—mostly the commercials. He'd seen a little while at Denazen, but nothing extensive. He couldn't believe there were so many products for the same purpose. Seven kinds of soda. Three kinds of bathroom cleaner. A hundred different kinds of cars. He couldn't understand why people needed more than one of something.

At lunch, breakfast, and dinner, a cart of food mysteriously found its way to the hall outside our door. Each meal was something different and new for Kale, and each time he'd find something that fascinated him. By dinnertime, his favorite was the watermelon Jell-O.

And of course, there was me. Another thing Kale couldn't seem to get enough of, which worked out because I couldn't get enough of him.

"Tell me this is different," Kale said sometime after dinner. We were curled up on his bed, snuggled close. He played with a strand of my hair, twirling it between his fingers while his other hand traced feathery circles across my arm. "Tell me this is something special."

"It's something special," I said, twisting to look at him.

TV, good food, kissing, cuddling—and a lot more touching. Each time Kale would marvel at the softness of my skin. He would insist it was all a dream because nothing in his life could be this good. For a while, I forgot we were on the verge of something major. Something life-altering. Something dangerous.

For a while, I forgot about the nagging voice in the back of my head. That voice came with warning bells. Warning bells and big, bright neon signs. I ignored them, even though they were always the elephant in the room.

Ginger said she'd help Kale learn to control his power. But she'd screwed us. Her promise of handing over the Reaper had been a lie. Sort of. For selfish reasons, I hadn't questioned her about her other promise. The one to help Kale. In the dark, self-serving corner of my brain, I wanted him to stay as he was. *Exactly* how he was. I wanted strings. If Kale never changed, then those strings would never choke me. The way I saw it, I'd had to suck face with a lot of frogs to find my prince. I deserved a little happy.

In the end, though, my conscience won out. I'd have to find Ginger—as long as things didn't go south—and ask for her help with Kale. He deserved a choice. If that choice in the end wasn't me, I'd have to live with it. I loved him. I wouldn't cheat him out of living his life because I wanted him for myself. That's what Denazen had done. What Dad had done.

Early the next afternoon, we bid Misha good-bye and set out to gather the costumes we'd need for tonight. Only one costume store stayed open all year round, but I refused to shop there. They were overpriced and the selection was a joke. French maids, gorilla costumes, cowboy hats…nothing original. But I was a resourceful girl. I could improvise. I'd had a killer idea last Halloween, but I'd come down with a wicked cold and never got to follow it through. Now was the perfect chance.

The costume idea for the rave served two main purposes. The obvious one was it'd be easier for Kale and me to hide in plain sight. They knew we would be there because of the information Mercy had given us, so by being harder to spot, at least we'd be able to move through the crowd more freely. The other reason? The chances of Mercy and Dad not finding out about the last-minute change in theme were in our favor. Knowing Denazen, there was always a possibility, but it was slim. We'd be hidden, and they'd stick out like sore thumbs. Win-win.

Thanks to a pair of scissors, a pad of paper, and a borrowed twenty in my back pocket, there was enough cash to get us whatever we needed.

Since it was summer, my costume had been fairly easy. A quick trip to the mall—Target, then Toys R Us and CVS—and I was set. Kale proved a little harder. When he saw what I'd bought, he got nervous about skin exposure, but I assured him I had something different in mind for him. We managed to track down most of what we needed at the mall—black jeans and T-shirt, dark sunglasses and boots—but the leather jacket was a problem.

"I have a question," Kale said as we made our way to the leather shop a few blocks away. The sun was starting to set and we needed to hurry if we were going to make it before the store closed.

I took his hand. "As long as it doesn't involve a midget and some whipped cream, I'm game."

He stopped, eyebrows raised.

"It's a joke, go ahead."

We started walking again. "What's going to happen after?"

"After?"

"This party. When it's over, then what?"

"What do you mean, then what?"

"What will happen to me?"

"Happen? Nothing's going to happen. You're free to live your life now. You can go wherever you want and do whatever you like."

"Go?"

"Yeah, like travel."

His eyes sparkled.

"There's an entire world out there, Kale. Things you can't even imagine. Fascinating sights to see, interesting people to meet…" Pretty girls to kiss. Damn it.

He smiled. "I want to see all the places I've read about. I want to sail on ships and feel sand between my toes." The smile got wider. "I want to sleep under the stars and swim in the ocean."

"Good goals," I said quietly.

He nodded. "Goals, I like that. I have goals now. It feels nice! What about you? What are yours?"

I laughed. "Mine? I don't think I've ever really had any. Other than pissing off my dad, I'm pretty unmotivated."

"So you can make some. When this is over, we can travel to all these places and you can come up with your own list."

The look on his face could have lit the corners of the darkest spaces on earth. It made my words taste bitter. "Kale, I don't know if I'll be able to leave when this is over. Someday, yeah, but I'm not sure how soon. You might have to go without me."

Kale stopped, grabbing my arm. "All these places I want to go don't exist without you. All my goals come from one place. You. *You* are my biggest goal. That's not wrong, is it?"

"No." I hesitated. "But you can't stop living your life for me. I don't know what's going to happen with my mom. I got cheated out of seventeen years. I want to get to know her… That won't happen if we manage to free her and I run off."

A few moments of silence ticked by, and the leather shop came into site. Thankfully, the lights inside were still on.

"But we can still be together, right? Even if we stay here?"

"Of course. I'll be here as long as you want me, Kale. And when possible, I'll follow you to the ends of the earth if that's where you want to go. I just need to square things up first."

"As long as I know this"—he lifted our joined hands—"is *mine* to hold, I'll wait for you forever."

I hoped so.

The clerk hadn't been happy about staying late. She glared daggers at us until I slapped down the three hundred and forty-two dollars cash I'd mimicked from several pieces of toilet paper back at the hotel. She'd closed the day with a nice sale, and we left with a gorgeous black motorcycle jacket.

Now, all the parts of our costumes collected, we needed a place to get ready. Kale wasn't thrilled with the idea of trekking all the way back to the hotel, but we didn't have another choice. The same woman sat behind the desk when we walked in, this time her smile slightly more genuine than before. Slightly.

"I hate to be a pain, but could we go back up to the room and get ready?"

She held out a set of keys. "Go to room 309 instead. There's someone up there waiting for you."

No one knew we were here, much less coming back again tonight. I was instantly suspicious. "Someone waiting for me?"

It must have been obvious, because the woman said, "Not to worry. He's a friend." She frowned. "Sort of."

Now I was curious. Still a little worried, but curious.

"Wait," Kale said as I reached for the door. "Me first." He sidestepped me and pushed the door open, stepping inside. I was right behind him.

On one of the beds, tossing back a cold one and watching TV, was Brandt's friend Sheltie. He saw us and smiled, waving. "Thank God. I wasn't sure you would be coming back."

Kale still stood in front of me, shoulders tense. "Who are you?"

"Christ, you're still here?" The guy peered around Kale and crooked a finger at me. "I need to talk to you."

I turned to Kale. "This is Sheltie, he's"—I swallowed and corrected myself—"he *was* my cousin Brandt's friend." Turning back to Sheltie, I asked, "What are you doing here? I thought you were leaving town."

"That's a good question—one I'd be glad to answer, but it's complicated."

Kale snorted. "Have you not heard? Everything is complicated."

I glanced back at the door, and then to the clock on the night table. We had a little less than two hours. "It's not gonna take long, is it? We kinda have somewhere to be."

He nodded. "I know." Taking a deep breath, he launched into it. "It's me."

I stared at him. "You're high, aren't you?"

"Look at me. Really look. Don't you see it?"

I tried to take a step toward him, but Kale grabbed my arm. "What am I looking for exactly?"

Sheltie frowned. "If anyone can see it, it'll be you. Try. Look harder."

I scanned his face, his clothing, everything looked the same as before. "Sorry. Don't know what you're talking about."

"Brandt. I'm Brandt."

My eyes started to water and I turned away, horrified. "You're a sick puppy, you know that?"

"Dez, I know how this sounds. You have to trust me.

Technically, I'm Brandt. And now Sheltie, too."

"Wow, you Denazen assholes must lock yourselves away in a room with a bottle of Jack and a bag of really good weed to come up with this crap." I jerked free of Kale's grasp and stepped forward, fingers itching. "Was it you? Did you kill Brandt?"

When Sheltie didn't answer, Kale snapped. "Answer her."

Sheltie jumped off the bed, ignored him, and backed toward the window. "Dez, *listen* to me, I'm serious. It's really me."

"Do you think I'm an idiot? I saw them taking Brandt's body away that morning. Uncle Mark saw him. *Dead.*"

"It's not that simple. I told you back at my funeral. I'm a Six. Something called a soul jumper. We're rare, there's only like four of us out there. When my heart stopped beating, my soul jumped into the body of the closest person. Sheltie."

"I don't believe you."

"When we were little we went on that camping trip. You and I got lost in the woods."

Kale stiffened. "Couldn't anyone get that information?"

He was right. Anyone, especially people with connections like Denazen, could find a ton of tiny, intimate details about my life. Hell, the newspaper had done a big story on it. Sold a ton of copies. They'd touted Aunt Cairn as a neglectful parent, leaving young children to play in a dangerous area unsupervised. Later they retracted the statement, but the damage had been done.

I needed solid proof. "The tree house in your backyard. There was a metal lockbox. What did we keep in it?"

He smiled. "A blue Hot Wheels car and your Hello Kitty notebook. Our most prized possessions."

I felt sick. Only two people knew that. One of them was supposed to be dead. "So where did Sheltie go?"

Smile gone, he bent his head and pulled the damn skateboard wheel from his pocket. Tossing it into the air, he caught it and said,

"Dunno. He was just gone—not that I'm sorry. Bastard offed me. He showed up at the house saying he had info on Denazen. I let him in and *boom*. No more Brandt. As soon as my heart stopped, I jumped into his body. I've been trying to decide if I should tell you or not."

"This is not happening…"

"The other catch is, apparently each time I jump into a new Six's body, I keep their gift. Sheltie had the ability to visit people's dreams. I tried to warn you in a dream, but it didn't come out right. I was disoriented, still fresh from the jump."

"That was you?"

He nodded again and my stomach churned. This was the biggest mind-screw ever.

"Yep. I'm still *me*, though. The same guy you've known your entire life. It's weird, I have all my old memories, but I have all this guy's memories, too."

"This is really messed up."

"Want to talk about messed up? I remember Sheltie killing me. It was like killing myself. Try that on for size."

I couldn't imagine having to live with that kind of memory. "That's horrible."

"No, horrible is, you're my best friend—my *cousin*—and all I can think about is how hot you look right now."

"Oh my God…"

Next to me Kale snarled.

I grabbed his hand and gulped. "I think I might puke."

"Right back atcha."

"So what about Sheltie?"

"He was working for your father. After I left the Graveyard, I started digging. It's amazing what you can find if you look hard enough. I guess when I found too much, though, they sent Sheltie. He said I'd officially crossed the line and my time was up. Dude pulled out a knife and that's the last thing I remember until I woke up in his body. I didn't know what to do, so I tracked down Misha and explained what happened. She's been helping me gather information about Soul Jumpers."

He turned to Kale. "This is your fault. If you hadn't gone home with her that night, things would still be normal."

I smacked him upside the head. "Normal? What they're doing at Denazen isn't normal!"

Kale nodded in agreement. "Denazen needs to be stopped."

He glared at Kale then turned to me. "You know what I mean."

"So now what? What are you going to do?"

"I'm leaving. I want to help you find your mom, but I just can't. Ya gotta understand... Your father had me killed... If they found out what I was—what I could do... I don't fully understand it yet, but seems to me that he could do a lot of damage with someone like me."

I shook my head. "It's okay, you don't need to explain." It'd be better this way. Brandt was right. Killing him off, tossing him from body to body amassing other Sixes' gifts, he could easily become a weapon far more powerful than Kale. I couldn't allow that to happen. I'd sleep easier knowing he was far away, and that my best friend was alive and safe. I threw my arms around him. "Will I ever see you again?"

"Like you could ever ditch me?" He gave me a quick squeeze and pulled away, reaching for a green bag on the floor next to the bed. "You have the list I gave you, right?"

"List?"

He gave the bag a shake and sighed. "The one I gave you at my funeral."

I'd totally forgotten about it. "It's at my house. I never even opened it."

"Don't lose it, Dez. It's a list of every known Six in the country. They're all on Denazen's bag and tag list. Being monitored. You're on there too, Dez."

"Me? How could I be on it? You gave me the list before I told Dad what I could do."

He shook his head. "Like I said before, this is bigger than you know. Don't lose that list."

I'd left it in the pocket of the jacket I'd worn to the funeral. "It's safe. I'll go back for it as soon as I can. I promise."

He nodded and stuffed the skateboard wheel back into his pocket. "I'll leave word with Misha when I get where I'm going. Don't worry, this isn't good-bye forever."

He turned to Kale, eyes narrow. "You better make sure nothing happens to my girl."

Kale squeezed my hand. The look he gave my cousin wasn't exactly friendly. "She's *my* girl."

28

I was used to wearing short skirts, but for some reason, the shorts made me feel self-conscious. Or maybe it wasn't the shorts. It could have been the hair. I'd done the unthinkable and traded my trademark two-tone locks for a simple reddish-brown shade very close to that of my favorite video game heroine of all time, Lara Croft, the Tomb Raider herself.

Kale's costume was perfect. The Terminator getup would keep most of his skin hidden, not to mention he looked *hot* as hell. He kept the collar of the jacket flipped up so only a small portion of his face was exposed. We were like polar opposites. Me in a skimpy tank top and short shorts, and Kale covered from tip to toe.

When I stepped out of the bathroom, gun holsters strapped firmly in place, and looked up at Kale, I couldn't help but smile.

His gaze appraising—and *appreciating*—he reached out and fingered my long braid. "How did you do that? Change the color?"

I ran a hand over my hair. "Do you like it? I know, it's different, isn't it?"

It didn't make sense. For some reason I was sad to see it change. I'd been rocking the blonde and black stripes for almost a year now. Hair color didn't define you. Spirit and soul did. Yet, I felt naked. "The character that I am has dark hair. We need to blend in and Dad will never assume I'd go as far as to dye my hair."

"Dye?"

"It's a goop you put in your hair and wash out. It changes the color."

"Will it change back?"

"To blonde? Not unless I bleach it."

He touched the shaggy black strands of hair that fell into his face. "I can change the color?"

I laughed. "Welcome to technology." I reached down and picked up a neon blue notebook, holding it out. "You could dye it this color if you really wanted to."

"Don't put the goop in to change it back. I like it," he said, stepping closer. He brushed his lips against mine and pulled away.

That wasn't going to work. I pulled him back and kissed him again—properly.

"I'm never going to get used to that," he said, smiling.

"Used to what?"

"The way I feel like I'm going to explode every time you come close. The way my head fills up with just you when you do that."

. . .

When we arrived at the party, things were already in full swing. The air crackled with energy. Whether it was the party or the excitement of knowing something huge would go down soon, I had no idea. I was edgy and ready to go.

I was relieved to see most people got the upgraded costume info. There were French maids, alien slave girls, and a handful of scantily dressed witches—when would people come up with something original? Obviously, they'd all gone to that same slutty costume place.

On the men's side, I saw everything from several cowboys bunched up in the corner of the room stalking a group of sorority girls, to cavemen and lifeguards. I passed at least four "Edward and Bella" pairs.

Kale was nervous, even though ninety percent of his skin was covered.

"You ready?"

He nodded and grabbed my hand. We made our way through the crowd, weaving in and out of the grinding, already semi-drunk dancers. So far, I'd only seen two or three people out of costume—I'd known them all—and no sign of Alex or Dad.

From the questions Mercy-as-me had asked Curd, I guessed Fin was one of the targets Denazen would be after tonight. We had no idea who the other was, but at least we could shadow Fin and try to keep him safe.

"It's still early. Maybe they're not here yet," Kale said, surveying the room. He'd pointed out on the way over that he probably wouldn't recognize my mom because she would have already mimicked before coming in, but Alex would be easy to spot.

"Maybe," I said, standing on my toes to see over the crowd. *Score!* Fin stood alone by the edge of the bar, tossing back a beer. "That's Fin, come on." I dragged Kale along behind me, through the crowd.

"Wow!" Fin let out a sharp whistle. "You look *hot*, Dez. You can raid my tomb whenever you'd like."

"Aww, you're sweet," I forced out with a smile. "Fin, this is Kale. My boyfriend."

Fin's face fell a little, but he recovered. "Boyfriend, eh? But Curd told me—"

"It's, um, really new."

Kale made a growling sound deep in his throat, towering over Fin.

"Okay, then," Fin said, inching away from Kale.

I nodded to the dance floor, about to suggest we dance, when I saw Alex's white-blond head bobbing through the crowd. "Thank God!" I turned to Kale and said, "Stay here and get to know Fin. I'm gonna go grab Alex, okay?"

As I walked away, I heard Kale tell Fin to stop staring at my ass or he was going to *punish* him. I couldn't help but smile.

Up the stairs and through the crowd, when I reached the top, Alex was leaning against the railing, talking to a tall redhead. "Alex," I said, out of breath. He wore normal blue jeans and a black button-down shirt. No costume. They hadn't found out!

Alex turned to me, a look of relief on his face. The girl was forgotten. "Dez, we have to leave. This whole thing is a setup."

"I know. It was Mercy. I'm not sure if the information is true or not, but they might be after Fin Meyer and someone else."

Alex groaned and grabbed my arm, pulling me off into a dark corner. "You don't know anything," he hissed. "You walked right into this. They needed you to mimic Mercy so she'd look and sound like you. They needed the party location and they needed someone to lure Fin."

"Wait, you're telling me Mercy's still wearing my face?" The idea that someone out there was walking around with my body made my skin crawl.

He paled slightly. "What, did you think it would wear off? Does anything else you change wear off on its own?"

Idiot. I hadn't even blinked when Mercy left me the note saying the mimic had worn off. I automatically assumed because it was a bigger, more complicated thing, it wouldn't last. I should have known better. "Where is she?"

Alex shook his head. "I have no idea. It doesn't matter. We need to get the hell outta here."

"Wait. How did you know *I* was *me*, if Mercy is wearing my skin?"

"There's only one you. Easy to spot a fake." He gave me a small smile. "Plus, you're in different costumes."

"Shit," I cursed. "So you guys *did* hear about the costume thing. What's she wearing?"

He grabbed my arm. "Does it frigging matter? We gotta bail."

I pulled free. "I can't leave. Kale's downstairs watching Fin, and my mom might be here. I'm not gonna miss the only chance I might get to save her."

"Your mom is here, but you won't be able to get near her. That's the point. Why else do you think Mercy *told* you she'd be here? To make sure you'd come. Did you ever think *you're* the second target?"

Again. Idiot. The thought had never even crossed my mind.

"That'd be stupid. They had me already, they wouldn't need to lure me here. Dad could have locked me up any of those days at Denazen."

"I heard them talking. They wouldn't have taken you while you were at Denazen because they're looking for Ginger. Been looking for her for a long time. They were hoping you'd lead them to her. Besides, your dad knows about you and 98. They want him back and they knew he'd come with you."

"Kale," I seethed. "You know damn well his name is Kale, not 98. Don't call him that."

"I don't care about him or his name." He tried to pull me

from the corner. "You and me. Let's get out of here."

I stared at him. "I care about Kale, and I'm not leaving without him. Or my mom."

"Screw Kale!" he snapped. On the railing behind him, a half-full glass of orange liquid shattered. "I love you, Dez. I always have. I'm sorry for what I did, but I know we can fix this. We can make it work. But you have to get out of here before they collect you like a science project."

I didn't need this. "Alex, don't. Not now. I told you, I had to sort through my feelings for Kale. I did and—"

I couldn't believe he was arguing about this here. Now. "There's nothing to sort through. We're perfect together. I know it and so do you."

"I love him, Alex. I love Kale."

His eyes went wide. "You—what about the other day at my apartment? It didn't feel like you were in love with him while you were kissing me!"

"I'm sorry! I was upset and you were there, and I wasn't sure—"

Alex shook his head. "It doesn't matter. Please, get out while you can. I've had a glimpse of what Denazen does to its Sixes. That place is a horror show, Dez. They've got half the Sixes there thinking they're doing everything from *God's work*, to super-secret government missions to make the world a better place. The other half are walking zombies living in cages with no minds of their own."

He tried to pull me out of the shadows, but I wasn't budging.

"Please, you're never going to get near your mother. Cut your losses and go."

"Want to bet?" I grabbed his face and held tight. In a matter of seconds, my own frame too heavy to keep itself up, crumpled to the floor. Alex caught me right before I hit the ground.

"No," he whispered, staring at me. "Don't do this, please. It's not part of the plan."

Still shaky, I climbed to my feet. The pain in my head was there—and sharp—but it was almost tolerable. On the plus side, I didn't feel the immediate need to puke up everything I'd ever eaten. Maybe the more I did this, the easier it would get. "Plan?" Suddenly I couldn't breathe. "What plan? What are you talking about?"

He tugged on my arm again, pleading. Pointing through the railing to the front he said, "Look, there's the door. We can be down the stairs, thorough it, and on our way to a new life in twenty minutes. I did what I had to… If we don't leave now, you're gonna fuck it up!"

A cold sweat broke out across my forehead and under my braid as I backed away. "It was you." All the air drained from my lungs and my vision swam. No. It couldn't be. "*You* told Dad about me and Kale."

I turned to scan the room. The bar where I'd left Kale and Fin was crowded now but neither were there. Mercy-as-me had told Curd I wanted to hook up with Fin. Curd, in turn, passed the message along. Fin, being the dog he was, jumped at the idea. While I was wasting time up here talking to Alex, Mercy-as-me had probably swaggered in and snatched Fin up. He would have gone along like a puppy begging for a treat after finding out I was on for him. Sure, I'd already told him I had a boyfriend, but with my rep, that wouldn't mean crap. My only hope was that Kale had been intimidating enough for Fin to back off in search of more promising prey.

I turned back and grabbed the front of his shirt. "What the hell did you do?"

"It's too late for him. If your dad doesn't have him yet, he will soon."

"How could you do—"

"The way you were kissing me the other day—then you pushed away. It killed me. Then you said it was because of *him*… When you went out to the car at my place the other day, I called your father back. I told him I'd make a deal. You for Kale. I told him you were infatuated with the little freak. He wasn't surprised to see me at the coffee shop, Dez. He already knew I'd be with you."

This person standing in front of me was a complete stranger. This heartless, selfish, cold thing that wore the face of someone I'd once cared about. "How could you do that? Knowing what they did to him—what they're *going* to do to him?"

"I did what I needed to—to make sure you were safe." He stood straighter now, jaw set. "That freak was going to get you killed. He was going to get us all killed."

I couldn't believe he was actually defending his actions. Trying to justify what he'd done. Even if his intentions had been good, he knew how I felt about Kale. He knew what they did to Sixes at Denazen. To knowingly hand one over…

"You disgust me." I spat in his face and turned away.

I left him in the corner and went to find Kale and my mom, wearing my ex boyfriend's face.

29

I'd been looking for signs of Kale, or my mom—even though I had no idea who to look for—when I spotted myself by the lower bar. I was wearing a pale pink bikini with a fluffy pink cotton ball tail attached to the back. My hair—in its former glorious blonde and black incarnation—hung in loose ringlets spilling from a pair of long pink ears pointing skyward. A playboy bunny? Seriously? I'd kick Mercy's ass from here to Jersey for that alone.

I made a beeline for the bar with a sudden burst of renewed energy. The mimic had still taken its toll, but my anger gave me a second wind. And a third. Plus, if one more trampy girl threw herself at me-as-Alex, someone was getting hurt.

"Hey," I said, leaning close. I hoped I could channel Alex well enough to make her believe I was him. "What the hell are you doing lounging around? We have work to do."

She shrugged and sipped her green drink. "Fin's been taken. It was so easy. I walked up to the kid, blew in his ear, and he followed me like a starving man."

"What about 98?"

She shrugged again and downed the rest of her drink. "He wasn't with Fin."

Her hand snaked out and caught me by the waist. After a moment it slipped down to my ass—Alex's ass. I'd never get over this as long as I lived, no matter what Denazen did to me.

"We'll find them. Her mother's here and she knows it. I made sure of that. That will be enough to bag her. And once we get Dez, 98 will be a cinch." She squeezed my ass. "We can kill the time by waiting for them in a dark corner somewhere."

It took me a minute to figure it out. My gag reflex kicked into high gear and I stumbled away. "Ew!"

"You didn't think that when you had your tongue down my throat last night," she snapped.

Wow. Just…wow. He was *that* warm for my form that he'd screw this cheap imitation?

She reached for my arm, and I let her take it. This whole thing was creepy and disgusting in an epic way. But *ick factor* aside, I could usually see the possibilities in any situation. This might actually work to my advantage. I wanted her out of my skin, and to do that I had to get her alone. "Fine, let's go."

She led me around the back of the bar. The door to the storage hall was open and, thankfully, empty. I didn't waste any time. Unfortunately, neither did Mercy-as-me. She pawed Alex—me—trying to back him up against the wall the second the door closed. "I know you were mad when you found out I wasn't her, but it was good, right? Something about that little tramp's body—it makes me bolder." Her hands were everywhere, grabbing and squeezing parts of me that triggered an intense need for eternal therapy.

I shoved her off and growled. No amount of scrubbing would ever scour the memory of this moment away. Brillo. Lufa. Boric acid. Nothing.

As she rounded for another pass, thinking it was all part of the game, I punched her in the face. She went down like a sack of textbooks. "You and Alex? That is *so* gross."

She stirred and I didn't wait. Falling to my knees, I grabbed her hand. Like back in the woods when we'd escaped her office, I concentrated on mimicking Mercy back to Mercy. Focusing on what was on the inside rather than the outside. A rush of warmth spread throughout my limbs, accompanied by a slight prickling in my temples.

When I opened my eyes, Mercy was back to a forty-something-year-old woman with mousey hair and a *way-too-tight* pink bikini. I was right. It was getting easier. Like a muscle needing to be conditioned. All these years I was afraid to mimic because of the effect it had on my body, and it could have been avoided. I could have been living it up all this time.

I jumped to my feet and was out the door, locking it behind me before she came to. Even if she yelled and pounded on the door for the rest of the night, the chances of someone hearing her over the music were slim.

With Mercy out of the way, I had to figure out how to find Kale and my mom. I also needed to find Fin. I had no clue what his gift was, but he was obviously important. I debated shifting back to myself, but for the moment, I was less noticeable as Alex.

With the dance floor full now, crammed like veal into a small wooden box, it was hard to see across the room. I pushed and shoved my way through, trying to see over the crowd. No sign of Alex. I hoped he'd tucked himself away somewhere—or better yet, left—but knowing him, the chances were slim.

"Dude, that's not a costume," a voice said from behind me. I turned to see Dax smiling, thrusting a beer into my hands. "I've been looking for you for days. Dez said you'd gone to Denazen?"

I smiled and shrugged, trying to walk away. The jig was up as soon as I opened my mouth.

Dax wasn't having it. He grabbed my arm and spun me to face him. "What were you thinking, running off to Denazen? You did it for her, didn't you?" Dax groaned and pulled me off the dance floor. I may have had Alex's body but not his coordination. "I thought you were over her."

I shook him off. "I don't have time for this now."

Dax hesitated for a moment, but let go of my arm. "It won't work," he called.

I didn't look back.

I searched the entire first floor and didn't see any sign of Kale. By the time I'd reached the second floor, I starting to get worried. I found a dark corner and shook off the mimic. If Alex didn't know what my mom looked like, the chances of her seeking him out were probably nil.

People yelled and hooted as I passed in my skimpy white tank top and tan short shorts, trying to get my attention. *Want to dance? Need a drink? Head to the back room with me!* I ignored them all.

When rounding the back corner on the second level, I caught site of Kale making his way out of the crowd. I was relieved to see he hadn't been picked off by one of my dad's goons. Calling out to him would be pointless. I didn't want to draw attention to myself, and he wouldn't have heard me above the music anyway, so I simply followed. I got right about to the edge of the crowd when I realized there was someone else following him. The blonde girl stayed far enough back not to be noticed, but she was definitely following. Kale veered off into a hallway past the restrooms. The girl followed. I brought up the rear.

Kale neared the end of the hall.

And just as he lifted his hand to open a door at the other

end, the girl must have called out to him, because he stopped and turned. I sped up.

The two, lost in conversation, didn't see me approaching. "Kale, don't move." I called, starting to run. He didn't hear me. Arm extended, he reached for her and it was at that moment she looked up.

Or rather, *I* looked up.

I forced my feet to move faster, trying to drive my voice above the music the entire way. "Kale! Stop!" Inches. That's all that separated their hands. Inches. And the distance was closing fast. "She's not me!"

"Stay where you are. I don't want to hurt you," my imposter said, turning to me.

I laughed—I couldn't help it. "You don't want to hurt me? Do you have any idea who I—"

"Dez?" Kale looked from her to me, understanding flashing in his eyes. Then horror. He'd almost accidentally killed my Mom.

"What happened? Where's Fin?" I asked, while at the same time, the other me said in a truly horrified voice, "Kale? It's really you?"

Kale took another step away from her. "Who did you think I was?"

She was pale and her voice shook a little when she spoke. "They told me there was another shifter here—a traitor. They brought him here for termination. I was told they'd instructed him to look like you. They gave me a picture of her"—she pointed to me—"and said to engage you in conversation. That the shifter knew this face." She looked around. "There was supposed to be someone here to apprehend you. They—"

She was speaking fast, not coming up for air, but Kale interrupted her. "It's okay Sue, this is—"

"Cross is here to capture two new Sixes. If he finds you, you'll never get another chance at freedom."

He stepped back, giving her an impossibly wide berth, and grabbed my hand. Her jaw—well mine—fell open. "Sue, this is Deznee Cross. Your daughter."

30

She said nothing at first, only stood there, blinking. When she did speak, it wasn't what I'd hoped to hear.

"You're—a Six?" she asked, horrified.

"I'm a Six. I can mimic, like you—only a little different."

If possible, she turned even whiter. "He told me you were a Nix—that you had *no* abilities," she breathed, turning away. "I thought you were safe!"

Not quite the heartwarming, long-lost-daughter welcome I'd hoped for. "He didn't know. I've kept it a secret." I let go of Kale's hand and took a step forward. "I only told him after I found out you were alive and trapped at Denazen. I did it so I could get you out of there."

"I can't believe this is happening!" she cried. "You kids have to leave this building now!"

"I agree," Dad said from the doorway. "Why don't we all leave together?"

"Dammit," Mom cursed, and with an eerie shimmer,

mimicked. She was no longer me, but a beautiful, tall blonde woman with a pixie-like face and long, flowing hair. Her eyes, the exact same shade of honey-brown as my own, darted from me to Dad. "Please Marshall, if you ever loved me, let our daughter go."

For a second, he hesitated. I had the insane notion that he might actually step aside and let us leave. Silly, I know, but there was something there. Something I couldn't remember ever seeing before. A flicker of emotion—a small twitch of his right cheek and the subtle flexing of his fingers. The equivalent of an emotional breakdown, considering the source.

"Please," Mom urged.

More hesitation. He'd taken several steps into the room and was watching her with a mix of annoyance and something else. Regret? For a moment it was as though he'd forgotten all about me and Kale. He opened his mouth, then closed it again. A sharp intake of breath and a step back. Then, as suddenly as it appeared, it was gone.

The little cracks in his armor, giving me a glimpse that there might be an actual person inside, vanished, and he was his old self again. A cold, clinical, Denazen monkey. "You were an experiment. An *enjoyable* one, but still, one of many." He grinned, but something about it seemed a bit forced. Or maybe I simply wanted it to be.

Mom sighed and shook her head. When she spoke, her voice was like a soft, barely there brush of a feather. "Does that make it easier? Telling yourself it was all about the job?

He ignored her, but I swore he flinched. "We found a way to enhance the abilities of Six offspring. The chemical boosted the abnormality of the sixth chromosome, making it, in ninety-nine percent of the trials, ten times stronger. While not every gift manifests exactly the same from parent to child, there's always a similarity. The project was called Supremacy."

Supremacy. That's what Dad and that Vincent guy mentioned in the emails. "Deznee is the result of that project. As is Fin."

Experiment? Like mold in a Petri dish? And one of many? That meant there were more than me and Fin? How many had Dad... conducted personally? God. I might have siblings out there somewhere. Maybe stuck inside Denazen.

He pointed from Mom to me. "Sueshanna's ability to mimic someone else was highly useful, but sadly limited. Nothing more than a simple illusion. Deznee, on the other hand, has far greater range. I imagine with age it will continue to increase unless..."

"Unless what?" I whispered, sick.

Dad sighed. He avoided making eye contact with Mom. "You're second generation. Your predecessors were amazing. The perfect employees with abilities greater than we had ever imagined. They didn't need to be coerced or lied to. They didn't need to be motivated or threatened. They were *raised* to be the perfect Denazen soldiers. They knew how special they were and that there were great things in store for them. But we must have made a mistake with the chemical composition. One by one, as the children turned eighteen, they became irrational. Impossible to control. All remnants of the first phase of the experiment were retired."

"Retired? You killed them?"

He glared at me like I was an idiot. "They were uncontrollable. In the end, nothing more than animals. We did them a favor."

"So you're telling me I might lose my shit when I hit eighteen? Go bonkers?" Really, it was the least of my problems at the moment, but if I made it out of this alive—and free—it'd be a major concern sooner rather than later. I'd be turning eighteen *in eight months.*

He shrugged like it didn't matter. "It's a very real possibility, yes. The first of the second trial Supremacy group turns eighteen next month. It will be exciting to see how it turns out."

Exciting? Not quite the word I was thinking.

"We started over again. Picking those we found most useful, and injected the improved chemical into the amniotic fluid. Once the babies were born, they were placed with Denazen employees. Most showed signs of their gift before the end of their first year. They were the easy ones. A generation brought up to believe in what we stood for right from the start."

I thought about Flip, the guy I'd met in the cafeteria on my first day. The things he said. The total and complete conviction that he was a *good guy*. That Denazen was out there making the world a better place. He was devoted, and he hadn't been raised there. Imagine what lifers would be like.

Dad's expression twisted into some horrible, distorted version of the controlled, blank one I'd known my entire life. "Two never developed gifts—unfortunate, but it does happen. When, by the age of five, you showed no signs, I chalked it up to a loss. You and Fin were our only failures. But you were sneaky, weren't you? You developed abilities and kept yourself well hidden. Tell me— when did you first get them?"

"I was seven when it happened the first time." Not like telling him mattered. It actually made me feel warm and fuzzy. He'd obviously been watching for it and I'd still managed to keep it a secret. Score one for me.

"All the other subjects in Supremacy showed early signs. Fin, we believe, only developed his abilities a few months ago. We found him purely by accident last week. He's quite remarkable. Most element throwers can only manipulate their element. Fin can actually create it. Because of his advanced age, bringing him in willingly was questionable. Especially with Ginger and her people spreading the word through the Six community. We didn't know if her people had gotten to him. Until we know the success rate of Supremacy past the age of eighteen, we still need to obtain and retain employees the old-fashioned way."

"You mean kidnapping," Mom spat. "Ripping families apart and forcing them to steal and kill for you."

Dad ignored her, laughing. "You never wondered? Denazen? Deznee? I named you for the company you'd one day serve."

Kale took a step forward.

"Stop right there, 98." Dad's smile got wider as he pulled out a small pistol from the folds of his jacket. "To prove to you I'm not quite the bastard you think I am, I'll give you a choice."

Kale froze. Maybe he knew what Dad was going to say, maybe he didn't, but when he turned to me, the terror in his eyes made the tiny hairs on the back of my neck jump up.

"Give me Ginger's location, and I'll let you pick one."

Kale looked from me to Dad, confused. "Pick one?"

"By having Sue mimic Deznee, I hoped to kill two birds with one stone. You see, Sue was the one who instigated this entire mess. *She* was the traitor I brought here to be retired. She had every comfort at Denazen and she abused it. She began feeding our residents ideas and dangerous thoughts. She told them we were using them. Keeping them locked away as prisoners."

"Um, you *are* keeping them locked away," I said.

He slapped me. It wasn't hard, but the blow surprised me. I stumbled back and Kale caught me before I could topple over. He didn't dare make a move on Dad while the gun was still in his hands. Instead, he stayed at my side, clutching me almost painfully close.

"We had an increasing level of problems stemming from disobedience that all came to a head when 98 managed to escape. The news traveled fast, causing further problems." He waved the gun in a small circle, then pointed it at Mom. "I discovered Sue was the root of the issue, and then this little party came together so nicely, I saw it as the perfect opportunity to take care of the situation." He turned to me and frowned. "Unfortunately, as usual, Deznee ruined my plans by getting in the way."

"Me?" I hadn't managed to accomplish anything. Mom and Kale were, as of that moment, still prisoners of Denazen, and I was about to join them.

Dad turned to Mom, who stared at him with pure, unadulterated hate in her eyes. "98 was compromised when he took off with our tramp of a daughter. I didn't *want* to destroy him, but the board already put in the order. They gave me one last chance to fix things, and this was supposed to be the perfect plan."

"This?" I asked.

"98 grew very attached to Sue. So attached that we were able to use her to control him in the beginning. My plan was to let that work in my favor one last time."

And then I got it. With a horrifying chill, I understood. She'd seen Kale, thinking he was the shifter she was there to target, and followed him down the hall. Kale thinking it was me, would reach out to take her hand… "You wanted Kale to kill her."

Dad nodded. "It would have been perfect. He would have been so destroyed by what he'd done, he'd be pliable again."

Mom laughed. "You're underestimating him as usual, Marshall. He's stronger than that."

"Unfortunately, I did underestimate him. I also underestimated the hold our daughter had on him."

Kale's mouth hung open in horror. "How did you know I would touch her?"

He gave a chuckle and nodded toward Mom. "It was a safe bet. One I'm sure would have worked if you hadn't been interrupted." He sighed. "I'm giving you a choice. If you tell me where Ginger is, I'll let you keep one of them. Sue or Deznee."

"No," Mom cried.

"Ticktock, 98. Choose quickly or I'll choose for you."

"Don't listen to him, Kale," I said. "He's not going to shoot me. I'm too important."

Kale looked from me to Mom, eyes wide. He stood between us, frozen.

"Kale," Mom said, voice sharp. "There is *no* choice here. Do not let this bastard hurt my daughter."

She reached out and pulled me close, wrapping her arms around my shoulders. Kale came with me, stepping dangerously close to mom. She smelled like lavender and cigarettes. I breathed in, committing the scent to memory.

"You are beautiful," she whispered into my hair as her arms tightened. "I am so glad I got to see for myself what an amazing young woman you've become."

I opened my mouth to respond, but I couldn't. This sounded like good-bye. I pulled away and turned to Kale. "Don't…"

Fists clenched at his sides, Kale let out an anguished howl. The muscles in his jaw twitched and his fingers flexed. In and out. In and out. He stared at us, clinging together like the world was about to come to an end. Shaking, he took a small step closer to my mom. "Dez, I can't lose you…"

Dad raised the gun and released the safety.

I spread my arms wide, standing in Kale's way. "You can't do this. It will make you no better than them. And you *are* better than them, Kale. You are." I reached out and took his face in my hands. Tears welled in his eyes. "They *do not* control you. You don't kill for them anymore."

His voice came in soft, cracked rasps. "No, I don't. But I would kill for you. Only you."

Seconds ticked away in silence.

Finally Kale spoke. His voice had turned icy—the same cold, dead tone he'd used the night we met. When he told Dad he would kill me. "I've made my choice, Cross."

"Who will it be?"

Kale stepped away and turned to him. I could see the wicked smile spread across his face. "It will be you."

Kale shot forward, fingers curled for Dad's throat. Almost as if he'd anticipated it, Dad wrenched himself to the side. Kale sailed past, but managed to jump to his feet before I could call out a warning. The gun was pointed at him now.

He didn't seem to notice. A shot rang out as he rounded for another pass. Kale's body was a blur of motion as he pivoted and ducked. The bullet ricocheted harmlessly off the wall, sending plaster and debris exploding all over the hallway. I rushed forward to tackle my dad, but stopped short when I caught sight of the other end of the hall. A dozen or so Denazen suits gathered, watching us.

I turned back to Dad, who was now pinned and fighting hard to keep Kale's hands away from his face. Kale struggled but was having no luck connecting with skin. His fingers, straining inches away from Dad's face, hovered, frozen. After a few seconds, Kale's fingers advanced an inch. Then two. Just when it looked like Kale might be gaining the upper hand, I saw Dad's lips move. Something he'd said caused Kale to hesitate. He scanned the room until he found me, eyes wide. Dad used this to his advantage. He kicked up, knee connecting with Kale's gut. As Kale curled from the blow, Dad followed it with an elbow to his throat. Kale choked and gasped, trying to catch his breath.

With Kale distracted, Dad shoved him aside. Climbing to his feet, he said, "There's only one way this is going to end."

I readied myself to surge forward, but Mom beat me to it. She flew at my dad, knocking him to the ground as the suits at the other end rushed us.

"Move!" I screamed and pulled her off him. She'd gotten in several well-placed blows and didn't look like she'd be stopping anytime soon, but we needed to bail. I hauled Kale to his feet and the three of us bolted to the other end of the hall.

"There's a staircase leading to the first floor beyond that door," Mom cried. "I saw it when we came in."

We burst through the door and, sure enough, there were the stairs. Flying down, two and three steps at a time, we were back in the main room, bodies grinding and music pounding. Unaware. All of them. Through the crowd, I could see more suits gathering by the entrance.

I was about to ask Mom if she'd seen another exit, but someone snatched my arm.

Alex.

"What the hell are you *still* doing here?"

I pulled away. I hadn't forgotten what he'd done. "There are suits everywhere," I yelled over the music. "Dad's upstairs and he's got a gun."

To the right, across the room, we could see several Denazen men shoving people aside as they stomped down the main stairs. I turned to my right, where a sheepherder danced suggestively with a scantily clad cat-woman. "I need this," I hissed, ripping the thick wooden walking stick from his hands. Whirling, I jammed it through the latch to stop the door from opening.

The men on the other side of the room were halfway down the stairs now, and they'd seen us. At the bottom, partygoers began to scatter when one pulled a gun.

"It's real!" someone screamed.

And chaos erupted.

"We have to find Fin and get the hell out of here!" I called over the bedlam. Turning to Alex, I asked, "Any ideas?"

For a moment he hesitated, but then gave in. "The bar in the corner by the front door. The chick is a Denazen employee. Fin is with her."

"You knew where Fin was the entire time?" I seethed. Did Alex know about Supremacy? "Did you know *what* Fin was? What *I* was?"

No answer.

Mom stepped up, eyes locked on the bar. "Is she a Six?"

Alex didn't answer, but I could see him glaring at Kale out of the corner of his eye. I slapped him across the back of the head. "Pay attention. Is she a Six?"

"No," he snapped as someone on the upper level screamed.

Another rush of people flew by and then I smelled it. Smoke. "Is something burning?"

Kale pointed to the bar by the door, where Fin was fighting off three Denazen men—with fire. "He's an element thrower. He's going to light the whole place up if he's not careful."

Mom didn't waste any time. She shoved through the crowd and took the furthest suit by surprise, grabbing a handful of his hair and landing a sweeping kick to the back of his knees. When he landed on the floor, she brought her boot down into his gut.

Holy shit. My mom was a badass!

I picked up an empty bottle of Bacardi from the bar and crept forward. As I was about to smash it against the head of the suit closest to me, he turned, narrowly missing my attack. He shoved me backward and I lost my footing, toppling over just in time to see the third suit overcome Fin and wrestle him to the ground.

"Mom," I yelled as I dodged a badly aimed kick. "Get Fin!"

She whirled around, opponent forgotten, but it was too late. The suit had Fin pinned on the bar, a needle plunged deep into the skin of his neck.

"No!" Mom wailed, hair swaying back and forth as she shook

her head. Her focus on Fin, she backed up too far, tripping over the guy she'd grounded. He grabbed for her, but she didn't fight.

Fin's struggles were starting to fade. His eyes, once a fierce and fiery hazel, glazed over. The Sixes on level nine. Kale's blood. They'd dosed him.

The suit nodded to the one I'd missed with the bottle. He launched himself at me, swinging a brutal kick at my side. I saw it coming and rolled away. Growling, he rounded for another assault, but again I skirted out of his reach, finally on my feet again.

"Stop playing and tranq her already," the one by the bar snapped.

Familiar green eyes gleamed with indignation as he said, "Who are you going to call this time? There's no security to save you."

The guy from the mall. The one we'd called security on. Someone didn't look happy to see me. He advanced a few steps, backing me up until I hit the wall with no place to go. Hands shot out, gripping my shoulders and hauling me forward. Bringing my knee up, I nailed him right between the legs. With a muffled *umpf*, he released my shoulders and staggered back, clutching himself.

Satisfied, I turned and started for the bar where Fin and Mom were. I got halfway there when someone tackled me. The air left my lungs with a whoosh as something wedged into the middle of my back. A knee.

"If you cooperate with them, Denazen isn't such a bad place for your kind." My attacker grabbed both my arms and yanked them back.

My kind? Next he would tell me I'd get my own suite with an ocean view and all the mint chocolate chip ice cream I could eat.

Um, no.

When I felt him lean forward, presumably to bind my arms,

I threw my head back, catching him off guard. A resounding crack filled my ears as a sharp pain throbbed across my skull. He loosened his grip enough for me to push myself off the ground. But no sooner was I on my feet than someone else grabbed me from behind. This grip held tighter, though. More solid. This grip wasn't going anywhere.

Dad stepped forward as the man behind me moved away. "I'm disappointed, Deznee. I'm always disappointed in you, but I thought this might have been different. We're not as bad as you think. We really are doing a lot of good in the world. You could have lived a normal life."

I kicked him. Childish? I know. Useless? Pretty much. But it made me feel a little better inside and that's all that counted.

"Well, if you're done, we need to proceed." Dad gave me a dismissive wave and turned to Mom. Kale was nowhere in sight.

Mom watched him, eyes pleading. "I'll go back without a fuss, I promise. I won't make any further trouble. Let her go."

Dad folded his arms and tapped his chin. He looked like he might be considering her request, but I knew better. The man had no conscience and no soul. "As much as I'd like to grant your wish, Sueshanna, I don't think it would be wise in the long run. You don't know our little girl very well. She's a troublemaker." He raised his gun, placing it against her forehead. "Exactly like her mother."

Dad clicked the safety and ground the gun further into Mom's temple. He turned to the nearest suit and said, "Take Fin and Deznee outside."

"Drop the gun, Cross."

31

We all turned to see Ginger standing inside the doorway...with about six others. Dax and Sira—the woman from the hotel—as well as a cluster of others I didn't know. How they'd entered the building without any of us seeing them blew my mind—until I caught the eye of the younger bouncer from the party. He saw me looking at him and winked.

Ginger stepped away from the crowd, eyes locked with Dad's. "Now," she demanded. The command in her voice was comforting and also a little bit scary.

Dad complied and lowered the gun with a sly smile on his face. "Fin, would you mind?"

Face still blank, Fin stepped forward, arms ablaze and poised to fire.

"Barge," Ginger called. A tall, thin boy no more than fifteen years old literally hopped out from behind Dax. He smiled at me, eyes glittering with mischief, and opened his mouth wide.

For a moment, nothing happened. Then I felt it. The

temperture in the room seemed to drop. In awe, I watched as the flames, previously devouring everything, swirled together in one large mass of smoke and fire and rushed at us. No, not at us. At Barge. The guy's mouth still open, the flames danced and swirled above his head for several seconds before, with a single breath, they were sucked into his mouth. Once they were gone, Barge closed his mouth, a wide smile on his face. He stepped back and burped, a small tuft of smoke escaping thorough his sealed lips.

There were several seconds where no one moved.

Then chaos.

Dad snapped something to Fin and yanked him behind the bar. The few remaining bottles of alcohol scattered and crashed to the ground, echoing through the room in the last seconds of silence.

With the smoke now clear, Dad's monkey-suited morons surged forward, and Ginger's group dove to meet them. Denazen versus Six.

One could argue that Sixes against a few guys with guns was a joke, and that would have been right—if Dad hadn't thought to bring reinforcements.

A figure appeared in the doorway and Sira screamed, "Move!"

She must have recognized the woman, because as Ginger's people scattered, the newcomer smiled and, with a slight twist of her slim hips, liquefied. Now an angry, swirling mass of water, she sliced through the room, straight at Sira.

I was about to rush forward to help her, but someone grabbed me from behind. I wrenched my right arm free and snapped it back into the gut of the suit. Surprised, he released me. I whirled on him—he was leaning forward to grab me again—and snagged a handful of his hair. A girl move? Totally. But he sure as hell wasn't expecting it. I yanked down, bringing my knee up at the same time. It connected with the side of his head in a very satisfying thwack.

Dad's voice rang out over the din. "Don't let him bleed on you."

It was that moment I heard the clatter of another struggle. Craning my neck, I saw Alex, bloody knife in hand, circling a fallen Kale. He lumbered to his feet, unsteady.

I didn't think—I ran. Swinging blind as I cut through the chaos, my fist connected with something soft. There was an anguished scream. A yelp. I didn't look back.

Something hot rushed past me. A fireball. It clipped Kale in the shoulder, sending him back to the ground. Behind me, Fin stood on the bar, face as blank as the Sixes I'd seen back in the Denazen cages. Dad was beside him. Fin's hands glowed a fierce red, smoke rising in waves from his arms. He fired another, this time missing Kale by a fairly wide margin. The flame sailed over his head and hit the bar clear across the room, bottles shattering and flames erupting.

Sira's gift was a mystery, but I hoped she could hold her own. I needed to get to Kale. I caught sight of Mom out of the corner of my eye—just as she mimicked into a man wearing one of Denazen's trademarked blue suits. I could technically do the same, but the change would take what little strength I had left out of me. I'd be useless.

I was halfway to Kale when something hit me. A chair. Someone had thrown a *chair* at me. What the hell was this, WWE? Air expelling from my lungs in a single whoosh, I crashed into the wall. While nothing screamed *broken*, there was the distinct snapping and cracking of limbs as I stumbled upright.

A few feet to my left, Barge went down. Fin was Dad's best weapon at the moment. In order to use Fin, they needed to bench Barge. He collapsed in a heap, a tranq dart protruding from the side of his neck. The suit who'd shot him aimed at me and fired, but I managed to duck out of the way. The dart embedded itself in the wall a few inches from my head.

Cursing, the man advanced. Mall guy again. "You're starting to piss me off, kid."

"Then my life is complete," I said, stepping closer to the wall. Fingers splayed against the brick, I looked for anything I could use as a weapon. Scattered bits of glass and wood. Nothing useful. I might as well throw my sneaker at him.

My sneaker!

I couldn't help it. A grin spread across my lips as I reached down and yanked off my shoe. This was one pair of Vans that would be lost to a good cause. Someone needed to knock some sense into this jackass. Pressing my right hand into the brick wall behind me, I clutched my sneaker with the left. The rubbery sole of the shoe hardened, tiny, sharpened bumps popping up along the surface. The pain was minimal. A quick, sharp jabbing in my temple and a dull ache in my neck. The weight increased, and instead of a shoe, I now had a handy, dandy brick.

Perfect for throwing.

My aim wasn't perfect, but I hit him. He went down like, well, a ton of bricks.

My attention went back to Kale. He was climbing to his feet again, shrugging off the remains of his singed jacket. I was relieved to see the blood on the knife came from a superficial slice on his left forearm. Alex faked a lunge forward as Kale jumped back in anticipation. Alex laughed and looked at the ceiling. The large light fixture above him began to shimmy and shake. Kale dove out of the way as the thing came crashing to the ground, sending bits of glass and metal bouncing across the floor.

Beyond them, Water Girl had backed Sira into a corner. Kale looked like he was holding his own with Alex. They circled each other, Alex making an occasional swipe with the knife and Kale expertly dodging him without steady concentration. They seemed okay so I darted across the floor to help her.

I got to Sira as Water Girl liquefied again. She reached for Sira, pulling the older woman in and engulfing her in a swirling tomb of churning water.

Skidding to a stop in front of them, I yanked off my other shoe, grabbed the top half of a broken Bacardi bottle and concentrated. The pain was almost a joke now, and after a few seconds, I had two matching, broken bottles. I hurled them, one after the other, at Fin's head. "Hey Smokey, over here!"

Without so much as a second's hesitation, Fin launched a barrage of fireballs at my head with perfect precision. I dove out of the way in time—for the most part—and the flames hit the real target. Water Girl.

An agonized, gurgling scream, and she resolidified, stumbling away from Sira. This was all the edge the older woman needed. Taking a deep breath, she exhaled. It was like a tornado had ripped through the building. Everything in her path—Water Girl, and two of the Denazen suits—flew backward, crashing against the far wall. Each slid to the ground, motionless.

Something hit me, knocking me sideways. "Down!" An older boy—one of the Sixes who'd come with Ginger. We crashed to the ground as a rush of heat soared over our heads.

"Thanks." I coughed. Above our heads, only a thin trail of smoke lingered.

He helped me off the ground, smiling. "No worries. This is fun, aye?" He had a thick Australian accent, brilliant smile, and deep brown eyes that screamed troublemaker. "I'm Panda."

"Dez," I said, ducking to the side as more darts sailed by.

Panda frowned. "Not nice to fire that thing at a lady, mate!" He turned and started across the room. With each step, his skin seemed to shimmer. His body widened in bulk and shortened in length. Skin paling, his sandy blond hair darkened until it was black. One final shimmer, and Panda was, well, a panda. With a snarl, he leapt at the Denazen man as he fired off another shot. They went down, and I had to look away. The man's screams and the ripping flesh was bad enough. So didn't need a visual.

Back to Alex and Kale. They were further away now. Still circling each other like caged animals. Alex was getting annoyed. Each time he'd make a swipe, Kale skirted effortlessly out of reach. Like a child playing *keep away*.

I rushed forward. Over a fallen Denazen suit. Around Barge's sleeping form. An entire room of carnage in between us. "Alex, stop this!" I called, tripping over a fallen chair.

Kale turned toward the sound of my voice, and Alex, being the sneaky, dirty fighter he'd always been, used the distraction to his advantage.

On my feet again, I ran. The distance seemed impossible. All the noise was gone, leaving an empty, sucking vacuum of silence. All I heard was the pounding of my bare feet as they hit the floor frustratingly slow. Something tugged at the shoulder of my shirt. A Denazen suit as I passed. Spinning, I twisted out of his grip and kept going. Almost there.

Alex lunged forward, burying the knife deep in Kale's stomach.

Something exploded behind my right knee. The smell of burning denim and flesh filled the air, but the pain barely registered. All I saw was Kale. All I felt was cold.

Still watching me, Kale crumpled to the floor. Alex stepped away, pale and looking sick. The knife had fallen to the floor at his feet. Something inside cracked. Barreling past Alex, I slid across the last few feet on my knees.

"Get up," I screamed, shaking his shoulders. The stain

spreading across his black shirt was only slightly darker than the shirt itself, but undeniably there. No matter how many ways my brain tried to tell me differently.

Kale's eyes opened, but they were unfocused. Dim. He looked up, but I could tell he didn't see me. "My blood…"

I looked down at my hands, coated in red. Like his touch, Kale's blood seemed to have no effect on me. His hand found mine, and he pulled it over his chest—over his heart and right above the wound. The thumping under my palm was too fast. Erratic.

"Do you see?" he whispered. "What you do? It shouldn't do that anymore." His grip on my fingers went slack as his eyes closed.

32

Kale's name a whisper on my lips, strong arms pulled me back and dragged me away. Dad. So the coward had finally come out of hiding?

On the other side of the room, the bar was completely engulfed in flame, and the fire had begun creeping through the rest of the room. The tables along the edge were starting to catch, as well as the overturned chairs scattered about the floor. One of the fallen Denazen suits was lying close to the edge. As I watched, the corner of his jacket caught fire. None of his co-workers moved to help him.

Alex stood to the side, staring from Kale to me, looking sick. After a moment, he cleared his throat. He was still pale, but his I-don't-give-a-shit-about-anything mask had slipped back in place. Tone even, he said, "As interesting as this has been, do you mind if we hit the road now? Dez doesn't need to see this and I have no desire to be baked alive."

Dad adjusted his grip on my arm and waved at the door.

"You're free to go, Alex."

Alex took a step closer to me, but Dad's hand shot out. "Alone."

Alex's eyes went wide for a moment before narrowing. "We had a deal."

Dad shook his head. "If you remember correctly, I never agreed to anything. You offered your aid in reacquiring 98. He hasn't been 'reacquired'. He's dead."

At his sides, Alex's fists clenched. Several chairs on either side of us started to rattle. The two suits left standing glanced at each other nervously.

"It's done, Cross," Ginger said, coming up behind Alex.

She and Dad eyed each other. Gesturing behind her, she said, "As you can see, I have an army at my back."

Dax flanked her on one side, bruised but still standing tall, and the bouncer from the party that I'd flirted with stood on the other. Sira was behind them, soaking wet, but with a satisfied smile on her face. I didn't see Water Girl anywhere. Next to her, Panda growled quietly as Ginger rested a hand atop his head, scratching behind his ear. One of the men I didn't know stood to the side, Barge in his arms. His fingers sparked, tiny currents of electricity skating up and down his body.

Dax smiled. "All you have is a few firearms and a single human matchstick. I think it's fair to say we have the upper hand."

Dad laughed and gave my arm a rough shake. "You won't touch me as long as I have her."

"They don't have to," Alex's voice came, cool and dangerous. The gun flew from Dad's hand, shot into the air, then hovered for several seconds in front of us. "Let go of her and get out before I kill you with your own piece." The gun shot forward, jamming itself into Dad's forehead.

Dad hesitated, but I could feel him tense. He knew he was

screwed. Letting go of my arm, he backed away. The gun followed him. "This isn't over."

"Lemme guess—you'll be back? Fire whoever is writing your material," I snapped, glancing over my shoulder. Kale still wasn't moving, but that didn't mean he was dead. He *couldn't* be dead.

Mom came up beside me. She was wearing her own skin now and looked a little worse for the wear, but she was alive.

I expected Dad to put up a fight, but he only smiled. Not the expression you'd expect from a man who'd been one-upped and lost a few of his favorite toys. "Enjoy your freedom, Deznee. Because make no mistake, it's temporary."

The two suits were out the door with Fin, Dad right behind them. He didn't look back.

Ginger stepped up to where Kale lay motionless. "Daun," she called. A small-framed woman emerged from the crowd, barefoot and wearing a simple white shift. I'd seen her come in, but hadn't seen her when the fighting started. I was relieved to see she appeared unharmed. She reached down and, to my amazement, lifted Kale into her arms as though he weighed nothing more than a sack of potatoes.

She placed him on one of the remaining tables and turned to me. "I may be able to help him," she said, tilting her head to the right. "But you must first understand something. I am a healer, but I do not give my gift easily. In one week's time, I will be forty-two. In all my years, I have healed exactly three people."

An icy lump formed in the pit of my stomach. "Why?"

"In order to heal someone, I must give them a part of myself."

"A part of yourself?"

She nodded. "A side effect. An *exchange*. There is no telling what it will be. Something as simple as a memory, or"—she tapped her left ear—"my hearing."

She looked from me to Kale. "In this case however, things

are a bit different."

"Different?"

"To heal someone, I need to touch them. Contact with skin must be made."

The lump in my stomach exploded, numbing me from the inside out. "So then you *can't* help him…"

"I believe I can heal him through your touch."

"Then what's the problem? Hurry, before it's too late!"

Her eyebrows raised, she frowned. "So it is acceptable?"

"Huh?"

"You can touch him, so the side effect, the exchange, will be with you, not me."

I fell to my knees beside them. I had no idea what I'd lose, but did it matter if I didn't have Kale? There was no way I would let him die. Not if I could do something to prevent it. "I'll give anything for him."

Daun nodded. "Place your hands on his skin. No matter what happens, do not let go."

I reached out and cupped the side of his face. Beside me, Daun took my hand. The sensation was instantaneous. Warmth. It felt nice at first. Tingly, like the summer sun kissing my skin on a day at the beach.

Then it changed. Stifling and humid. Choking. Daun's fingers tightened on mine as a spasm racked me to the core. "Just a bit more," she said.

The room began to spin. I leaned forward into Kale, trying to steady myself. As the heat started to ebb, I said a silent prayer, thanking God it was finally over.

Only it wasn't.

The room began spinning again, this time so violently, everything mashed together. Daun, Kale, the charred remains of the party—all swirled together in one massive blob of color.

Vomit rose in my throat as a loud keening sound filled my ears. Several times, I almost let go of Kale to shield myself from the sound.

Then, as abruptly as it all started, it stopped. I collapsed on the floor, unable to open my eyes. In the distance, I heard a faint sound.

Thump thump. Thump thump.

Steadily, it grew louder. Stronger. My heart.

Thump thump thump. Thump thump thump.

I listened to it, still unable to open my eyes. Well, maybe not unable. Possibly unwilling. The rhythm sounded strange. Unnatural. Something in the back of my mind told me I should be concerned, but I wasn't. Every bone in my body ached, and each one of my nerve endings vibrated like a guitar string ready to snap. Had it worked? Had I managed to save Kale in time? A sick feeling washed over me. Surely it hadn't worked. The room was too quiet.

Then I heard it. Not one beat, but two.

Thumpthump thumpthump thumpthump.

Something warm and soft slid over my hand. Kale. With a squeeze of his hand, I had the strength to open my eyes.

"You did it again. You saved me."

33

"It doesn't look like anyone's home," Kale said. "We came all this way for nothing."

He rubbed his chest, below his heart. The wound had healed months ago, but he said it still *tickled* sometimes.

I squeezed his hand. "It wasn't for nothing. We've had an entire two days of peace and quiet. Besides, they'll come home eventually." I checked my watch. "They're probably still at work."

We settled down on the steps of the bright yellow Victorian, Kale on the top step, me on the bottom, leaning back. The summer had been rough at first. Two weeks after the disaster at Sumrun, the Denazen *law building* burned to the ground. Dad had disappeared, along with Mercy and Fin and the other Sixes, but I had hope. We could still save them. Even if we had to do it one at a time.

Ginger told us Denazen had seven major branches throughout the world, as well as forty-two smaller facilities in the US alone. It wouldn't be long till they started snatching Sixes from the street again—there was no way Dad was letting me go. And eventually, if not already, he'd find out Kale was still alive. He wouldn't stay underground forever.

When I'd gone back to the house to get some of my things, I'd also retrieved the list Brandt had given me. The one with the names of all the Sixes on Denazen's hit list. Most of the summer, Kale and I spent traveling from state to state, tracking them down. Out of a total of fifty-one, we'd found and warned—and in several cases recruited—twenty-one. The last stop on our summer tour of fun would be 8710 Fallow Street. Once we'd tracked down the owner, a Mr. Vincent Winstead, listed as a telepath, we'd be on our way back home.

Home. That meant something different to me now. I had no idea what living with my mom would be like, and although I'd dreamed about it since I was a child, the idea scared me now. We had a lot of time to make up for, and a lot of things to work out.

Like Kale, it was there in her eyes. She was just as damaged by her time with Denazen. Mom was living at Misha's hotel, where I would go once we returned home. Kale would also be staying there too—in a different room. On a different floor, as I was very pointedly informed by my mom.

Kale. He was slowly starting to get acclimated to the outside world. Seeing things through his eyes had been an eye-opening experience for me. His first sunset, the first time he'd tasted mint chocolate chip ice cream, his first trip to the movie theater, all these things breathed new life into me. Simple things, things the rest of us take for granted, they were all new and exciting to him. In turn, they felt new and exciting to me.

There was still a lot he didn't understand—the first day of our trip he'd tried to attack a man giving a woman choking on a scone the Heimlich. Kale thought he'd been trying to hurt her. And a few days later, he'd taken it literally when I got frustrated and said I wanted to jump off a bridge.

He still wouldn't use an elevator and would probably always insist on checking under the bed each night, but he was learning. He had nightmares from time to time, waking up in a cold sweat or with a scream ripping from his throat. He refused to tell me what they were about, but promised me someday he would. I believed him. He had to heal in his own way.

No nasty side effects had surfaced as a result of Daun's healing. For weeks after it happened, Kale panicked with each new day, terrified he'd find me missing a limb, or a memory—the memory of him was his biggest fear. But nothing had happened. Before we left to track down the Sixes, Daun had warned us that sometimes the exchange took a while to surface. We still weren't out of the woods yet. It didn't matter to me, though. I had Kale, and I had no regrets.

"Look." I pointed to the street, where a black Ford Explorer pulled into the driveway.

The man behind the wheel hopped from the truck, light brown hair, bright green eyes, and a friendly smile. "Hello there."

We stood and made our way down the walkway to meet him.

"Vincent Winstead?" I called, bringing my hand up to shield my eyes against the bright noon sun.

"Call me Vince." He smiled, friendly and welcoming, and extended his hand. "Can I help you?"

I took his hand. "My name's Dez, and this is Kale. Do you have a few minutes?"

Vince fished into his pocket and pulled out a set of keys. "I'm expecting company in a little while. Is there any way you could come back tomorrow? I have no problem supporting our local school—"

"We're not from the local school," Kale said. "You're in danger and we've come to warn you."

While Kale and Vince talked, I found myself distracted. The one thing that scared me more than Daun's trade-off was the Supremacy project. No new, awe-inspiring abilities had surfaced, but that didn't mean they wouldn't. I was six months away from eighteen. That meant eight months away from a possible, inescapable bout of the crazies. Ginger and the others had already begun searching, but without knowing what chemical Denazen had used to enhance us, we were pretty much sitting dead in the water.

I was determined to find the others—they needed to know the truth—but I had no idea how. We didn't have much to go on other than they'd all be about my age and have unusually strong gifts. Dad said most of them had been raised thinking Denazen was the good guy, so they were probably already working for them. I just had to find them, and convince them they'd been lied to. Yeah. No big there.

Sighing, I glanced toward the street. Bright purple flowers with cool white swirls lining the driveway caught my eye. They'd make a killer nail polish color. Bringing my hand up to examine the peeling remnants of my two-week-old manicure, I gasped.

The previous chipped red paint was now bright purple with cool white swirls.

Shit.

Keep reading for bonus scenes from TOUCH, as told in Kale's point of view...

KALE MEETS ALEX

We approached the building by way of the back entrance. The dark alley was littered with garbage, and Dez had her hand over her nose. The smell wasn't that bad, but I guessed after spending weeks at a time in the holding cells at Denazen, there weren't many smells that would bother me.

I followed Dez as she wove between drink cans and stepped over discarded, black plastic bags, until she stopped in front of a white door labeled *Employees Only*. Her right hand shook slightly as she took a deep breath, hesitating a moment before turning the knob and pushing through.

The first thing I heard was a rythmic sound, accompanied by a man screaming. I tensed, ready to fight, but Dez didn't seem concerned. Still, it put me on alert. Anything that sounded *that* angry was surely dangerous. As we walked down a short, narrow hall, I kept my eyes peeled for anything that might become a threat. But nothing happened. The angry man continued to scream, but no one attacked.

When we got to the end, the hall opened into a large room with bright lights and strange looking tables that had multiple holes in each. They were covered in green cloth, several with people standing around them pushing shiny balls across the top with long, thin sticks. They seemed entranced by the little balls. One man in particular was lost in intense concentration as he nudged a red one into one of the holes. When it went in, he jumped up and down, pumping his fist in the air and cheering. This was a source of happiness? Poking objects into holes in a table? It seemed silly, but suddenly, I wanted to try it for myself.

We made it several steps before a thin, redheaded boy whistled and charged Dez from the right. I prepared to fight, but she smiled and laughed, and returned his greeting—though less exuberant. As they spoke, I took the chance to survey the rest of the room. Two doors at the front, plus the one we came in through in the back. Several large windows and multiple things that could be used as a weapon. We would be able to defend ourselves here.

Dez finished with the boy and continued on, heading straight for the boy standing at the back of the room. I stayed close. There was something about him I didn't trust. He'd been sneaking glances at Dez from the moment we entered the room.

Now, as we approached, he was pointedly averting his eyes, focusing on anything and everything but Dez.

"I need to talk to you," she said, tone icy. Her posture was stiff and her jaw taut.

He didn't respond, watching her for a moment before shooting me a suspicious glare. I knew that look. It was meant to intimidate. But this boy was in for a rude surprise. I straightened my spine and clenched both fists.

After a moment, he nodded his head to the right, and began moving toward the closed door in the corner. We followed him through, and he finally spoke as he closed the door behind us.

"You look good."

Dez bristled. She clearly didn't want his compliments. I didn't know why, but this made me happy. "Cole Oster sent us."

Sent us? To him? *This* was Alex Mojourn?

He tried to hide it, but surprise over the name flickered behind his eyes. "Cole Oster?"

Dez seemed annoyed by this for some reason, but she continued as though she hadn't noticed. "We've gotten into some trouble with Denazen, and he said you could help us find the Reaper."

Again the boy tried to act unaffected. He looked me over, then casually leaned back against the wall. "You a Six?"

Dez looked angry. "You know about Denazen?"

He ignored her, eyes still on me. "What'd you do to get on their radar?"

"Radar?" I asked, confused. "Like an airplane?"

Dez stepped between us before I could say anything else. "He escaped."

"Escaped?" This was a surprise to him, and I got the feeling he wasn't very smart. He kept repeating things.

He lashed out, hand locking around Dez's arm, and yanked her forward. The dark bubble—anger from so many years of life at Denazen—churned in my chest. I didn't think about the consequences, or worry there was no clean up or surveillance team with me, I simply reached for him.

"NO!" she cried. Impressively fast, she pulled away from him and yanked back on my shirt simultaneously. "No," she repeated, looking a little pale.

Her actions left me confused—and more than that—angry. "He was hurting you," I snapped. Didn't she understand that I was trying to protect her? "He was going to strike you."

"Strike her? What the hell is wrong with you?" He wore a

horrified expression, but I wasn't fooled. "I'd never *hit* her!"

"You were hurting her." I advanced on him, the urge to close the distance and wrap my fingers around his bare throat almost overwhelming.

"It's fine, Kale. Alex wasn't going to hurt me." Her warm fingers, still wrapped around my wrist, squeezed. "He was just surprised, that's all. Right, Alex?"

Alex frowned. "What's his touch do?"

Maybe he wasn't so simple.

"Death touch," Dez said, letting her fingers unwind from my wrist. But I wasn't ready to lose the feeling. As her hand slid over my knuckles, I took it, lacing my fingers through hers. The sensation was exquisite. It made me think of the hotel. The *kiss*. I wondered if it would be inappropriate to kiss her again. Now…

Once, on a particularly bad day, Sue told me that for every moment in life we suffered, we were rewarded double later. Of course, I hadn't believed her. Sue was always saying things to make me feel better. But now, after meeting Dez, after *touching* her, I was beginning to wonder if Sue might have been right.

"I guess I owe you an apology," he said to Dez.

Dez looked away, and I didn't think she realized it, but her grip on my hand tightened even more. I didn't mind. "Yeah. You do." She took a deep breath. "How do you know about Denazen?"

Alex hesitated, and I knew the answer before he even responded. There were only two explanations for knowing about a place like Denazen. You either worked for them—or they owned you or someone you knew.

He proved me right by stepping to the side and, with a sharp flick of his right hand, sent a can shooting across the room and into the wall.

"Telekinetic," Dez breathed.

She seemed upset about this, but Alex was oblivious. He was giving her a cocky grin, and since I couldn't wipe it from his face, I decided to inform him how unimpressive his display was. "There are many of you," I said. "When one disobeys, they *retire* you and pull in another. There is nothing special about you."

Expression loaded with challenge, he said, "Yeah? Well at least I can touch—" His eyes fell to our joined hands, and he faltered. "Wait, didn't you say—"

Dez squared her shoulders and flashed him a little smile, and my heart raced. "When he tried to kill me, we found out I was immune."

Alex's eyes went wide. "Tried to kill you? Dez, what the hell have you gotten yourself into?"

I didn't understand much about things outside of Denazen, but this boy's behavior was disturbing. One minute he acted as though Dez didn't exist, avoiding her eyes and pretending she wasn't here. The next, he acted as though she was something precious to him—upset that she had fallen into a dangerous situation.

She ignored his question and a jolt went through my system. I liked when she did that. I could tell from the look on his face that it irritated him, and that made me happy. "We need to find the Reaper."

"I don't know where he is, but I know some people who might."

We waited. When he didn't say anything further, Dez tapped her foot and said, "Well?"

More irritation. "You're not going to tell me what's going on?"

There was disgust in her voice. "Why should I? You didn't feel the need to tell me you were screwing that college girl behind my back."

Her voice. The way she was glaring at him—like she wanted to hit him. I realized that not only did she know him, but he'd hurt her somehow. From what she'd said, he'd done something behind her back. Knowing that, it was even harder to keep my hands to myself. But I did.

For now…

DEZ AND KALE'S
FIRST KISS

The woman crossed the room, and when she reached the door, turned back to me. "Because of the dangerous nature of your gift, I'm afraid I'll need to insist you stay in this room at all times. I do not wish to see any of my guests harmed."

I gave a small nod to let her know I understood and had no intention of harming anyone. At that moment however, I would have said anything to get her to leave. As soon as the door closed, I moved to sit beside Dez. "Okay."

"Okay?" she asked.

"She's gone."

Dez glanced up at the door and shifted on the bed. "Yes, she is."

I couldn't help the smile that split my lips as I reached across and brushed a single finger over her cheek. It was so incredibly soft. Being near her made my head spin, but when she'd touched her lips to my cheek? It was… I didn't know the words to properly describe it. "That was nice."

She inhaled sharply. "Was it?"

The kiss. She'd said there were different kinds. If the one she'd given me earlier was anything like the others, I was eager to experience them. "What's another kind?"

Her smile widened as she faced me, and I couldn't help myself. I took her hand and held it tight against my chest—directly over my heart. "Why does my heart pump faster when we're close? How is it you do that to me?"

"Nerves, excitement, fear? Could be a lot of things," she said.

"Nerves?"

"Like when you're worried about something. Nervous."

"I know what nervous is." I removed my hand from over hers and placed it on her chest. Over *her* heart. The steady rhythm that drummed beneath my fingers nearly matched mine and gave me pause. "Yours is doing the same. Are you nervous?"

A flush of color rose in her cheeks. "Yeah, I guess I am, a little."

I left my hand where it was. Her words were surprising, but more than that, made me worry. The last thing I wanted was to cause her distress. "Nervous because of me?"

"Yes," she said then frowned. "No, I mean, it's complicated."

I leaned back a bit, irritated. "I don't like that word. Complicated."

She laughed. "No one does, trust me."

I didn't want to ask, but I needed to know the answer. "Do I make you afraid?"

There was no response. Surely her silence meant yes. I couldn't blame her. She'd seen what the simplest touch of my skin could do when the agents attacked us at her friend's house. She'd watched the man crumble into nothingness. In a single beat of his heart, he was there then gone. That would frighten anyone.

After a moment, she took a deep breath and moved my hand from over her heart. I started to back away—I had my answer—but she did the unthinkable. Reaching forward, she took hold of my chin, and without a word, pressed her lips to mine. Every muscle in my body stiffened in response. It was sensation overload. She was warm and soft, and if at all possible, my heart was beating even faster than before. A scorching heat bloomed across my jaw as she trailed her fingers up the sides and into my hair. Still, I didn't move. I *couldn't* move. The only explanation for something so amazing was that I'd died and this was my payment for a life of hell. If that was the case, then I'd gladly live a thousand lifetimes of hell.

The air in my lungs suddenly disappeared, and I had to grip the edge of the bed with my left hand to keep myself grounded. With my right, I grabbed her hand and pressed it tight against my chest. She needed to know. To understand what she did to me. "It's even faster now."

She smiled and leaned forward, mouth moving over mine once again. A sigh escaped my throat and everything went from standing still, to moving very fast. I reached for her with both hands now, slipping my arms around her waist and dragging her close—and she let me.

For the first time in my life, someone *wanted* to be close to me. To *touch* me. The thought was almost as amazing as the feel of her pressed tight against me. *Almost.*

"We should really get some sleep," she whispered, pulling away.

Sleep? Was she crazy? There was no way sleep would come to me now. Not after this. My entire body felt alive, nerves humming and muscles twitching. I could do this all night. I *wanted* to.

"I'm not tired." I ran a finger along her bottom lip and

suppressed a shiver. "I'd like to do that again. Please?"

She chuckled and slipped from my arms, moving to the other bed. The room instantly cooled with the loss of her and I had to fight the urge to drag her back. "You're a lot more normal than you think."

"That was like nothing I've ever experienced before. Does it feel like that every time?" I leaned back and kicked both feet up without taking the borrowed boots off.

"With the right person, probably." She smiled, bending low to pull open the laces on her shoes. Once they were off, she tucked both feet onto the bed and pulled the covers tight up around her shoulders. Shifting, she rolled onto her side so she was facing my side of the room, and for the longest moment, simply laid there staring at me.

Had it affected her like it had me? I couldn't tell. "What was it like for you?"

She hesitated, and I could see she was trying hard not to smile. Turning out the light, she said, "It was...different..."

Different. I didn't know why, but something tickled in the pit of my stomach. For the first time in as long as I could remember, when I closed my eyes, there was peace.

Acknowledgments

There's an African proverb that, until recently, I never gave much thought to. *It takes a village to raise a child.* This book is like my baby, and without my village it would still be a small, horrifically punctuated thing hidden in the deepest recesses of my hard drive.

First, to my parents, who never once gave me the *get a real job* speech. You've been supportive and enthusiastic from day one, and there's no way I'd be where I am—or who I am—without you. Some days you may not want to take credit for me, but really, ya did good!

To my husband, Kevin, who insisted I chase this to the end. For all the dinnerless nights and hours spent alone in front of the TV while I hung out with people who didn't really exist. I don't know what I did to deserve your unending love and faith, but I thank God for it every day.

And to my brother, James, who sat in front of the computer for hours to learn flash so I could have an awesome website. Thank you!

To Heather Howland, my very first CP and a true friend. My sounding board, plotting partner, and savior of my sanity (what little there is). Your faith and encouragement were key in getting *Touch* off the ground. If this book was a child, you would be its Godmother.

To Liz Pelletier, my editor—and friend. Your dedication and enthusiasm for this book got me through many moments of self-doubt. For loving Dez and Kale as much as I do, and helping me to share them with the world, thank you. For you, I would brave an entire army of commas.

To Katy Upperman and Christa Desir. I consider myself unbelievably lucky to have your amazing talents in my life. For always making time for me, and for your constant faith and friendship, thank you. It means more than you'll ever know.

An unending thank you to my agent, Kevan Lyon. For seeing the potential and possibilities ahead. Here's to many books in our future!

A huge thank you to my publicist, Cathy Yardley. For insisting I just *be myself,* and doing all the dirty work so there was nothing left for me to do except write.

To Lori Wilde, for making me more aware. I'm a better writer because of you. Thank you so much for your encouragement and moral support.

And to my first readers, Mom, Aunt Nina, Leslie Dow, and Melissa Karvecky. Your suggestions and enthusiasm were invaluable.

A heartfelt thank you to Jennifer Armentrout. For taking an interest and spreading lots of *Touch* (and Kale) love. Thank you so much for all your help.

Last but so far from least, to my family at Entangled. Thank you for your support and friendship. You leave me truly honored to be a part of such an amazing community.

A LUX NOVEL, BOOK ONE

OBSIDIAN

They're not like us...

Starting over sucks.

When we moved to West Virginia right before my senior year, I'd pretty
much resigned myself to thick accents, dodgy internet access, and a
whole lot of boring…until I spotted my hot neighbor, with his looming
height and eerie green eyes. Things were looking up.

And then he opened his mouth.

Daemon is infuriating. Arrogant. Stab-worthy. We do not get along. At
all. But when a stranger attacks me and Daemon literally freezes time
with a wave of his hand, well, something…unexpected happens.

The hot alien living next door marks me.

You heard me. *Alien.* Turns out Daemon and his sister have a galaxy of
enemies wanting to steal their abilities, and Daemon's touch has me lit
up like the Vegas Strip. The only way I'm getting out of this alive is by
sticking close to Daemon until my alien mojo fades.

If I don't kill him first, that is.

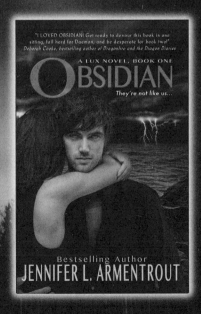

Available online and in stores everywhere.

Death doesn't fall
in love. Usually.

Coming to a bookstore near you

08.07.2012

inbetween

a kissed 1 by death
book

tara fuller

HE'S SAVED HER.

HE'S LOVED HER.

HE'S KILLED FOR HER.

HUSHED
KELLEY YORK

Eighteen-year-old Archer couldn't protect his best friend, Vivian, from what happened when they were kids, so he's never stopped trying to protect her from everything else. It doesn't matter that Vivian only uses him when hopping from one toxic relationship to another—Archer is always there, waiting to be noticed.

Then along comes Evan, the only person who's ever cared about Archer without a single string attached. The harder he falls for Evan, the more Archer sees Vivian for the manipulative hot-mess she really is.

But Viv has her hooks in deep, and when she finds out about the murders Archer's committed and his relationship with Evan, she threatens to turn him in if she doesn't get what she wants... And what she wants is Evan's death, and for Archer to forfeit his last chance at redemption.

HUSHED

AVAILABLE ONLINE AND IN STORES EVERYWHERE

GRAVITY
Melissa West

In the future, only one rule will matter:
Don't. Ever. Peek.

Seventeen-year-old Ari Alexander just broke that rule and saw the last person she expected hovering above her bed—arrogant Jackson Locke, the most popular boy in her school. She expects instant execution or some kind of freak alien punishment, but instead, Jackson issues a challenge: help him, or everyone on Earth will die.

Ari knows she should report him, but everything about Jackson makes her question what she's been taught about his kind. And against her instincts, she's falling for him.

But Ari isn't just any girl, and Jackson wants more than her attention. She's a military legacy who's been trained by her father and exposed to war strategies and societal information no one can know—especially an alien spy, like Jackson. Giving Jackson the information he needs will betray her father and her country, but keeping silent will start a war.

Gravity
drops
10.09.2012

Pretty Amy

a novel by Lisa Burstein

Sometimes date is a four-letter word...

Amy is fine living in the shadows of beautiful Lila and uber–cool Cassie, because at least she's somewhat beautiful and uber–cool by association. But when their dates stand them up for prom, and the girls take matters into their own hands—earning them a night in jail outfitted in satin, stilettos, and Spanx—Amy discovers even a prom spent in handcuffs might be better than the humiliating "rehabilitation techniques" now filling up her summer. Even worse, with Lila and Cassie parentally banned, Amy feels like she has nothing—like she is nothing.

Navigating unlikely alliances with her new coworker, two very different boys, and possibly even her parents, Amy struggles to decide if it's worth being a best friend when it makes you a public enemy. Bringing readers along on an often hilarious and heartwarming journey, Amy finds that maybe getting a life only happens once you think your life is over.

Coming to a bookstore near you

05.15.2012